CIRCLE
WALKER

CIRCLE WALKER

P. R. BROWN

DB PUBLISHING

By the same author

Non-fiction:
The Gods of Our Time
Dreams and Illusions Revisited
The Mountain Dwellers

Fiction:
The Mirror Men
The Treadmillers
The Shadow People

First published 2021 by DB Publishing, an imprint of JMD Media Ltd, Nottingham, United Kingdom.

ISBN 9781780916217

Printed in the UK

The geometry of our lives is seldom straightforward; what might at first sight appear as a straight line may turn out to be a very small arc on the circumference of a very large circle.

1

Red Snow

'The white man knows how to make everything, but he does not know how to distribute anything.'

Tatanka Yotanka – 'Sitting Bull', Hunkpapa Lakota Sioux

~ ~ ~

Sitting Bull's pithy observation, made without the benefit or assistance of any Marxist diatribe, has been attributed to the great chief on a visit to Washington, when this hapless 'savage' was shown the achievements of civilisation in an effort to impress him into subservience. As it turned out, he was far less impressed with the way in which the white man dealt with the city's poor as they crouched in doorways begging for bread. Were he alive now he might despairingly apply his insight to the great cities of the civilised world and wonder how this much-vaunted 'civilisation' could possibly have taken such a wrong turning.

Be that as it may, it is most unlikely that much later, in the early 1940s, Robert Eagle-Sees-Him, a name truncated by an irresistible mixture of custom and ignorance to 'Bob Eagle' for the benefit of the white American administration, knew what Tatanka Yotanka had said, let alone ruminated upon it, even though he was, like his great ancestor, Hunkpapa Sioux. Bob Eagle was impressed by the contrast between life on the Pine Ridge Reservation of South Dakota, where he was born, and that in the burgeoning city of Billings, Montana, which he'd had several occasions to visit ; and he'd heard that life further east had even more to offer than Billings, and that in fact Billings was considered by people further east to be little more than a backwater town.

East is east and west is west, but they had, Bob had heard, streets of gold back east, in contrast to the mud-tracks of Pine Ridge. And that place, further west, called Los Angeles was nothing short of a haven for those with a love of life and a desire to live it to the full, if the stories about it were even only half true. No love was lost between east and west, and Bob wouldn't live long enough to become acquainted with eastern books with such titles as, *Los Angeles: Capital of the Third World.* For Bob, as for most of us, the grass is greener on the other side of the hill; in his case, he would willingly have exchanged the desolation of Pine Ridge for the thick trees of the Black Hills (known to the Lakota Sioux as Paha Sapa), and, in turn, these lush Black Hills for a house of stone, east or west mattered little, and a job that paid well.

The moth follows the light, even to its own destruction; men may follow the promise of new life-starts, refusing to believe that their pursuit may be no more life-giving than that of the moth in its deadly flight. Wisest of all were those who followed the American Dream with the words 'Lead kindly Lord' repeatedly on their lips and the sentiment they expressed constantly and uppermost in their minds.

Bob's frustration was shared by the love of his life, Ruth Plainfeather, for a couple in love tend to project what they feel inside to the hopes they share on the outside. Well, it has to be said that, even now, in 2020, you would be hard-put to paint a more poignant picture of emptiness and hopelessness than that of Pine Ridge, with its dilapidated huts and mud-tracks, its worn-out automobiles which some use for shelter, and the sheer bone-shaking temperatures of winter, as though the whole place is reserved for those who merit the lowest regard while they live as a foretaste of their eternal damnation in the afterlife.

Statistics can be trusted to under-estimate the levels of poverty on Pine Ridge, though it is generally agreed that two of the poorest communities in the United States of America are to be found there, Allen and Wounded Knee; tuberculosis is said to be 800 per cent higher than in the rest of the United States, infant mortality 300 per cent higher, and teen suicide 150 per cent higher, while 85 per cent of Lakota families are affected by alcoholism. Floods, storms, snow and ice, and searing temperatures in summer all contribute to grave discomfort. All this, and an unemployment rate of 90 per cent, readily explains a festering sense of futility and a school drop-out rate of over 70 per cent.

Back in the early 1940s, when Bob and Ruth were busy making each other promises they could never hope to keep, the picture was much bleaker. Little wonder then that Ruth's misty dreams extended far beyond Pine Ridge. Her people sometimes called her 'wichinchala', literally 'little girl' but in common parlance 'pretty girl'. And she was pretty, as pretty as those half-baked dreams of hers. Neither she nor Bob had heard of such a thing as 'economic growth' so could not have wondered about its disastrous shortcomings when taken too far and regarded as the accolade of human achievement. There was no such thing as economic growth on Pine Ridge, for there everything was and still is static, or, if there is movement at all, it's decidedly retrograde. The follies of going too far with simplistic definitions of GDP were as far removed from the minds of Bob and Ruth as it is now from those of much more sophisticated, intellectual pretensions.

So it was that when the couple decided to live the rest of their lives together they both agreed without question that there was no future in the past. Sad to tell, however irresistible this adage seemed at the time, and still seems to those most determined to make something of it, they and the only child they were to bring into their world were destined to learn that, on the contrary, the only future worth having lay precisely in the past; a civilised future lay not in turning their backs on the past, but in learning from it – in discarding what is useless but preserving what it had to offer. But such wisdom does not come easy, often comes too late, and then not without disastrous limitations.

These lovebirds decided they had to leave Pine Ridge far behind and head for pastures new. But the road out of Pine Ridge was indicated by an event no Lakota could have predicted. The attack on Pearl Harbor on 7 December 1941 brought the United States into Hitler's war, when Winston Churchill is said to have literally jumped for joy when Uncle Sam declared war on Japan. Churchill regarded it as a bright beacon of hope. Well, neither Bob nor Ruth jumped for joy either literally or figuratively, and little did they know at first the opportunity that a declaration of war offered them – against an enemy they had never imagined and could not imagine still.

Japan and the Japanese were just words in the white man's language for a people and a culture as mysterious as the greatest depths of the wide ocean. They must have felt the same kind of puzzlement as that of the poor Irish and Italian immigrants after their processing on Ellis Island and their almost immediate recruitment into George Armstrong Custer's regiment to fight the red men; who were these 'red devils' who were said to be savage, ferocious, primitive, barbaric, and how come they were red? How such delineations must have seemed to the average Irish or Italian Roman Catholic one can only wonder; surely they were called upon to confront the agents of Satan himself! Were they not on a divine mission? The Irish and the Italians who had suddenly become infinitely more apprehensive of their scalps than ever before must have been swept off their feet by the sheer speed of events and perhaps the knowledge, quickly gained, that they had a primary duty to serve Uncle Sam, especially when the prospects of gainful and meaningful employment as civilians were as chimerical as streets paved with gold. Better to serve their new country than starve on its back streets.

Irrespective of who or what the Japanese were, Bob reckoned that by fighting for the United States he could become sufficiently white to lift himself and his beloved and his future children plumb out of the desolation of Pine Ridge and into the east lands or the west lands, it mattered little which, and so into pastures mightily greener. This glorious transition, once made, meant the way was open for a job and all those conditions necessary for raising a family with decency and a modicum of hope for a brighter future.

Since he had no idea who the Japanese were, he had nothing against them except the word of the white men that they had to be stopped; in fact, if anything, he was grateful to them for the opportunity they had presented. Putting a stop to the imperialist designs of the Japanese meant that Bob and Ruth could make a real start; stopping the yellow man was a start for the red man, thanks to the undying gratitude of the white man – he actually said as much to Ruth, and it made him smile. Ruth smiled, too, but it wasn't the same kind of smile. Soon after Pearl Harbor, Bob enlisted in the marines and was assigned to a special unit of Code Talkers. Anyhow, that's how Robert Eagle-Sees-Him became Bob Eagle.

What Bob could not have predicted, in company with just about all his military comrades, those who were truthful anyhow, was the sheer ferocity of modern warfare; the Japanese were well prepared, sure enough, and no walkover. After coming home on short leave, Bob was sent to Iwo Jima, a small Japanese island just off the mainland which the Japanese defended with the greatest zeal, since it was their homeland. If Bob had had time to give the matter some thought, he might have compared the desperation of the Japanese with that of his own people in defending their land against white incursion, except that all his ancestors wanted was to be left alone, while the Japanese didn't want to leave others alone, much like the whites. But he had no time for such thoughts, because he had no time for such luxuries as thinking.

The fighting for Iwo Jima lasted from February to March, 1945. The 21,000 Japanese defending the island had been ordered to kill as many Americans as possible before being killed themselves, for there was no such thing in the Japanese code of conduct as honourable surrender. Bob was in the thick of things as a Code Talker; his job was to send messages from the front lines about enemy movements and strengths. These messages would be sent in Lakota, a language the Japanese didn't understand. The American armed forces readily employed tribal languages in this way – Lakota, Navajo and others; not for the first time, for the way had been paved for such work by the Cherokee and the Choctaw during the First World War. The irony did not strike him that it was only the American engagement in two world wars, as distinct from peace-time American government, that was responsible for focusing attention on the importance of tribal languages. Between these wars and after the end of the war in the Pacific, there must have been a mysterious lapse in attention, because it was not until 1990, with the passing of the Native American Languages Act, that government policy which had been designed for the previous 200 years to eliminate all indigenous languages in the USA was finally reversed – thanks to the Act's sponsor, Senator Daniel Inouye.

***

Code Talking was highly dangerous work, and by the end of February, Bob Eagle was no more. Mortar fire upon mortar fire had strewn his body parts over such a wide area that nothing discernible was left, and he was simply pronounced 'Missing in Action'; he had gone much further east, west, north and south than he could ever have intended, but not in one piece. So ended his dreams, and those of Ruth Plainfeather.

The battle for the island was successfully concluded by 26 March 1945, and it is grievous to reflect that the successful conclusions of battles relatively few in number are tragic ends to the innocent dreams of so many, whoever the protagonists may be.

Back home, prayers were offered up in memory of Robert Eagle-Sees-Him, both in the ramshackle Christian church on Pine Ridge, and by Running Deer, a Lakota 'medicine man'. Many more words were spoken in the church than by Running Deer, since it was regarded by the Lakota too unseemly and quite unnecessary to say much, it being more important to feel than to speak; speaking your feelings could be false, especially when you speak too much and may lose track of the very feelings you're supposed to express. No, Running Deer said very little. He smoked the sacred pipe, which was the holiest thing he or any other red man could have done, allowing the smoke to join the material world with the world of the spirit, the world of men with that of Wakan Tanka, the Holy Spirit or Great Mystery, and then, after a while, he ended with the customary phrase 'mitakuye oyasin' (all my relatives) as a mark of respect for all things that live, for it is the spirit that is life that unites us all and makes that life sacred.The white priest in his simple, dilapidating wooden church spoke, and many of his words were incomprehensible to those few in attendance, and Running Deer in his cramped and smoky tipi spoke little, but Ruth was grateful to both for the respect they showed Bob who was now in the hunting grounds of the White Buffalo. What seemed to link priest and medicine man was the idea that we should honour the unsatanic dead at least as much as we sometimes praise the unsatanic living, for the dead once lived and did their poor best, as the living do theirs – and after all, the dead are only those who quit the stage before us, trailblazers into the world of the spirit.

But Ruth considered that her own life on earth was over and that she should make every effort to join her beloved in the land of the White Buffalo. She could comfort him there. Without him, there could be no escape from Pine Ridge, especially now that another heart beat inside her alongside her own. She decided to take her baby with her into the hunting grounds of the White Buffalo and place it in the hands of Bob Eagle, who without doubt was eagerly awaiting them both. It was with this most solemn and irreversible undertaking that Circle Walker first saw the light of day in the early hours of Sunday, 4 November 1945.

Circle Walker turned the snow red that morning, for he was born on an ice-cold white carpet. But we must be allowed to digress to show that he was not the first Indian baby to make the snow red. Red snow seems to mark the history of the red man.

The forced relocation of the Cherokee nation between 1836 and 1839 is remembered as 'The Trail of Tears' (Nu na da ul tsun yi – The Place Where They Cried), with the deaths of an estimated 4,000 souls from exposure and starvation. Then the Cheyenne and the Arapahos painted the snow red when they were massacred at Black Kettle's camp at Sand Creek on 29 November 1864 by John M. Chivington and the Third Colorado Cavalry. Black Kettle's Southern Cheyenne camp was attacked again, on the banks of the Washita River on 27 November 1868, this time by Lt. Col. George Armstrong Custer, when the majority of the dead and dying were old men, women and children, including

Black Kettle himself – despite the fact that he had flown the stars and stripes on the top of his tipi with the solemn white reassurance that by so doing his village would be safe from attack. Chief Joseph of the Nez Perce surrendered to General Nelson A. Miles on 5 October 1877, tantalisingly on the fringes of the Canadian border for which he was aiming; his people had been decimated by fighting, and those who remained were seriously threatened by starvation and exposure.

And to crown this brief catalogue of events, the Massacre at Wounded Knee, South Dakota, sometimes misrepresented as The Battle of Wounded Knee, took place on 29 December 1890, when Chief Big Foot's Lakota Sioux camp was attacked, amid shouts of 'Remember Custer!' by units of the reconstituted 7th Cavalry Regiment of the now deceased 'General' Armstrong Custer; several hundred Lakota were killed that day, including Big Foot himself, who, already feeble with disease, died in a sitting position where he quickly froze and, like the rest of the dead, turned into a block of ice. Almost half of those who were killed were women and children. They were all interned in mass graves in their macabre frozen postures, while on one of the wooden carts on to which the corpses had first been piled was written, with sombre, not to say wicked, irony, 'The Season of Goodwill to All Men'.

The Massacre at Wounded Knee is given as the last engagement between federal soldiers and the Lakota Sioux, and, in the interests of historical veracity and moral integrity, it must be said that about 30 soldiers died at Wounded Knee, many, however, in their own crossfire, perhaps from the army's terrifyingly efficient Hotchkiss guns that had been placed strategically on the heights surrounding Big Foot's camp. The Lakotas themselves had already been stripped of most of their poor arsenal of rifles.

Time and again, red snow symbolises the fate of the red man in his dealings with the white man.

In contrast, the Battle of the Little Bighorn took place on 26 June 1876. It was a hot day, so hot that Custer would have folded his buckskin coat and placed it behind his saddle. Custer and those who were with him died making a last stand, although it was a hollow victory for the Sioux and the Cheyenne who fought together that day against the military incursion of the whites – in fact, it was their last stand, too, and, no doubt, Sitting Bull felt it in his bones; from then on every Indian, whether he had taken part in the fight or not, was a marked man.

Circle Walker's father, Bob Eagle-Sees-Him, was born in 1915 when his own father was 45. So, Circle Walker's grandfather was only six years old in 1876. After the battle at the Little Bighorn, Sitting Bull took about half the tribe with him to Canada, while Crazy Horse continued on the warpath, refusing to surrender the victory he had already won. Circle Walker's grandfather went with Sitting Bull on the long trek north, towards the snows that would once again risk their purity at the hands of the white man.

2
Colours

'Black represents the west; red, the north; yellow, the east; white, the south.
Black is night, darkness, mystery, the sun that has gone down. Red is the
earth, the pipestone, the blood of the people. Yellow is the sun as it rises in
the east to light the world. White is the snow. White is the glare of the sun
in its zenith.'

Lame Deer, Lakota Sioux medicine man

~ ~ ~

Sure enough, cold, hard facts can often be stranger than the fictions of
the white man.

Ruth Plainfeather had resolved to die, taking her baby with her, and set
out for a cold space in a grove of trees that stood in a dark corner of Pine
Ridge Reservation on that snowy morning in early November – not really
trees, more a bunch of bushes with a space in the middle, their thorns icy
sharp in the dark, small hours. She was accompanied by Little Star, an
old woman who knew a thing or two about bringing babies out of bellies.
Little Star would sit with Ruth, and when the baby came she would wrap
it in the folds of its mother and leave them both to die, for that had been
solemnly agreed between them, and Little Star knew the power of grief.

But Little Star hadn't reckoned on the power of a mother's love, for
when the man-child was born Ruth begged Little Star to take it to the

white man's church where the good Reverend Jeremiah Bate had lit the stove late on Saturday night so that the little church would be warm on the following morning for his red congregation. Reverend Bate had never managed to understand that the warmth of the stove was largely for his own benefit and was of no interest to his small flock. In return, his red brethren never did understand how white men could have killed the son of their God, that same son that they now revered above all other men. Much of his sermons went either unheeded or were considered unfathomable mysteries, more incomprehensible, if anything, than the Great Mystery, Wakan Tanka itself. But they seemed content with the teachings of the Sermon on the Mount, for the good Reverend took infinite pains to translate it into simple English, the kind of English that Christ himself would no doubt have applauded.

Ruth instructed Little Star to take the man-baby to the little wooden church, place him near the stove, then wait for Reverend Bate and offer the baby to him as a gift from the Great Spirit. For it now seemed clear to Ruth that the Great Spirit had not intended Bob Eagle's child to enter the hunting grounds of the White Buffalo, and this she would explain to Bob when at last she met him there. Whether she explained as much to Bob must remain unknown, but she did not have long to wait for the opportunity. Exhausted by the birth, with a significant loss of blood; the bitter cold; and months of grieving after the death of her beloved, during which time she ate little, with a stoicism towards her own determined demise that would have won the admiration of the ancient Greeks, she finally breathed her last, leaving behind her a son who one day would be called Circle Walker.

But not yet. This name would need to be acquired, and to be acquired it would need to be earned, and it would be given him by those who knew the meaning of the sacred circle of the Lakota Sioux. It was not a white man's name, and in answer to the Great Bard's question, 'What's in a name?' we may, in this case, reply, 'Much – everything! The whole man! The essence of his being!'

The snow was still red long after Ruth's body had been carefully wrapped and taken away, and it was still red when the Reverend Bate stood perplexed, looking now at Little Star, now at the small bundle, at the same time noticing how uncommonly and deathly pale the baby's complexion seemed – after all, despite the stove, it was still uncomfortably cold in that draughty wooden box of a holy place.

***

The snow into whose bosom Circle Walker was delivered was light, powdery and in appearance resembled cotton wool. But looks are nothing to go by, and he would have done much better to have been born in a bed of feather down, such were the immediate thoughts of Reverend Bate. His reasoning was predictable enough. According to the canons of white custom and plain white common sense, he was right. The Reverend reflected on the pity of it all, for there was no good reason for Ruth to do what she did, and 'Thank the Lord!', she'd had a change of heart and not taken the baby with her as well.

Lots of men die in war, white men, too. And it was not really relevant that Bob had died in a white man's war – ironic, perhaps, but, no, she might have honoured his memory by giving birth in a white man's warm bed. The baby was as much Bob's as it was hers, and she had no right to give away life, not even her own, especially not her own, for she had responsibilities as soon as the baby was conceived. Grief, like everything else, should be disciplined by duty. True enough, in days gone by, the women of warriors felled in battle might burn or otherwise dispose of the possessions of the deceased, including some of their own, not forgetting the practice of self-mortification, like cutting hair, gashing arms or legs, and chopping off bits of fingers. But such professions of grief must clearly stop short of suicide and infanticide, however genuine and however profound that grief may be.

But what was clear to the good Reverend was not at all clear to the Lakota Sioux; the words 'suicide' and 'infanticide' have an immediate negative connotation for those who speak the white man's tongue, those brought up in the white man's cities, and those who have written the white man's history. How come these things should be condemned by those who killed the son of their God and so often disobey his teachings, thereby killing him every day? No wonder the people of the Lakota, and most others, had trouble being taught the ways of the white man, when all was misty contradiction. Even the Reverend Bate questioned the validity of his mission. Gone were the days when he was touched by the enthusiasm of youth; now he went about and gave his sermons like a modest spectre in a crowded room, unseen and unremarked.

Be that as it may, Reverend Bate concluded generously that, as far as grief is concerned, we could never hope to plumb the truth depths of the tortured soul. Less generously he entertained the idea that Ruth's grief had been over-long and had gone beyond the bounds of customary decency. He lamented the fact that he hadn't had the opportunity to speak with her; had they spoken together he might have understood better, and maybe, just maybe, he would have changed her mind. The Reverend was a good Reverend, and not one of those bigoted Bible-punchers who had been so often in evidence in those parts, Bible in one hand, whisky bottle in the other; and because he was good, his thoughts vacillated this way and that, dictated by the ambivalence of his feelings.

Because he was a good Reverend he was uncertain of the conclusions he should reach in his deliberations. He needed to come to terms with the fact that when Ruth, already almost doubled up in labour pains, lay down on her bed of snow, it was not to give birth with the kind of stoicism attributable to an almost primeval indifference to pain, the cultural legacy of the tribe, which had baffled and frustrated white men in their attempts to inflict pain on red men in greater measure than that which they had themselves received, but to die and to take her newborn with her to the spirit world where she might meet again her warrior king.

Besides, that particular brand of cultural stoicism had not extended to the outdoor delivery of babies in the cradle of winter. Stoics, if the word is correctly applied, are not fools. The white men, who she preferred to call 'wasishun' in compliance with customary Lakota terms of disrespect, had taken her man from her in their war, not the red man's war, with the yellow man. Yet the belief in an afterlife, shared by both the red man and the white man, promised to reunite them in the next world: husband, the lover/father; wife, the lover/ mother; and child the lover/father-to-become. Why, the Reverend Bate had told them as much, promising that all would meet again in what he called 'Heaven', or what the red men called the land of the White Buffalo. Her sentiments did not lie with the white man's idea, among a confusion of others, that you should follow your own star and live your own life, and live on alone if your warrior king should die or if fate decrees it. It seemed clear to her that if you love another, your life can never be your own. Without her warrior king she had to decide which was more to dread, the end of her life or its continuation?

Slowly and painfully, as though, it seemed, through a glass darkly, Reverend Bate at first interpreted her decision to end her life as a rejection of all that the white man offered, for all that the world of the white man could offer was hollow without her warrior king. She seemed to be rejecting much. Had not the white man created a new and infinitely better kind of motherhood? He had built immoveable square tipis made of wood and stone to live in, warm beds with slats and springs to sleep on, penicillin to heal the wounds of childbirth, and even movies to watch, if only you could manage to turn a blind eye and a deaf ear to all that Hollywood stuff about bugles in the afternoon, bluecoats, yellow braid, glistening sabres and Custer's 'GarryOwen' – all that good box-office material. Tipis were ice boxes in winter, ovens in summer; the ground was hard to sleep on, and childbirth was a precarious business. And what was there to do before the white man brought civilisation, but dance and sing and tell tales? No, the white man had brought civilisation and nothing had been the same since – may the Great Spirit be thanked! How irrational of her to reject the boons and advantages of civilisation!

But, reasoned Reverend Bate, her rejection was also a reproach, a shaking fist against everything that the white man called 'civilisation', a civilisation which the white man considered to be his 'manifest destiny' to achieve at whatever cost to the red man. She was counting coup against those who had become again the enemy of her people, though they had never been anything other than false friends at best. But she counted coup with her life, not with a coup stick, because her warrior king had been killed in a white man's war. Why, that's it! Reverend Bate concluded very nicely that it was simply a cocktail of grief and anger that had led Ruth to take her own life, grief and anger plain and simple, as plain and simple as the Reverend Bate himself.

She had been overcome with grief and despair, and her action had not been a rejection of all the white man could offer. Her motherly love was inextricably linked with hopes for a better future, for her baby – if not for herself. What Bob Eagle-Sees-Him could not now do, perhaps the Reverend Bate might do instead; her baby would need to become white, for if there was one thing worse than being a red man in the land of the whites it was being a red orphan as well. True, there had been sympathetic voices in Washington, and even Hollywood would soon begin to paint the red man in more sympathetic hues, but he was still essentially persona non grata. It would take many generations to straighten the record, even if there was a will and a way – and history shows that there's too seldom either. Many tears would need to be shed in high places in the land of the free before the red man was given a level playing field, and people in high places weren't given to weeping easily. So, if Ruth was determined to pass over to the land of the White Buffalo, it would seem natural to take her baby with her rather than leave him behind in a world where all the cards were so heavily stacked against him that it was hardly worth taking his place at the gaming table. Unless, that is, her baby became white.

Her own parents had long since passed through to the other side, joining the spirits that reside in every cloud and blade of grass, in every mountain and in every stream. Her grandmother had outlived them easily, and now the old woman was no more. Ruth had spent more time with her grandmother than anyone else, and she believed what her grandmother had told her, that both her parents had died before she reached her infancy. This was true, but the old woman herself passed on before the whole story could be told, and Ruth never did get to know it, for no one else could tell it. Perhaps the truth would have been, though less wholesome, infinitely more instructive. As it was, her grandmother was as frugal with the truth as the white man is said to be in his perception of the world of the spirit.

***

The truth is that Ruth's parents, Jack and Elisabeth Hawk, were one of the earliest examples on record of Washington's policy of relocation. Indian couples had been invited to pilot the scheme, which consisted in finding jobs and accommodation in white cities far removed from the reservations and hence from everything the red man had been brought up to know and to believe, where 'everything' included, first and foremost, each other. The idea was to integrate the red man so well into white communities that he would become a lighter shade of red, possibly pink, and eventually as white as everyone else.

The rationale behind this policy was anything but altruistic. On the contrary, Washington could not only save itself all the greenbacks formerly devoted to the funding of the reservations, which after all was less than a drop in a mighty ocean, but further release vast tracts of reservation land for speculative development and hence further white encroachment, thus adding enormous sums to state coffers. Why, there was no much to be had for so little or nothing; the possibilities were enormous – perhaps culminating in the creation of Disney Lands, one for each and every former reservation. The commercial potential was mind-blowing, compared to which the contribution of red workers in white cities to the GDP paled into insignificance.

Of course, the policy of large-scale relocation also possessed a moral dimension, and moral dimensions are extremely useful weapons in political arsenals: it is wise to want to kill as many birds as possible with one shot expended, but the killing of red men those days was a more doubtful matter – you had to think of your electoral chances, and so it was better to be seen doing one's utmost to assimilate the red man than to be hauled up in the United Nations on charges of extreme neglect. Calling the red men 'Native Americans', a sop to early expressions of political correctness, would hardly be sufficient.

And there were worse places than the United Nations. Dissident voices at home, usually from Democrat sources, could also be silenced. In short, one could solve the red problem by simply removing them – not with a Winchester .44-40, the gun that had allegedly 'won the West', but with a policy of relocation, integration and eventual assimilation. The red problem simply dissolves away, while the greenbacks multiply to infinity; Machiavelli would have found the solution so admirable that he would have turned green with envy. That the red man stood to lose everything, including his very soul, seemed not to arise.

And on the question of greenbacks, which the red man was supposed to create and himself learn to covet, there was little respect for the irony that the greenbacks taken by the red victors from the pockets of dead soldiers after the Battle of the Little Bighorn were simply given to little red children to play with, maybe to use as blankets for toy horses made of dried mud. The red men had no use for greenbacks or for the yellow stone the white man called 'gold'; a pocket watch taken from a dead white man would be thrown away when it stopped ticking, because when it stopped ticking, it stopped speaking and had lost its soul and had become a mere bauble. Greenbacks, gold and pocket watches were the white man's trifles; discarding them seemed a judgment upon his world. A man who carried such trinkets in his pockets carried his whole world with him, and when he died his whole world died with him. Only the mountains and the Plains and the rivers and the Black Hills would outlast him, things for which he had had no respect. Mother earth would laugh at him as he lay lifeless.

A stroke of political, economic and dubiously moral genius though this policy of relocation was, it failed signally to improve the lot of the red man. Red men, once relocated, were totally forgotten. Attempts, when they existed at all, to monitor their progress were half-hearted. Out there in the white man's stone wilderness, it only needed the advent of hard times, loss of job and consequent loss of square, stone house, to restore all the old mistrust towards the white man, he who speaks with forked tongue.

Unsurprisingly, Ruth Plainfeather's parents succumbed under the twin hammers of white city poverty and neglect. Jack stole a bowl of sausage meat from an American-Italian butcher who had turned his back for an unlucky instant. Jack had to run. But the city isn't much like the Great Plains, and there was no swift Sioux pony for Jack to ride like the wind. True, he managed to out-run the white man. But it's hard for a red man to stay hidden for long in a white city. He was due to be thrown out of his ramshackle apartment anyhow, but now they had no time to pack. The butcher, accompanied by two stout Italian friends, burst in on Jack and beat him so well that the White Buffalo seemed to be knocking on his door. While Jack lay in a stupor, the buffalo snorting in his ears, these fine gentlemen made themselves known to Elisabeth. She could not have delighted in their company, for they left her dead, though it must be said to their eternal credit that they believed her to be simply unconscious. She would not bow to their lusty demands and had to be rendered pliable with a blow to the head which proved much more efficacious than intended.

And as these gentlemen made off down the stone staircase of that stinking tenement building, fearful now that the noise they had made might attract the wrong kind of attention, they were totally oblivious to the cries of baby Ruth as she lay in a makeshift cradle in a shadowy corner of that shadowy room where her mother lay and her father was beginning to rise from the floor, the blood in his eyes making it harder still to make out anything clearly. Ruth was naturally ignorant of what had taken place, except that it was time for her feed and she was getting no response. How the babe hadn't responded earlier in all that din takes some believing, except to say that it is lamentably possible to frighten a child into silence, just as silence can frighten it into a scream.

The fact that the Italians were relative newcomers in the boiling pot of nationalities didn't inspire sympathy among them with the lot of the red man; they themselves were a persecuted breed and clung together for mutual protection in a land that had not yet learned to welcome them with open arms, so much so that it was as late as the early 1970s when the Italian-American Civil Rights League was formed in New York with the purpose of improving the image of Italian-Americans among the rest of the white populace. So, even whites couldn't get along with each other; the elements in this vast cultural cocktail refused to come together and there seemed to be no sustainable catalyst capable of performing this task. Their combined efforts under the banner of the stars and stripes in two world wars failed to make much headway, and with the sediment at the bottom of the glass lay the red man, too low to merit even a mention. True, he had earned a place in Hollywood Westerns, but there he was depicted as an inexpressive, unsmiling moron capable only of expressing himself, in English, with short, clipped sentences. 'Me good Indian' allegedly brought forth the response, 'The only good Indian I ever saw was dead,' from General 'Little Phil' Sheridan. If this was meant as a joke, it was in the poorest possible taste, but , unsurprisingly, it caught on as though it were a corollary of the Doctrine of Manifest Destiny, 'The only good Indian is a dead Indian.' The fact that the red men had languages of their own was passed over in silence, or remarked upon only as obstacles to their progress in a civilised world. Jack and Elisabeth Hawk had, therefore, been treated by those three Italian gentlemen with the respect generally accorded to them, by those who were themselves disrespected by everyone else.

Jack covered his dead wife in a blanket, head to foot, in the manner in which a Sioux warrior of old might have honoured the fallen in battle. He sang no dirge. There were no tears, either. He left her there, but he picked up baby Ruth and he ran. Maybe he thought the whole white race was after him, out to finish him and his child; it was just like Sand Creek and the Washita all over again. It was crazy to believe what the white man promised. Chief Red Cloud knew that when he said, 'The white man made us many promises, but kept only one; he promised to take our land, and he took it.' He was right. The old men were always right; Jack reproached himself for not listening more closely to them round the campfires during the long, winter nights of his youth.

Well, it was too late now, and all he could do was run. When he had been selected for relocation, he had been selected to die; had he lived long enough to hear of the extermination camps of the Second World War, his anger and his grief, a heady mixture, might have led him to compare the promises of relocation with those made under the slogan 'Arbeit Macht Frei'. But that is what he repeated to himself over and over again: he had been selected to die, he and his loved ones with him. That is what he told himself on the freight train he managed to jump, or as he ran and walked, walked and ran all the way back to Pine Ridge – all the way, and never leaving baby Ruth out of sight, no, not even for an instant.

He would have a long list of sorrows to tell his mother and all the others but, above all, he would tell them that their grandfathers were right and that whatever the white man said he was not to be trusted, that the white man had it in mind to dispose of them all, for either they learned to live as non-persons, or there was nothing; either they learned to live with abuse, or there was nothing; either they forgot to be red, or there was nothing; either they were white, or they were nothing. Trouble was, this meant that either there was nothing, or there was nothing.

He told his mother everything, but without making the long speeches that a white man might make. The Lakota Sioux are not famed for making long speeches. It was just as well, for his anger stamped a time limit on his stay at Pine Ridge; what he had to do meant that his time was not his own. Leaving baby Ruth in the loving care of her grandmother, he made his way back to the white man's city of stone, first to avenge the death of Elisabeth and then, well, after that nothing mattered. As it turned out, even the sweet taste of vengeance was denied him. He was recognised and arrested on his way to punish the butcher – arrested for the brutal murder of his own wife! Insufferable irony. And just a moment later he would have been charged with the attempted murder of the butcher himself – an infinitely more serious matter – as distinct from simply punching him in the face, for the knife he then pulled was not meant for peeling potatoes.

A white man might have found it hard to talk himself out of this one, but a Lakota Sioux would find it next to impossible to talk their way out of anything, much less a charge of murder when the circumstantial evidence was so compelling. Jack's lawyer provided a perfunctory defence; it was not altogether his fault, since all Jack could do was to repeat his innocence and blame men he could hardly describe and who could not in any case be found. The butcher confessed to having chased him to his apartment, but to nothing else. If we feel obliged to use the word 'luck' at all, we might say that Jack was lucky to be given no more than a 15-year spell in the state penitentiary; the evidence against him was sufficiently damning, the jury readily agreed, yet not entirely conclusive. The sentence was also justified, the judge explained, on the grounds not only of what he had in all probability done, but in terms of what he might go on to do; in fact, he went on, sending him to prison was as much for Jack's own good as it might be for the butcher's.

When the State awarded him free accommodation for a term of 15 years, it was therefore made out to look like a favour accorded him with his best interests at heart. Implausible though it may seem, Jack found it difficult to express appreciation for the generosity of the State, and gave none. The irony is that sending Jack to prison, instead of the chair, did in a sense amount to an act of generosity. It was in the early 1920s, the Era of Prohibition, the 18th Amendment having been passed in 1920, which lasted until 1933 when the general consensus was that 'the noble experiment' should be renamed the Error of Prohibition, since the policy of making the sale of alcohol illegal had failed miserably and had to be repealed by Congress in the 21st Amendment.

The whole enterprise had foundered on the hard rock of human nature, like most noble political enterprises: the attempt to improve the physical and moral wellbeing of the nation simply opened the doors to corruption on a murderous scale, while it proved counter-productive to efforts to curb the consumption of alcohol, by simply forcing it underground. The whole idea of Prohibition was to improve the physical and moral health of the nation, with the expected result that prison populations would decline, thus saving Uncle Sam money. After all, keeping people in prison is expensive and taxes are unwelcome. Jack was therefore fortunate to be offered the opportunity of rehabilitation with all expenses paid. It was rumoured, falsely as it turned out, that he didn't survive the process and was found dead, hanging in his cell with a rope round his neck – though how he obtained the rope was never explained; but, according to the rumour, his end was in keeping with his heritage, for no red man can abide iron bars, much less so than any white man; many of his ancestors would have chosen to hunt the White Buffalo in the spirit world rather than rot in confinement, even if their resistance to bluecoat cavalry charges would be counted crazily suicidal by whites.

Be that as it may, Jack Hawk was unable to return to Pine Ridge until many years later.

***

Ruth Plainfeather was left in the worn but capable hands of her 'kunshi' (grandmother), who gave her granddaughter this name and began to pick up the pieces. Maybe Grandma planned to tell her the whole truth one day about her parents, but as the years passed, the girl seemed content to believe that they had been killed in a truck that had overturned on an icy road. She asked the kind of questions a child might be expected to ask, and Grandma could tell her everything else she wanted to know without upsetting her; on the contrary, she painted both parents in loving hues, as was appropriate and right.

Ruth and her grandmother lived together in a small wooden hut which always seemed dark on the inside. Ruth used to walk around it wishing the walls were made of glass. It was dusty, too; you could smell the dust, or was it the wood? There were cupboards, with doors that refused to close shut, and cracked cups and blackened kettles. There were even knives and forks, which had seen much better days at some white man's table, together with rickety chairs, threadbare curtains and cracked glass jars – everything the worn-out paraphernalia of white civilisation. Grandma's clothes were white, too – or had been. She always dressed in the same way, in a thin, stained, woollen top which she kept buttoned up to the neck in winter, with a headscarf tight around her crown, tied up at the back of her neck, her ears uncovered, an apron under, not over, her top, and two or three pairs of socks, one of which she always seemed to be darning. Short, stocky and in her mid-to-late 70s, she hobbled along with a stoop, and since she was heavy she seemed to risk falling flat on her face with every step she took, so far forward did her body seem to incline.

But that was the only indication she ever gave of going places, for everything else spoke of her having been places already, so worn did she look, so lined her face that it resembled the cracks, fissures and crevices of the Badlands, so wrinkled her hands, so shrivelled her stature – not at all the lithe, well-proportioned squaw of her youth who had attracted the young men and inspired at least one to play his siyotanka (flute) in the hope that he might win her and take her under his wing. She'd had a hard life, sure enough, for on Pine Ridge there was nothing but a hard life to look forward to. In fact, she was lucky to have lived so long – the same kind of 'luck' as that enjoyed by her son who had rotted in jail for free at the white man's expense. Ruth knew that Grandma had more stories than she had either time or inclination to tell; she vaguely considered Grandma to be a leaning tower of tribal stamina testifying to the sheer power of endurance of the red race in the face of overwhelming odds; there was a strength in Grandma's silence, and Ruth found speculation about the stories she didn't tell more intriguing that those she did.

During the day Grandma would sit in that part of the living room which pretended to be a kitchen, in a crude wooden chair, her arms resting on the small, plain, square table, one hand cupped in the other, while she stared out the window to the grey-green, grey-brown hills beyond, staring but unseeing, her hair white, her face deeply lined, her cheeks hollow. She would sit like that for hours, motionless, her mind full of everything or of nothing. It's not that she objected to talking, only the day didn't seem to be the time to do it. When, at night, she did talk, it was as though she were talking to herself, thinking out loud. But she knew Ruth was listening to her and hanging on to every word. She knew she had an audience – maybe she wouldn't have spoken otherwise.

Yes, nights were different. They would sit together in that wooden tipi, either side of the spitting wood fire, which gave the only light, the glow forming dancing shadows on the walls. Grandma would always sit in the same place, on a rocking chair close to the hearth, which creaked as she rocked, and as she slowly rocked to and fro, the shadow behind her rose and fell in slow motion like the wings of some mute, gigantic black bird. She sat so close to the fire that when sparks flew they would land on her lap, and she seemed to know instinctively when to brush them away and when to let them die of their own accord; they might land on her withered hands, but she would be content to give them a gentle rub occasionally. It never seemed to occur to her to retreat further back into the shadows.

Ruth loved these nights. On nights such as these the woody smell of dust didn't bother her at all, and the place was so dark and the fire so red that she and Grandma could be anywhere and long ago, in a forest, on the Plains, sitting round a campfire inside a real tipi when the men were away on a hunt, or raiding the villages of the Pawnees, their old enemies, or scalping wasishun. Not that she could have had any memory of these things, but they were all there somewhere, deep down in her psyche, pulsing away like the beating of a drum and the singing of songs for the hunts to be and the many hunts to come, and maybe just as the Great Spirit, Wakan Tanka, flowed through the rivers and the hills and through everyone and everything that lived.

''T ain't right,' the old woman would say in her long drawl and squeaky voice – a phrase she had acquired from her white conquerors along with her cotton apron and viscose headscarf. 'No, sir. 'T ain't right. Tried to make me Christian. Don't know what for, though. First they nail 'im up, then they praise him. No red man do that! No, sir! 'An see where we all are now! Turned us crazy. Crazy! Tryin' to find ourselves and getting all mixed up. All mixed up. You know why? 'Cos all red men wanna be Sioux. All Indians wanna be Sioux!' This she mumbled to herself now and then, maybe when she wanted to make herself laugh, because it would make her chuckle – 'All Indians wanna be Sioux!' Ruth thought Grandma herself was crazy, touched by age and decline. But Grandma had heard some talk about the Six Nations Iroquois in Ontario who would dance for tourists, or maybe just for themselves. They would dance in feather headdresses of a type never worn by their ancestors but were copied from the war bonnets of the Plains Indians, typified by the Sioux and their allies the Cheyenne and fully exploited by Hollywood. Someone said the war bonnets were one step further removed from authenticity, since they had been made in China! No wonder Grandma chuckled to herself: the Iroquois had no right to wear war bonnets meant for the Sioux, a felony compounded by their being made by yellow men. But it all really came back to white men, because the Iroquois wanted to please the white tourists: a kind of appeasement, one which meant changing the kind of red man you were for a red man you were not, and all with the help of the yellow man. Yes, everything was mixed up, alright! Yes, it was sure hard to get away from the white man, even in the attempt to assert your own identity, an attempt which was doomed to failure if you happened to be an Iroquois pretending to be Lakota Sioux.

The very fact that very different kinds of red men were using the same symbolism was not only a tribute to the all-pervasive power of the movie industry but an indication of the seriousness of their plight. 'All Indians wanna be Sioux' struck Grandma as a pitiful 'cry for help' – a phrase she would almost certainly have used had she known it. Nothing was sacred when it came to the power of Hollywood, for even the contours of the land were simplified, and then the simplification became a vast over-generalisation and coloured the perception of the white man beyond recognition. John Ford's preference for filming Westerns in and around Monument Valley gave a fragmentary view of the land against which the so-called Indian Wars had been fought, since the place is only about six squares miles with a terrain untypical of everything outside it; his fascination for the place, though understandable, gave a very partial, and therefore unreliable, depiction of the topographical canvas on which the red man's story unfolds.

The white penchant for simplicity, generalisation, drama and spectacle spread its tentacles far and wide. In their most sacred ceremonies the red man cannot even now escape the bemused gaze of tourists. The sun dance was banned by the United States government until the late 1970s, partly because it had been assumed to be something it was not. The practice, a solemn religious ritual of self-purification during which prayers were said in aid of the whole community, was, and still is, erroneously believed by many whites to be a primitive display of brazen courage, but after the official ban was lifted it began to bring in the tourists and still plays its part in preserving and promoting a misleading identity. However, some white onlookers might be somewhat confused at the sight of a red man enduring the hell of a sun-dance only to jump into his Toyota next day and go for a hot-dog and an ice-cold glass of Budweiser, as if in celebration of an alternative and entirely white culture.

One 'obvious', and characteristically white, conclusion to draw is that the sun dance is simply endured to show off and to humour the prejudices of the white man, which consist in the view that the red man featured by Hollywood is no more than a barbarous example of God's creation – a primitive conundrum, if you will. It's enough to make some white onlookers believe that sun dancers might at any moment turn on them and lift their scalps. To a white, maybe even to some reds, it certainly is confusing – enough even to confuse the Great Spirit himself. Had Grandma lived into the era of the deadly mix of Toyota and Budweiser, she might have shed a few tears through her chuckles, tears more of sorrow than of joy, to see how that cocktail ruined the lives of red men before their prime.

Grandma did do her fair share of chuckling. Not a day went by when she failed to chuckle about something, for the whites were mighty persistent in pursuing their policy of eventual assimilation. It seemed the American Dream, if it meant equal opportunities for all, implied sameness; but sameness implied force, and force implied inequality of treatment. The contradiction was built-in. The whites had tried to exterminate the reds or oblige them to become white, and they had succeeded in doing neither. That posed a problem for the whites – and as long as it did so then it was a problem for the reds – which kept her chuckling at nights and Ruth bemused. So, here were all the red men trying to be the same as the Sioux, for the badge of the Sioux was their answer to the white demand for assimilation. All red men wanted to be Sioux, simply because no red man wanted to be white. The symbolism was easy to understand, and also the need for it. If things were the other way round, if the red men had sat in the Red House in Washington forcing assimilation on the whites, then maybe every white would want to be the same as all other white men; not Southerners, Northerners, Virginians or Texans – no, just plain white! If the whole planet were threatened by aliens, maybe divisions between countries would be placed on the back boiler, to be resurrected in better times if at all, and everybody would be just plain 'human'. Maybe it was thoughts like these that kept Grandma amused and Ruth bemused. If all red men wanted to be the same, they were crazy; but they were crazy because the whites made them that way. Maybe Grandma was crazy. Maybe there was something that made the whites crazy, too – but what could that possibly be?

In the years to come, whenever Ruth wanted to think of something agreeable, she thought of Grandma chuckling away in those warming nights by the speaking fire when the old woman voiced aloud her favourite self-made slogans, mainly in English but with an occasional smattering of Lakota, as if to further the cause. Which was another thing – because the younger generations didn't speak their own tongue at all well, if at all, and most of the older generation had given up trying to make the language obligatory, especially when Uncle Sam was trying his best to eliminate all indigenous languages across the United States. The whole national environment was pro-sameness and against cultural individuality; to insist that a red person should speak Lakota was like insisting that a man who doesn't need a walking stick should nevertheless use one. Technology was progressing and communication was expanding: radio, television (invented in 1927 and broadcasting the first drama a year later), newspapers, official communications, story books, school books – all were in English. Hollywood was in English; Hollywood had set the stage, and it had decided the language, too.

Ruth recalled Grandma saying that two white college students had come calling on the wooden tipi, wanting to practice Lakota. She said they wrote things in notebooks and recorded the sounds of words, though they had sounded mighty strange when they tried to repeat things out loud. The old woman said this was crazy, too; because it seemed crazy that white people should be trying so hard to speak Lakota when young red people were resisting it, and everybody else, including all other whites, were trying to close Lakota down, like an old, abandoned gold mine.

She said the argument against Lakota was part of the war against the Sioux and every other kind of red man, except maybe the Crow, Arikara and the Shoshone, three varieties of red men to which the white man had taken a particular shine. Custer had been fond of Bloody Knife, his chief of Indian scouts, whose father had been a Hunkpapa Sioux, his mother Arikara. The Arikara, or Ree, were enemies of the Sioux, and it seemed Bloody Knife had taken sides with his mother's tribe. Before the Battle of the Little Bighorn he allegedly told Custer, 'Today we shall go home by a road we do not know.' He died with Custer that day, and so his prophecy was fulfilled. As for the Shoshone, they must have decided which side of their bread was buttered, for they helped General Crook to avoid defeat at the hands of Crazy Horse. According to Grandma it was a crazy world altogether. Crazy Sioux to expect recognition and righteousness from the whites who even now as good as killed them, trying hard to complete what Custer had intended at the Bighorn fight by hiding them away on reservations instead, and not even allowing them to talk Lakota, like bad men burying their consciences.

Grandma said these two white kids, one boy and one girl, had come calling and sat respectfully at the small table, notebooks in hand, while she rocked in her chair. They had asked her to help them translate this or that word or phrase but had mainly come to practise Lakota. 'Well as long as they didn't come to gloat, I didn't mind too much. That's what I told them,' she said. 'I didn't want tears, either – and there weren't any of those.' Ruth didn't understand what she meant by tears, but she let it pass.

Grandma said she didn't know what to make of those two young wasishun. When they began to feel more at ease, they tried to apologise, first in broken Lakota, then with resort to English, for the deplorable attitude taken towards the Sioux and all red tribes all along. They said the government in Washington didn't represent the ordinary man, that one day the ordinary Americans would change things and finally set everything to rights, leaving Grandma to wonder who on earth the 'ordinary' Americans might be and how they might differ from all those Americans who filled the ranks of Custer's regiment and every other regiment that had provided the cutting edge of the Doctrine of Manifest Destiny, that 'weltbild' which set the white man so far above the red man that anything he might do to assert his superiority was perfectly acceptable to the white God.

But they were doing a mighty good job, these two young wasishun. They almost had Grandma on the edge of her rocking chair with their promises and hopes for the future and their anticipation of a time when the 'ordinary' white Americans would achieve amicably what Sitting Bull, Crazy Horse, Gall, Crow King, Roman Nose, Quanah Parker and Geronimo, among others, had clearly failed to achieve militarily, when the 'ordinary' Americans would prevail over the whole land and return to the red man what had been stolen from him. Would they return the buffalo, too? If so, they might also return the dead, and then the promises of the Ghost Dance would be fulfilled without taking a step. The medicine man Wovoka had invoked the power of the ghost dance to restore everything to the red men that had been lost; they had believed him, and they had worn ghost dance shirts, believing also they these would stop the bullets of the white man, which of course they did not.

But now, if these young wasishun were to be believed, there was a new magic on the horizon in the form of 'ordinary' Americans.

But afterwards Grandma got to thinking that those two young wasishun were themselves anything but ordinary. Listen to them speak and you would think they wanted to be Sioux, too, and there was nothing ordinary about whites wanting to be red. On the contrary, it seemed mighty suspicious. Another mystery. Maybe they would grow out of it when they grew older, though not necessarily wiser, and then they wouldn't try to be Sioux anymore, and the Sioux themselves would be no further forward than they had ever been.

Grandma smoked a pipe. It wasn't a 'chanunpa', the long red-stone sacred pipe of the Lakota Sioux, and in it she didn't smoke 'chanshasha', the customary red willow-bark tobacco of the chanunpa, or 'kinnickinnick', a mixture of tobacco and herbs. Her pipe was a white man's pipe, a simple corncob pipe which came to be known to whites as the Missouri Meerschaum, and in it she smoked a white man's aromatic Virginia mixture. Her pipe and tobacco were as white as the rocking chair she sat on; on summer nights she would place that chair outside the wooden tipi and sit there, rocking and smoking, smoking and rocking, occasionally producing one of her muffled chuckles. In winter she would hardly smoke at all. If Hollywood were to be believed, the red man smoked only when he wanted to celebrate peace with the white man, cross-legged inside or outside his tipi. Its spiritual significance and its role in religious ceremonies were hardly understood. And it seemed inconceivable that a red man might take a puff or two just for the simple pleasure of it.

Yet it was not unknown for the chief of the tribe to complain that his young men were imbibing too much of the weed and should cut back , because it was slowing them down on the hunt or lessening their effectiveness as warriors; chiefs might preach moderation as effectively as any 'nanny state'. As always, the preference of the white man for simplicity and generalisation meant that the only pipe associated with the red man was the pipe of peace. The practice of 'hupa gluza', of raising the pipe in prayer and as a salutation of 'tate topa' (the four directions of the universe) was passed over in ignorance. The idea that smoke was a spiritual instrument of unification, joining the material and the spiritual worlds, was and is hard enough for Sioux medicine men to explain, let alone white men, or those very few who had an inclination to understand more than Hollywood would have them know. A chief once tapped the ashes of his pipe out on the boot of General Custer as they sat together inside a tipi. Custer believed it to be a mark of respect; it was instead a warning not to pursue the red man, a warning of course that he failed to heed.

Grandma smoked her pipe for the same reason many red men smoked theirs – for relaxation and enjoyment at the end of a long summer's day, or to help them think, before a hunt or a fight, to reflect on what had passed and what was to come, to remember good days and learn lessons from the bad, or simply just to enjoy the taste. And while they smoked they had their pipe dreams, just as the whites had theirs. A red man might possess more than one pipe – one for ceremonial purposes, the other for general use – but his pipe was more important to him than his weapons. If he lost his weapons, he might lose his life as well, but if he lost his pipe, his soul was in jeopardy. The red man knew how to relax and to dream, just as he knew how to smile, which meant he was as human as anyone else, and maybe more human than many who made unquestioning claim to that epithet. But this didn't mean that the red man was really white, and it didn't mean that all red men were the same.

Well, Grandma died as she had lived. One warm evening in July she planted herself in her squeaky rocking chair outside her wooden tipi, puffing away with the regularity of some large, unstoppable pendulum. And in this manner she puffed and rocked herself into the land of the White Buffalo; Ruth found her next day and reckoned the pendulum had stopped swinging in the chill hours of the early morning when her heart had finally run its course. There she sat, her pipe in one hand, a faint smile on her lips, her eyes gazing skyward as though she had wished herself one of those bright stars and her wish had been kindly granted.

Whenever Ruth called Grandma to mind she remembered the rocking chair, the pipe, the fireside in the wooden tipi, the dancing shadows and the fires that made them, the smell of dusty wood, the smoke that curled from Grandma's pipe, and the words, 'All Indians wanna be Sioux.'

***

Maybe she recalled some of these images that cold day in November, when she lay in the snow about to produce Circle Walker. If so, they may have been of some comfort to her.

It was not just what Ruth might have seen in her mind's eye as she lay down; it was what she saw might have spoken to her – words of encouragement, maybe, or a warning. There was a chance that Grandma might have given her the go-ahead, that she would have sanctioned death in the snow for both Ruth and the babe about to be born. Death would be a final act of resistance to the white call for assimilation – because you can't assimilate what has ceased to exist. On the other hand, she might have counselled life for both of them, or at least for the baby, in the hope that the child wouldn't have to choose between competing with the whites for recognition or lying indolent with his fellows, demoralised and dead from the neck up in a place like Pine Ridge; or in the hope that there was maybe some middle way after all. But then, middle ways are so hard to find and so hard to sustain. She might have entertained the possibility in one of her pipe dreams, but this kind of possibility ranked with squaring the circle, and no red man would want to square the circle. Besides, in the land of the White Buffalo everyone retains the identity they had in the material world – no assimilation there, and no competition, either. Grandma might have been hard put to dissuade Ruth from her initial intention.

We shall never know. All we know is that Ruth had a change of heart concerning her baby. With that change of heart the wind began to rise and caress her bed of snow. Yes, and as the wind rose, at that very same instant, someone far away in Washington was talking about it, or something like it. A red man was addressing a convention of the National Congress of American Indians, an organisation founded in November 1944, almost exactly a year to the day before Ruth lay in the snow. This gathering was composed of delegates from many tribes in Uncle Sam's land, and he spoke words that bore testimony to the fact that Sam's 'assimilation or bust' policy was failing miserably. If the great white chiefs in Washington, and the much lesser white chiefs there and in every state of the Union believed that red men who rejected assimilation were guilty of persistent Indianism, they were quite right – the red men were guilty as charged. The hallowed Doctrine of Manifest Destiny was still undemonstrated after 500 years of attempted proof:

Many years ago we were close to nature. We judged time, weather conditions, and many things by the elements – the good earth, the blue sky, the flight of geese, and the changing winds. We looked to these for guidance and answers. Our prayers and thanksgiving were said to the four winds – to the East from whence the new day was born; to the South which sent the warm breeze which gave a feeling of comfort; to the West which ended the day and brought rest; and to the North, the Mother of winter whose sharp air awakened a time of preparation for the long days ahead. We lived by God's hand through nature and evaluated the changing winds to tell us or warn us of what was ahead.

Today we are again evaluating the changing winds. May we be strong in spirit and equal to our Fathers of another day in reading the signs accurately and interpreting them wisely. May Wah-Kon-Tah, the Great Spirit, look down upon us, guide us, inspire us, and give us courage and wisdom. Above all, may He look down upon us and be pleased.

These words were spoken in English, yet it was not the language of the white man. Maybe the Great Spirit looked down on Circle Walker that day and was pleased. He had been conceived through no choice of his own, but had he been saved by mere chance or through the natural love of a mother for her child? Or had Wah-Kon-Tah had a hand in it? Had the Reverend Jeremiah Bate been brought on the wings of the wind from the East whence the new day was born?

3

From Red to White

'One thing we know, which the white man may one day discover – our God is the same God. You may think now that you own Him as you wish to own our land, but you cannot. He is the God of man and His compassion is equal for the red man and the white.'

Sealth (Chief Seattle), 1854

~ ~ ~

Try though he did, and, truth to say, he didn't try as hard as he might have done, the good Reverend Jeremiah Bate never managed to equate Wakan Tanka, the Great Spirit, the Great Mystery, with his own God, the God of Christ, the God of the New Testament, despite the words of Sealth spoken just over one hundred years before. Wakan Tanta, he thought, seemed to have more in common with the Judaic God, God the Creator, the God of the Old Testament, or yet the God of the Koran, the Compassionate One, but also the One that punishes men through eternity for their earthly misdeeds or rewards the 'good' in something akin to the holy hunting grounds of the White Buffalo. More than this, the red man might think it possible to commune with the Great Spirit through ritual and the sacred pipe, but the good Jeremiah Bate, though not an obvious bigot, actually thought himself an instrument of God.

With the passing of Ruth Plainfeather and the arrival of her baby, Jeremiah Bate imagined himself presented with an opportunity to serve God in a way he had never before imagined. Little Star told him how Ruth had changed her mind and wanted her to take the baby to him, to be his guardian, if only temporarily. Here now was an opportunity to convert red into white, and, as if he needed a further indication of God's intentions, Ruth's baby really did look as pale as a white baby, pink and healthy despite its less-than-salutary mode of advent. So pink, indeed, that Jeremiah wondered to himself, despite the assurances of Little Star, whether his father had been white or part white; or maybe further back along the line of progeny there might have been a mixing of blood, red and white. After all, such things were not unknown; white men had intermarried with red and vice-versa. Of course there was the case of Quanah Parker, born of a red father and a white mother, and Quanah, despite his love, not to say reverence, for his mother, Mrs Parker, whose photograph he jealously guarded throughout his life, looked every inch a Comanche chief, there was no getting away from it, but still, one never knew, maybe Ruth's baby had some kind of white ancestry. Such thoughts were beguiling, but the delicious fact remained that the complexion of Ruth's baby was a good starting point, even a sign that a divine plan might be unfolding and that Jeremiah Bate might himself be instrumental in its full and happy realisation. Parts of a puzzle were coming together.

The pieces were coming together almost of their own accord, for Jeremiah called to mind the Bensons who, being themselves childless, had often expressed to him their heartfelt desire for a little bundle to bring up as their own, since the Lord had decreed, for reasons the Almighty had been careful to keep to Himself, that they would never have a child of their own flesh and blood, try as they might.

After a joyous call to the Bensons, it only remained for Jeremiah to jump into his old Buick and shake, rattle and roll the two-hour journey to the Bensons' place just outside Rapid City in the company of Little Star, who would tend to the baby en route. Soon God's Plan would be complete, and Jeremiah, though not the Divine Architect, could congratulate himself on the part he had played in bringing it to fruition.

Ed and Emma Benson, a kindly couple, were overjoyed with the 'little bundle' presented to them by Little Star and through the unbelievably kind auspices of Reverend Bate. 'Oh my! Just look at him, Ed!' was just about the only coherent sequence of words Emma could bring herself to utter on sight of the said bundle, while Ed, equally ecstatic, was somewhat eccentric: he just wagged the index finger of his left hand dangerously near the little bundle's nose, beaming all over his face as he did so – as if to reprimand the bundle for some kind of trifling misdemeanour committed in a former life. However, if the bundle could only have known it, Ed hadn't meant a single wag as a reproof; had the little fellow been older, Ed might have shaken hands with it instead

– as it was, the little hand was a mite too small to be shaken, and a wag or two had to suffice. Even so, Ed managed a ridiculous 'Howdy!' – which sounded as much out of place as a benediction in Wall Street. The Bensons were in their mid-50s and finally their prayers had been answered, though not a moment too soon.

Reverend Bate was then a bachelor in his late 50s and had never known the comforts of a home life, a loving wife and the patter of tiny feet. He had often wondered, and wondered now more than ever, how much he had missed out on, seeming to belie the notion that you can never miss what you've never had. He seemed to relate well enough to the Bensons and their needs. Besides, the Bensons thought the red man pretty hard done by in the history of the United States and had listened intently and sympathetically to what Reverend Bate had to relate concerning the living conditions, or the lack of them, on Pine Ridge. He and they both believed that the red man should be given a break, and here was a chance to do just that, if not for all red men, at least for this little bundle. The way the Bensons would feel was not at all second-guessed.

It was hard to say who had first expressed the idea to Reverend Bate a long way back, but most good ideas emanated from Emma, who planted them like seeds in good soil, which were thereafter carefully nurtured by Ed until they were in full bloom and ripe for the picking. When the Reverend thought of the Bensons as suitable parents for

Ruth's baby, the idea was in no way plucked from the air, for the possibility of finding a suitable orphan – red, white, black, or yellow with purple stripes, the colour mattered little – had been brought up in conversation several times over the past few years. Like good Baptists, the Bensons attended church regularly and had got to know Reverend Bate quite well, and he them, and they sometimes met up after his services, which were divided pretty evenly between the Baptist church outside Rapid City and the little dilapidating wooden hut which tried in vain to pass as one in Pine Ridge.

As he sat with the Bensons on this eventful day, he found himself lying for the first time in his long and austere ministry; or, better to say, he decided to economise on the truth. He told them that the little bundle was an orphan, which was of course true; he told them his mother had died in childbirth, which was tolerably true. But he didn't tell them what Little Star had told him, that Ruth Plainfeather had allowed herself to die on a bed of snow and had had it in mind to take her little bundle to the spirit world with her, that she had changed her mind at the last minute and entrusted him with the baby from the hands of Little Star. He no doubt felt that the story, already sad enough, was in no need of further and morbid embellishment; the joy of the occasion should be preserved as far as possible and no good could possibly come from further additions. So the Bensons were spared the more gruesome details of Ruth's departure from the material world and her entry into the spiritual. And it meant that when the little bundle grew into a big bundle, he also would be spared the whole truth about his advent, about how he had painted the snow red. In any case, neither the Bensons nor Reverend Bate relished in the knowledge or narration of the more unseemly and gory details of life; they, like the three wise monkeys, spoke no evil, saw no evil and heard no evil – Amen.

Neither the colour nor the gender of any offer they might possibly be made weighed anything with the Bensons. But as soon as they had discovered that the little bundle was male, they set about choosing a name, which really isn't all that difficult if your sights are sufficiently narrow. The Bensons looked no further than the New Testament. Mark seemed too Roman. John too commonplace. So it was down to Matthew and Luke. Luke had been a physician, and that was a good thing for any little bundle to become; more than that, he'd been a social reformer – and that clinched it. There can be no doubt that if Ed had had what very few are blessed with, namely a totally free choice of career, he'd have chosen to be a social reformer. As Ed saw it, there was some kinship between physicians and reformers. 'Well, they both try and put things right, don't they?' Emma had agreed with a knowing nod and a feminine grunt. It must be recorded that both Emma and Ed agreed on fundamentals, which is maybe one reason why their marriage had lasted so long and so happily in the absence of children to cement them together. It wasn't that they held to a complex creed. They both tended to feel that Christian love was as much, if not far more, than socialism could ever possibly mean or aspire to, that socialism was Christianity with all the superstition and all the ceremony and ritual left out. 'Feel' is the right word, because it's not as though they had sat down and thought everything through; they felt, not thought, as far as they did, and then stopped, because there didn't seem any need to probe further into matters irrelevant and too complex for words. It was a comfortable and comforting view of things – it felt right anyhow. They were philosophers, of a homespun and practical kind. The salt of the earth, some might say.

So the little bundle, much later to be given the name Circle Walker, now became little Luke Benson and was baptised accordingly by the very same Reverend Jeremiah Bate. In his name was all the whiteness the Reverend and the Bensons could have wished for him. In this name was the promise of assimilation; for if assimilation for the red man had been the aim of the White Fathers, then calling the little bundle 'Luke Benson' set the seal of authority and approbation on that purpose – the very act of naming almost seemed to suggest that that purpose had already been accomplished and that what remained was mere formality, a matter of going through the motions, of due process. The very act of baptism conferred on the little fellow a whiteness previously absent – though, we must remember, not altogether absent; after all, his pale complexion had already been noticed more than once by the

Reverend. But now the Bensons even began to see in baby Luke's face features that seemed to resemble their own: his nose, for instance, was said to look just like Ed's, while his ears were definitely Emma's. Things were already looking up for Luke, who could now look forward to his liberation from the yoke of 'Red in Pine Ridge' to the accolade 'White in Civilisation'.

***

But it has to be said that, in Ed, Luke had found a father in all senses, other than the biological, truly worthy of the name. First, if Irony could take on human attributes, it might well have taken the form of Ed. Ed was a bank clerk, and although he looked every bit like a bank clerk plain and simple, the inner and the outer man were deeply at odds with one another. Yes, he looked the part, sure enough: slim, clean-shaven, balding, steel-rimmed spectacles perched low on his nose – he needed them only for reading, but seldom took them off – a permanent stoop, sometimes called 'aristocratic' (though Ed was anything but aristocratic), and shiny black leather shoes, a three-piece suit, pocket-watch and chain, and briefcase completed the picture.

And the inner man? No better, sharper, cleaner contrast could possibly be imagined. For Ed was a rebel who exemplified rebellion. The little man who smiled at his colleagues on briskly entering the bank every morning with a cheerful 'Hi there!' would undoubtedly have earned for himself the label 'Public Enemy Number One' under closer scrutiny – if his feelings, as distinct from his mind, could have been revealed.

Ed was a human chameleon. In banking territory he was a bank clerk. At home he became a social reformer, a role in which he believed he was his true self. On reaching home each evening he abandoned the role of bank clerk, as he peeled off his grey three-piece suit, carefully hanging it away in the closet until the next morning – like a snake shedding its skin, or an oyster its protective shell, or like a bird flinging off its feathers, or, to use a simile Ed would certainly have preferred, like a phoenix rising from its ashes. Then came the nightly shower, when he seemed to be cleansing himself and disavowing some of the transactions he had performed during the day and bitterly regretting those he hadn't. Ed seemed to consider himself some kind of feudal serf, obliged to work on the Lord's manor during the day, but free to return home at night and be himself.

As already remarked, Ed and Emma were creatures of feeling and would not have been able to articulate their feelings in any way that might satisfy the intellectual requirements of a university degree in politics, philosophy or any of the social sciences. Such requirements are amply satisfied by university professors who spend their whole lives articulating without ever putting anything into effect, rather like the philosopher who, undecided whether to go up the road or down it, ended up standing in the doorway and going nowhere at all, or the philosopher Thales, who is said to have fallen down a well while pondering the mysteries of the stars – a joke, the point of which has been amply appreciated by many 'practical' men who sadly never bother to think at all.

Yes, but this is not to say that Ed was incapable of expressing anything at all in well-formed sentences. In fact, the shedding of skin and showering were part of a necessary ritual, an inevitable preliminary to Ed's nightly act of rebellion and sedition, which consisted in his writing his thoughts on this or that aspect of life, and doing so in highly polemical tones. What he wrote was almost always informed by what had happened during the day, what he himself had done or witnessed. There was the sad case of Old Man Granger, for instance, who had come into the bank pleading for an extension of the mortgage on his small holding; his request had been denied and he had left the manager's office almost in tears, leaning heavily on his walking stick, and arm in arm with his daughter, who was mentally deficient and dependent on her father.

It was the contrast that Ed found startling. There were cold, heartless foreclosures, but then there were the well-off who came into the bank all smiles, made large deposits and left with their pockets full of dollars they didn't know how to spend. Such things made a deep impression on Ed, who then felt he had to say something, or write something down, because he had gut feelings which wouldn't go away until they were somehow exorcised. So he wrote, always in large old diaries and always something critical – as though he was determined not to let somebody or something off the hook. He was one of those people who had something to say but don't quite know how to say it. He would let Emma read whatever he had written – in fact, he wouldn't rest until Emma had read and approved it, which she mostly did and with the minimum of comment, or no comment at all, just a brisk nod of approval, as though she had written it herself.Ed knew, he felt it instinctively, that without Emma there would be no consolation to be found in pen, paper and his cherry-wood pipe. Emma's very presence was a form of encouragement; her being gave sense to the senseless, meaning to the meaningless. When Ed finished one of his scribblings and let Emma read it, he would wait nervously for the verdict, which might be rendered in an approving 'Hm-Hm!' as she returned to her knitting, which meant that he could go on without further ado, or in a 'Well, I don't know' as she put down and picked up her needles, meaning that Ed might do well to reconsider or rephrase. Immediately such brief exchanges were made, the rhythm of the needles would be heard again, and the moving finger that writes would move again, for life goes on whatever the judgment of our seers might be. Such was the harmony that existed between these two, a kind of tacit conspiracy of the very best kind; the one could almost feel the approbation or disapprobation of the other on any subject that happened to come up, and with the very slightest turn of the head, as though there existed between them a kind spiritual osmosis. We may guess they were soulmates through and through. They both wanted to give the world a kick in the rear end, and they both seemed to agree where that rear end was to be found and how hard the kick should be. Trouble is, such kicks are not at all pleasant, and those who deserve them most shift their position to avoid them; even if both Ed and Emma instinctively realised the hopelessness of the task, the love between them held them together in a bond of mutual sympathy.

Ed spent his small change on diaries, pens and ink. He bought a diary every year and preferred large ones with lined pages. Many a night he would stay up late burning the midnight oil if he had something particularly pressing or heartfelt to say, and then he might use up several pages, so the dates on the pages meant nothing. Otherwise he might write only a sentence or two. But he just had to say some darn thing. He just couldn't let it be.

How he would have loved to peel off his three-piece suit forever, casting off with it so much else besides. But jobs were so hard to come by, and Ed was a man of limited marketable talents; besides, Uncle Sam was just about to put an end to the war with the yellow men of Japan and the whole country was on a war footing, and soon enough the Korean war would be knocking on the door. No, you had to look after whatever job you could find; if you didn't like what you did, you just had to steel yourself and get on with it – nothing else for it! Giving up his job and relying on Emma was not an option. She did what she could at home to supplement their income by knitting this or that or sewing here and stitching there and even making up the occasional dress, but it was peanuts. And since 'going on welfare' in Uncle Sam's land was the mother of all euphemisms, there was nothing for it but to work for the 'system' that Ed detested deep down in his heart, much as a feudal serf of limited means and an unlimited capacity for misfortune would have needed to serve his Lord, faithfully with his body if not with his soul – like it or lump it.

Ed therefore had to make do, like the vast majority of the population. His evening pipe seemed to help. Like Grandma, he smoked a pipe, Bull Durham in his cherry wood; better to say, he smoked matches, for he would light his pipe and forget to relight it, or relight it so many times that his ashtray was overburdened and then over-spilled with matchsticks, so that Ed consumed far more matches than tobacco – good news, for matches were cheaper. His cherry wood was so heavy and held so tightly between his teeth during his writing sessions that his teeth loosened in their sockets. Ed's teeth, amazingly still his own, seemed to hang on for grim death, but never did fall out, while his head inclined much further towards the lined paper than necessity would have dictated, making the act of writing even more entertaining to witness than to perform – when, that is, it could be witnessed at all, the smoke from Ed's cherry wood making its own contribution to his perpetual obscurity.

Not that his making do was always easy. No sir, far from it. Sometimes he would dress, have breakfast, flop down, almost fall down, into his armchair in the living room, wondering just how he was going to leave the protection of his house and face the day at the bank. It was making him ill, and he had a vague feeling that one day it would kill him. It was all very well trying to write things out of his system in the calming hours of the night, but he knew he had to get up the next day and do all those things people expected him to do, and do them all politely and respectfully. But on such occasions he had to remind himself that it was, after all, absolutely necessary to make do. He had his cherry wood to look forward to. But, above all, there was Emma. Yes, there were things to be thankful for, blessings to be counted, even when, especially when, the whole business of making-do no longer seemed possible.

If Ed's nightly scribbling was a necessary excursion from the dull, often objectionable, routine of daily life, it was just as well that he found some comfort in the journey itself, for he would never be in a position to test Stevenson's observation, 'To travel hopefully is a better thing than to arrive, and the true success is to labour.' The truth of this adage would have to be taken on trust, for, of course, none of his scribbling would ever see the glorious light of day. The only thing ever published with Ed's name attached to it was his own obituary, which was concise and written with a conventional taste for mediocrity, mediocrity taking up less space and therefore more affordable. Even the name on his headstone was miss-spelt 'Edward Benon', but was left intact, for it was too many dollars to put right. The best we can say is that Ed was a real-life Cyrano de Bererac, believing it morally necessary to wage war, alone if necessary, and whether it be won or lost.

***

To say, then, that Ed found an almost holy consolation in Emma's existence is an understatement of wild proportions. It helps to explain why Ed always held himself responsible for the fact that Emma was childless, though the cause did not, as they both well knew, lie with him. To have held himself responsible was irrational – just as irrational as it might appear to say that you can't believe to be true what you know to be true. But Ed was clearly prepared to sacrifice rationality on the altar of love – as if to suggest that Emma might have been more capable had she married someone else.

Anyhow, eventually the time came when to wait longer meant waiting forever. They would not allow that fellow Fate to gain more territory in this affair if it could possibly be avoided, so that heartless creature was finally brought to a halt through the endeavours of the Reverend Bate. Like so many of his fellow countrymen, the Reverend was an 'assimilator' and an 'integrationist', which is to say he believed in integrating the red man into modern, civilised, and that is to say white, American society. But unlike all those with-us-or-against-us whites, who were more than ready to bully the red man into submission or eliminate them militarily, Reverend Bate was, as we should expect, very much a man of peace and, to this extent at least, was faithful to his calling. His understanding of 'God's Kingdom on Earth' seemed to imply a huge society of mankind, one in which all differences might be dissolved away, so that nothing would remain except a kind of 'standard man', one capable of understanding his fellows on completely equal terms, free from the barriers of racial or any other kind of prejudice. Or it was as though White America was a warm house, and the red man lived outside it in the bleakness and the cold of a desert snow. It seemed only Christian to invite them in from the cold, the very least that should be done; and then they might become equals, a true brotherhood of man, and all under the kind and wise auspices of the Stars and Stripes. The only question remaining was how to achieve it. Integration was the answer, and, with integration, assimilation was bound to follow.

We know that when Ruth's child was delivered into his hands, Reverend Bate was given an ideal opportunity to put theory into practice, a chance to be the hand moved by his God towards this national brotherhood of man. No matter if his contribution was such a small one, he would have done his bit. It was not like sending a red man to live among the whites to do what the whites do; it was important to catch him young, and they couldn't get much younger than Luke. Luke could be brought up white, and with no memory of anything else. No, to all intents and purposes he would be white, with all the benefits and advantages attendant upon his being so. If Luke failed to walk the straight and narrow when he grew up, it wouldn't have anything to do with his being anything other than white, but everything to do with his being human, and no human is perfect. Jeremiah's theory concerning the virtues of assimilation was unassailable. No wonder he felt gratified at the opportunity now afforded him by Luke's advent into the society of the white man.

The obvious virtues of assimilation apart, there was the very human service he would be doing Emma. Wise, intelligent, gentle, Christian Emma. Yes, Jeremiah could serve his God twice over; three times yet, if he included the benefits Ed would derive from a fatherhood which was better late than never – to which we may add the alleviation of Ed's irrational sense of responsibility. Oh, Divine Providence! The divinity of the whole thing was shared by the Bensons, especially Emma. Indeed, one fragment of the conversation between them is worth mentioning here. 'Oh, Reverend! Y'know, Luke is all we could ever have wished for!' exclaimed Ed, during one of the Reverend's subsequent visits.

'Well now,' responded the Reverend. 'Well, I don't know. I don't know about that. It's said you should be careful what you wish for! No, no, say it's what you prayed for, Ed. Y'see, if your prayer's answered, what you prayed for is ordained by the Lord God Almighty Himself – and then you've got nothing to fear.'

'Yeah, that's right – now you make a note of that, Ed!' said Emma, smiling broadly.

'Instruments of the Almighty – that's what we are. Instruments of the Almighty!' said the Reverend a few moments later, as he wound down the window of his Buick before it rattled down that dusty dirt track of a road outside the Bensons' place. Thereafter, the phrase 'Instruments of the Almighty' became a kind of catchword, or password between conspirators – holy conspirators, of course.

The privileges conferred on Luke through Divine Providence proved to be every bit as expected. Apart from all the benefits he stood to reap from full citizenship and a sense of true belonging to that great community of Christian fellowship known to the world as the United States of America, he would be privileged meantime to listen to Ed's nightly scratching and the click of Emma's knitting needles; these sounds of virtue and industry married together in perfect harmony, the one an unceasing encouragement to the other. For after Luke's admission into the Benson household, Ed persistently continued to judge a world that adamantly refused to be judged, and Emma faithfully continued to sit in fond approval of the judge.

This is not to say that Ed found little time for his adopted son. On the contrary. On summer Sundays, in particular, he would take his little charge into the woods and into the fields, crazily running after butterflies, or feigning falls and tumbles, just to get the youngster to laugh. Ed was never slow to make a fool of himself if it might have the desired effect on Luke. As far as Luke's introduction to the Great Outdoors was concerned, the infant fared better than if he had been born a hundred years earlier in a tipi with both parents alive and well, since red fathers didn't have much to do with their offspring until they were old enough to ride, and fix bow strings, and old enough to kill intentionally.

Come Sundays, Ed had had enough of banks during the day and pen-scratching at night. In the middle of a field or on top of a hill and with both arms up-stretched towards the blue sky, he would breathe deeply and sigh – the sigh of one who truly appreciated the natural gifts of the Great Spirit. 'God's fresh air, son!' he would say. 'God's fresh air!' You might have imagined a red chief doing the same – maybe with a mite more solemnity and dignity of motion, but no less sincerity of conviction. But no red chief would have tumbled downhill as Ed did, or fall flat and roll over, losing his glasses in the process, and all to make Luke laugh – or so white men would think, and maybe they think wrong. Anyhow, the infant Luke never did know how to understand this strange creature; Ed was an irresistible clown, and Luke loved him for it. He loved his father.

So much for play!

As for Luke's more formal education, Emma was determined to put him well in front of white kids, without of course telling him this, for his red origins were a closely guarded secret; as far as Luke knew, he was white through and through and Ed and Emma were his natural parents. If at any time, through blunder or design, the truth about his origins ever did leak out, then at least Luke would have proved himself more than equal to any white kid in reading, writing and arithmetic. The trouble is, the truth is in the habit of declaring itself when discretion would be kinder. But the truth would never come out if Ed and Emma had anything to do with it, not until the time was right, if it ever was. If there was a right time, it would be right when Luke would know he was superior to most white kids and could protect himself with the armour of self-respect, for, as Emma knew, though it was a bad thing to look small in the eyes of others, it was much worse to look small in your own.

Wise, intelligent, gentle Emma would sit with Luke in the evenings before her ritual sewing and knitting began, and while Ed was still filling his cherry wood and settling down to scratch his way through a few lines of invective, like a termite bent on getting places, Emma would be educating Luke, taking the infant gently through the letters of the alphabet, or reading to him while smoothing his soft, dark hair. Then, when enough was enough, he would get him ready for bed, before picking up her knitting needles and clicking away in unison with Ed's fountain pen.

So, while Ed sought to instruct the world, Emma endeavoured to educate the young. There the similarity ends. For Emma was not just mildly successful but spectacularly so. While Ed's wisdom fell on deaf ears, other than Emma's, her own seeds of instruction fell on young and fertile ground; they took root, and they grew, and they blossomed. When Luke was old enough to start regular school he was way ahead of all the white kids, and pretty soon he could tell them of things they hadn't yet heard of, and may never have heard of at all were it not for Luke. His teachers were amazed at his accomplishments and of his knowledge of historical facts – names, dates, places. They decided that Luke was a good two years ahead of the other kids; they were full of admiration and wonder for Luke's knowledge and intelligence. And as for any physical evidence of his origins, it was as though the Good Lord had conspired with nature to remove them. Even as a baby Luke's skin was unusually pale, and continued to be so, while his hair, though still dark, had lost its raven-like depth and gloss.

So it was, then, that Ruth's baby, having avoided the initial tragedy of dying without ever having lived, not only survived his birth but had started life in the best possible way. He had acquired a father who would find real, unfeigned and enduring pleasure in his company from the outset. He was not a father who would take part in the sun dance, or teach Luke to bend the bow in anger, or even in play. He would not teach him how to hunt or show him the ways of the buffalo, nor would he see his God in a blade of grass; but neither would he dream of riches, as other white men so often did, or drink himself into stupors should he fail to attain them. No, but he was the best father the whites could possibly have produced. In many wonderful ways, Ed achieved manhood and suffered death without ever having grown up; for love was restless in his heart, making him one of the very best of men.

Maybe enough has been said in praise of Emma. But let it be noted that while she never did manage to do the ironing and the cleaning without a few grumbles, for these were not in her view the most rewarding of pursuits but, on the contrary, the most irksome of necessities, and while she held far more sway over Ed than red women dared do over their men-folk, her life was guided by the two men that were now in it; and as her goodness helped mould them, so they, in turn, were the objects of her deepest and most selfless affections.

***

It must be said that Ed was given about as much choice over his manner of dying as that of living – which is to say, precious little.

Luke had just passed 13 when Ed first started to complain of stomach pains. Tests led to more tests, and Ed found himself sitting in a hospital bed looking mournfully at Emma seated in a chair at the bedside. 'Doc said he wanted to see us both, Ed.' Ed nodded and said nothing – he didn't have time. The door swung open and in marched the doc, a man in his mid-30s or thereabouts and sporting a closely cropped ginger beard, accompanied by a nurse in her late 20s and looking no better or worse than she had ten years earlier; a solemn pair they looked, the nurse sitting herself down on a chair next to Emma and taking her hand in hers.

The doc remained standing. 'I'm afraid you've got cancer of the pancreas, Mr Benson,' he said benignly. 'And, er, well, I'm afraid it's inoperable.' Had the nurse's hand tightened any further, poor Emma might have passed out on that account alone; as it was, she seemed to swoon in her chair. 'Oh, God!' she mumbled, having turned as white as a sheet, and then she had nothing to say, as though shocked into silence. 'Nothing you can do, then?' asked Ed, feebly – it was more like an expression of resignation. 'I'm very sorry, Mr Benson,' said the doc. 'How long, doc?' 'Can't say, Mr Benson.' 'No, say something!' Ed pleaded. 'Don't know. Six months, maybe. Can't really say. Sorry,' said the doc, looking down, like some schoolboy forced into an admission. Emma remained silent, her free hand trembling slightly.

Whether the doc expected Ed to react differently, perhaps with expressions of disbelief, by foaming at the mouth with rage, or with demands for second and third opinions, can't be known. That he might have expected some such thing is quite possible, for he was quite unprepared for what did happen. Ed stood up out of bed, straightened himself up and dusted himself down, and, with face beaming, as though he had received some long-awaited good news, exclaimed, 'Well, now, thank you kindly, doc! Yes sir, the cloud's lifted at last. Yes, – grateful for everything, much obliged!'

The doc looked at Ed as though his patient had suddenly gone off his head – bringing fleetingly to mind an article he had recently read about several instances of sudden insanity having some unconfirmed connection with a virus carried by an African beetle. But the doc had no time to prolong such reflections. 'So, we'll be getting along!' said Ed in the next instant, taking Emma's hand and heading straight for the door. The suddenness of Ed's action dragged the doc out of his reverie – the African beetle would just have to wait. 'We'll set you up with some medication,' said the doc, as he quickly followed behind Ed and Emma who were making their way down the corridor towards the exit as though there wasn't a moment to lose. The poor doc looked as though he himself could do with some hand-holding, an office that was no doubt soon to be performed by the young nurse that accompanied him. 'Emma! You've got to be strong, woman! Strong! Who's gonna look after me if you go down? Eh?' said Ed, turning to Emma as they walked out into the fresh air.

Things moved apace, as though knowledge of the inevitable brought it closer. Within a week Ed was enthroned in his bed at home, determined still to spend his last six months kicking the world up its rear end even harder than before, leaving behind him, if not a carbon footprint, a moral footprint that no one could mistake for anything else. Ed was dead set on kicking out like a crazed mule, and he even said that he felt better than he had for a long time. However, it was not to be. Ed's condition deteriorated faster than the doc himself thought it might; not in six months, but six days. Ed suffered a series of minor strokes followed by a major, which deprived him of the ability to think straight, let alone write. Into those last few days, in fact, every malady under the sun seemed to be squeezed, like sounds in a concertina. Last to make its presence felt was pneumonia and Ed sank in to a coma, the noise of his troubled breathing seeming to pervade every nook and cranny of that house.

It was while poor Ed was breathing his last that something curious occurred – or so Emma thought at the time, though she kept it to herself. One night, when the moon was full, she made out Luke through the window of the darkened bedroom in which Ed lay. Luke stood in what passed as the rear garden of the house, really just a patch of grass bounded by hawthorn bushes here and there, and seemed to be looking skyward with both arms outstretched, as though addressing the stars. He held a long stick aloft in one hand, stood there in silence for a few moments, brought his arms down to his side and then threw the stick away aggressively into some nearby bush. For an instant it struck Emma that what she saw was not Luke at all but a red boy conducting some ceremony or ritual, as though Luke had become red, and as if in that one scene all her work had been undone, and the red boy, maybe even the red savage of 100 years earlier had finally broken through. It was an unpleasant experience, what with Ed's hard breathing in the background. Was Luke, or what had been Luke, saying goodbye to Ed in this strange kind of ceremony? No, it was crazy to think anything of the sort. She had to pull herself together, for Ed's sake, for Luke's sake, for her own sake.

It was only a fleeting impression and her attention was pulled back to the dying, for Ed's breathing now seemed louder and more laboured than ever. Nor did she know that Luke was most likely imitating Ed's own eccentricities, as when Ed stretched his arms skyward and breathed God's fresh air. It was natural for Luke to express his love for Ed by imitating him, even if the air he breathed now was more like the breath of the Grim Reaper than that of those sunny ramblings together in the fields or woods. Maybe, in the boy's confused and grieving mind it seemed that in appealing to what Ed had appealed to, his God, he might succeed in rescuing his father from the clutches of death and bring him home. Luke had tears in his eyes as he stood out there in the darkness with his arms held aloft – something Emma could not have seen. When he threw the stick away, maybe it was in anger – anger about Ed's dying, an anger that Ed himself was no longer capable of scratching on to the lined pages of his diary.

We shall never know. But if Luke's strange behaviour was intended to work some salutary magic, it did not succeed. Later that very night, Ed's hands grew cold and lifeless. The silence was deafening and it was hard to say what was worse; the laboured breathing or the silence that followed it. The night nurse covered up his head. A little later, Emma slowly uncovered it and looked down on the face of that beautiful mule that had at last been deprived of its almighty kick. The absence of all movement: the silence and stillness of the body that had just a few moments ago fought so hard to live – that kind of peace was so hard to understand, so hard to live with. But live with it she must.

Luke, as expected, had great trouble getting his head round the fact that he would never hear his father scratching paper or smoking matchsticks. Equally crazy was the burial: watching his father being laid into the ground, well it was like watching the impossible and the absurd. Not that he shed more tears, for not a tear had formed since that night in the garden. Likewise, Emma proved at least as strong as Ed said she would have to be. She and Luke would stick by each other and help each other through – same book, new chapter. Ed's clothes were soon given to the less fortunate, and, eventually, his cherry wood went the way of his poor, jumbled-up attempts to put on the outside the confused but well-meaning sentiments emanating from the inside: his pipe and diaries were boxed up and put into a dark cupboard under the stairway, and there they remained until forgotten and then discarded after Emma's own demise.

Ed was gone, having achieved nothing at all that could be described as the realisation of his ambitions. His life had had about it the beauty of a dream, but also the sting of a dream unfulfilled.

4

Whiter Still, and Whiter

'We do not want riches, but we do want to train our children right. Riches would do us no good. We could not take them with us to the other world. We do not want riches. We want peace and love.'
Chief Red Cloud, Makhpiya-luta, Lakota Sioux

~ ~ ~

Peace, love and riches. Well, Emma provided the first two, and both Emma and Luke had a notion that the third would come of its own accord, flowing naturally enough from success with his studies. The word 'riches' must be used advisedly. Both Ed and Emma prized the riches of heaven and true happiness far above the pleasures attendant upon high dividends in Wall Street; you needed enough to live with simple dignity, and the rest was just dross. Ed had taken the view that where there were high dividends someone somewhere had taken a dive, that one man's success story was another man's downfall. Emma was of a similar cast of mind, though a little more temperate, a little more reluctant to take the most jaundiced view.

While Ed's passing did Ed himself no good, it seemed to act as a kind of catalyst in Luke's own development, or else his father's death was just co-incidental with that development. Anyhow, because Luke was already beyond his years thanks to Emma's patience and persistence, and because she gave him the peace he needed at home for study, taking on all the household chores herself including those Ed had been accustomed to doing, it should come as no surprise that his education took off like a rocket. He would sit in a corner of that cramped living room, poring over his school books under the light of a table lamp. There were even times when Emma herself questioned whether Luke was over-doing things with studying so hard and intensely – so much so that she expressed her misgivings to one of his school teachers, who assured her that as long as Luke enjoyed the process, studying wouldn't do him any harm at all.

So Emma let things be and tried harder to look on the bright side – after all, Luke was now doing on his own account all those things, reading, writing, thinking, that she had helped train him do. He wasn't like most other teenagers. There was no need for coaxing or persuading, no need to drum into his head all that stuff about the value of a good education and the importance of getting on in the world. No, sir! If Emma had once led this horse to water, he needed no directions now and would drink deeply from the well of knowledge all by his lonesome. Go on like this and the world would be his oyster. Such reflections were a great help to Emma as she accompanied Luke with her knitting needles night after night, as if her output was hard put to keep pace with Luke's input of hard facts.

As for the hills and fields he had roamed with Ed in years not so long gone by, they became indistinct and distant. They hadn't moved an inch, but Luke had, so now they were like objects seen through the wrong end of a telescope. The rustle of textbook pages had replaced that of grass in the winds of early spring or of leaves in the fall, while the aroma of nature's fresh larder had been displaced by the stale odour of books. Ed had, in his own way, tried to teach Luke some kind of lessons – well, if they were lessons at all. In a field or on a hill, Ed would suddenly say, 'Now, boy, turn your back on all the familiar things, all the things you know – things like clothes, toys, tickets, things man-made. Look! Look around you! See the trees, grass, fields, hills. A real wonderment! Now doesn't it scare you, hey don't it now? – the magic of it all? Doesn't it freeze your blood, boy?'

If Emma had been with them on these occasions, she wouldn't have been much impressed. 'Now, Ed,' she would have said. 'Don't talk to the boy that way. Nonsense like that'll scare the child!' But she hadn't heard. Well, even if Ed had been trying to say something worth saying, the spectacle of his standing there, arms up-stretched as usual, like some half-demented soothsayer, would have been off-putting to adults, let alone children – though, come to think of it, a child might have had a far better chance of catching some sense from such episodes. What a funny man! And all the fun in it seemed to take all the sense out of it, as though you couldn't have fun and sense at one and the same time. What might have been serious to Ed was anything but to a child – and no doubt that's just how it should have been. So, Ed's verbal ejaculations were hurried away on the wind, as though inappropriate for young ears, so that only the eccentric postures that had accompanied them remained in the child's memory.

Emma's knitting needles clicked away while Luke sat in a corner writing his school essays and doing his math. It was so like old times when Ed was alive that Emma would sometimes doze off and awake thinking Ed himself was there scratching away with his pen, and when she realised he was not, she would console herself with the thought that Luke was amply justifying all the labour and kindness they had both heaped upon him.

But Luke's accomplishments were not confined to the intellect. He was also an achiever at sport. He seemed to be gifted with an innate stamina and single-mindedness which put him top in every school event. It was at running that he chiefly excelled, yet not through sheer stamina alone. He would plan his assault on the leading runners, having acquired, by some second nature, an understanding of their strengths and weaknesses. Strength and intellect worked hand in hand with a beauty and a mystique that seemed almost divine in origin. His skill at sport was a distinct advantage, for it's well known by those who know anything about anything that the United States of America has profoundly understood and wholeheartedly taken on board the unparalleled wisdom of the ancient Greeks in all matters military and civil, but particularly in the education of its young and the conduct of the same in the higher institutions of learning, for equal if not immeasurably greater weight is placed on physical attainment as on the achievements of the intellect itself. For example, and as a limiting case, a superior ability in American baseball may win you a scholarship even when your intellectual promise is next to zero.

But Luke was a limiting case par excellence, as academics might put it, for he was the perfect embodiment of both the physical and the intellectual and was therefore a model pupil. As such, he was ready to realise the American Dream, a success story in microcosm to exemplify the success story of the United States itself. He could not fail to attract the attention of all and sundry, including, of course, that of the opposite sex. He would not court such attentions nor in any way indulge himself in them – a fact which paradoxically guaranteed their continuance.

Vince was certainly attracted to him. At first a sullen bully-boy, he came to admire Luke, not so much for anything Luke could do for him, but on account of Luke's unassuming manner, which he found strangely disarming. Luke's silence in strength lent him a kind of strength in silence. Vince and Luke became firm friends. Luke would sometimes help Vince with his schoolwork, not because he could be bullied into helping him, but because Vince had actually asked, and since he had been asked and not forced, Luke truly wanted to give him a hand.

Not that Vince hadn't at first tried bullying, which was his customary technique with the other kids. But when tried it on Luke, that well-tested method was found woefully wanting since it landed him flat on his back in front of everyone else and with a temporary inability to return to his feet. Afterwards, while Vince was in the very process of devising some kind of vengeance, Luke not only offered him the hand of friendship but also help with his schoolwork, persuading him in the process that retaliation wouldn't work and that a little respect would go much further. Vince abandoned his faith in the argument of force and came to see that the force of argument had a lot going for it, for further attempts at violence were not only very risky but also unnecessary. Vince actually began, expectedly and contrary to habit, to admire the way in which Luke had demonstrated the simple efficacy of the olive branch over sheer coercion.

But it wasn't altogether the moral beauty of such a demonstration that prompted Luke to make it, but rather the beauty of Vince's sister, Laura-Lee. Luke and Laura-Lee, both in their late teens, were mutually attracted, and Emma might have seen in this the early beginnings of a step further along the road to red-white assimilation and a recipe for happiness everlasting, if things were cultivated and nurtured with care. But it was not to be. Vince's father, Grant, took an instant dislike to Luke, which was, on the face of it, irrational. Luke was, to all appearances, the American-boy-next-door, with perfection thrown in to turn an attractive potential son-in-law into a very sure and ideal thing. 'But he's such a nice boy,' Grant's wife, Rosie, would say, when

Grant paced up and down impatiently waiting for Luke to bring Laura-Lee back home from a drive-in movie or a school dance.

Well, the trouble was, as Grant seemed to think, Luke was nice, but he was too nice. That seemed to stick in Grant's craw; Luke's perfection stuck in Grant's throat like a small fishbone – uncomfortable, difficult to extract and unwilling to leave of its own accord. Grant had a hard time with perfection. Any prospective suitor for Laura-Lee would have improved his chances by cultivating a vice sufficiently clear, or bad, to be immediately observable. As it was, Rosie's repeated 'but he's such a nice boy' worked Grant up the wrong way and made him restless. Of course, the fact that underneath all that white perfection Luke was actually red, had nothing to do with Grant's discomfort, for that was something of which even Luke had no idea – apart from Emma and Reverend Bate, no one knew, and the secret was so well kept that even they had forgotten it.

Grant was in his early 50s, and if he was not yet quite over the hill, he certainly had a good view of what lay on the other side, and he didn't relish the prospect. It was all very well rewarding yourself with a gutful of beer on Friday and Saturday nights, but it was hardly much to look forward to after a week sweating under other people's cars. He didn't even own his own garage, and everything he ever really wanted seemed to belong to someone else. It had always seemed that way, but now he could add youth, looks and prospects to the long list of other people's possessions – and it could only get worse.

Luke could not only 'go for' things, he could get them, too. Try telling Grant that he himself had 'made it' and he would want to give you a sock on the jaw; what he wanted had always evaded him, and now it wasn't even on the horizon because there was no horizon left that anyone in their right minds would want to reach. It looked as though he'd had to make do with a bird in the hand and now regretted that he hadn't tried for the two in the bush, risk or no risk. Opportunities had come and gone, and there wasn't any second time round. As for Rosie, she was well past her prime, and the very sight of her reminded him he was also well past his own. Not that he harboured any bitterness towards her – in fact he wouldn't have wanted to live without her or even have known how to try. It was just that in recent years he'd thought more about lost opportunities, which were too high on the balance sheet, and what he'd achieved, which were far too low.

He could only look at his reflection in the mirror and see his beer belly staring back at him, keeping him as mindful of his predicament as a circumcised penis is supposed to remind the mutilated of their promises to their God – the difference being that with Grant the reminder actually worked, making him frustrated, irritable, and pathetic. Grant's cynicism was so marked that the symmetry of a rose in full bloom would have prompted at the very best a grunt of grudging admiration, and at worst a dismissive wave of the hand. In short, Grant saw nothing around him to be grateful for, a fact which cut off at least one road to God and left other, more dubious paths wide open.

Luke being red could of course have had nothing to do with anything. Grant had decided to take out his frustrations on those who seemed to have it all even before they had started out. As far as Grant was concerned, Luke always seemed to be up to something. Grant didn't even get on with his own son, maybe because Vince had youth on his side and saw his father as a beer-swilling stick-in-the-mud incapable of anything beyond the purely routine. Grant's outspoken mistrust of Luke drove Vince even closer to Luke and further from his father. Vince actually went behind his father's back as a go-between for Luke and Laura-Lee – not because Grant had forbidden them to meet but, because he was so tetchy about it, that what he didn't know, and certainly what he didn't see, wouldn't hurt him in the least. Their secret meetings were far more exciting for Luke and Laura-Lee than the more legitimate disco or drive-in – and there's no telling where they might have finally led had they not been brought to an abrupt and final halt by Luke's departure for fresh fields and pastures new.

***

Since Luke was summa cum laude material, he was awarded a rare scholarship at Montana State University at Billings to follow a Bachelor's degree program in Business Administration, of three years' duration; he had been selected as much for his ability to put one foot in front of the other with extraordinary speed as for his academic standing. After the successful completion of the Bachelor's degree, he might achieve even greater distinction. There was talk that Billings were preparing a post-graduate MBA course, so if Luke had a mind to do it, and he certainly did, he could also be one of the earliest recipients of an MBA at the College of Business, MSU. The prospects could hardly have been brighter.

More extraordinary yet was his announcement to Emma when the offer of the scholarship arrived. He saw himself as a major future contributor to and partaker of the world's business affairs and to this end he was committed to the Bachelor degree program, and, to follow, the MBA, on which, he said, his sights were firmly fixed. Luke was not slow to grasp the commercial value of a Master's degree in Business Administration. If an MBA was next to self-flight in the annuals of human possibility and aspiration, Luke could be trusted to know it. Why, even in curious and far-off places like Japan people were falling over themselves and each other to win that final badge of honour and distinction. Lovingly bestowed by Uncle Sam on all those who understood the divinity of making money and the physics of profit and loss.

Sure enough, Luke was good enough at figures and logistics, and the direction he now wished to take might have been predicted by more discerning and worldly eyes not long after Ed's demise, when he would help Emma to sort out the incomings and outgoings, expenses and bills, with a dexterity well beyond his years and an enthusiasm beyond comprehension. Emma had put down the dexterity to natural intelligence and the enthusiasm to his simple delight in at last being able to give her a helping hand in recompense for all the help she had given him. But, clearly, there was more to it. What better, then, than to aspire to an academic qualification in eminently practical matters, combining head and pocket in perfect harmony? Not for Luke the eternal stuffiness of academia or the thanklessness of teaching to ungrateful pupils, nor yet the blood and grief of medicine. Educated and qualified he would certainly be, but not in the dead letters of Latin or the inaccessible byways of philosophy. His perception of the commercial value of an MBA was just a further instance of the way in which Luke epitomised the American talent for combining the virtues of sound intellect with practical affairs – the Greekness, one might say, of white America. Since Luke believed himself to be as white as Uncle Sam himself, he thought as white Americans thought, which was entirely natural.

But alas, alack Emma thought it extraordinary.

She sat on a wicker chair on the porch, checking through some dress material. Luke stood tall, one hand resting on the wooden support of the porch. It was mid-summer and the early evening of a hot day. 'Your mind's made, then?' said Emma, suddenly flicking hurriedly through the material as though some minute trinket of great value might have dropped between the folds. Luke kicked a loose piece of stone across the porch with his right foot and sent it flying out into the grass beyond. 'Sure, it's the right thing to go for, Ma. BA first, and then an MBA opens all doors – y'know it's a competitive world out there; yeah, you've gotta get high grades, but then, once you've made it, well you're sitting pretty.' 'Well', said Emma, who had temporarily stopped flicking through the material and sat looking into the garden and the bushes that hid parts of the wooden fence, 'Well, you've done me, your dad and me, proud, mighty proud, Luke, and I know you're gonna go on doing just that.' It sounded slightly less than convincing.

Luke bent down, smiled and kissed her on her grey hair. Then he ran across the grass and jumped over the low fence, maybe to see Laura-Lee for the last time. Emma smiled as she watched him go. 'Wonder what Ed would say,' she mumbled, knowing full well what Ed would have said. Delighted as he would have been with Luke's progress at school and the scholarship, the very idea of his going for business qualifications, and the enthusiasm with which he pursued them, would have given the good-natured eccentric pause for thought. Had he the talents and opportunities enjoyed by Luke, Ed would never have opted for a career in business, and maybe he reckoned that Luke might aspire to something other than figures, numbers and dollar signs and achieve a kind of freedom that had been denied to him himself. It never rains but it pours, and what holds for rain holds for irony, too. There are times when irony knocks the door and takes it clean off its hinges. University business degrees and high-sounding business titles were all very well, but it all amounted to the same thing – figures, numbers and dollar signs.

'Boy's mind's made!' Emma said insistently as she arranged some sorry-looking flowers in a sorry-looking pot on Ed's grave, where the headstone still read 'Ed Benon'. She didn't even bother to look round to see if anyone was nearby and listening. She stressed each word slowly, nodding as she did so, as if in some debate with the dead and determined to come out of it on top. Emma had taken to visiting Ed's grave whenever there was anything of importance to report or think through. Anyone listening would have shaken their heads in pity. She was surely on the road to senile dementia – living in a world of her own, but harmlessly. 'Nope! No use you grumbling, Ed,' she went on, still arranging the flowers, over-arranging them so that they fell out of the pot almost as quickly as others were put in. 'We can't all be reformers, Ed. Reforming's part-time, anyhow – and it's an unreliable occupation, too. And little you did of it!' She paused, pulling the odd weed here and there. 'Yeah, I know, I know. Galls me, too. When I think, well, anyhow, the boy's mind's made! That's all there is to it. No!' she said, wagging her finger at Ed's headstone, 'Not another word!' Giving the stone one last, firm nod, she walked home. The matter was settled.

Yes, quite settled! For once again, Luke's ambitions were distinctively, though not uniquely, white. Emma had done a good job making him white, which is just what she's wanted to do all along. So it was perfectly natural that he should cherish white ambitions, just the kind of ambitions his red forefathers might have cherished had they only been taught how, for both red and white had at least humanity in common, with all its virtues and all its vices. For all Sitting Bull's admonitions of white capitalism, in particular his reproach that whites knew how to make everything but not how to distribute anything, he nonetheless ended up selling his autographs at a dollar a piece , in this way demonstrating a nose for good old white free enterprise – though it has to be remembered that the very humanity he shared with those ubiquitous white cousins meant that he too had to find ways to keep the wolf from the door. And, as he well knew, there was nothing more voracious than a white wolf.

Emma had done a good job, and she was sensible enough to know it. So what was there now to complain about? Complain?! Why, no! Ed's nightly invectives against the evils of American capitalism had omitted to say anything about its virtues. Yes, that's it! Emma now decided that it wasn't that she disagreed with what Ed had said, just that he had forgotten to say anything about the other side of the balance sheet.

She and Ed would launch heavy salvoes, strictly between themselves of course, against the evils and excesses of McCarthyism, and she was glad that it was all over at last. Good riddance! But on the other hand, and if only the truth could be known, maybe the 'Commies' were just waiting the chance to give their beloved creed a well-deserved kick in the pants and embrace the American way of life.

Well, it was a question of balance, and it was better to suffer the vices of capitalism than to endure those of communism. Why, who could tell? Maybe those commies, who she had never forgiven for the barbarous slaughter of the Romanovs, were waiting to pour through the gates of a capitalist nirvana at the break of dawn if it wasn't for the chains that held them tightly back! And maybe the Chinese were just trembling in their shoes with excitement and anticipation, just waiting to get their teeth into plates of longhorn steaks and french fries, followed by apple pie with lashings of maple syrup – for things weren't all that bad. Maybe it was just a question of time. Emma wasn't all that happy with her own reasoning. She wasn't around to witness 'perestroika' and 'glasnost' from the mid-1980s on; had she been, she might have felt a mite better about herself. As it was, she almost hated herself for crossing swords with Ed, who was no longer in a position to defend himself.

Meanwhile, Luke continued to reap all the benefits of a studious disposition, gaining his grades and satisfying the conditions of the scholarship he coveted. From here on, the battle for assimilation was all but complete. And whatever misgivings Emma might sometimes entertain, there was nothing more soothing than the observations of Reverend Jeremiah Bate. That good man, it need hardly be said, was a most keen observer of Luke's development, though his observations were made at a safe distance by letter lest any doubt at all were thrown on the legitimacy of Luke's origins, for Luke himself was better off knowing nothing at all about them; the Reverend would keenly await fresh news touching the progress of his 'experiment'. Usually by letter. But on one occasion, Emma attended church, just as Luke was about to depart, on the threshold of his undergraduate career.

'I am touched, Emma. Touched, dear lady!' he said, taking her hand firmly in his and kissing it. He meant it. He was touched, alright. 'To think we forced him from the Devil's grasp, from the very jaws of obscurity, and lifted him up, Emma. Yeah, lifted him up! Lifted him up to where he stands now, and the Lord knows where he'll end up standin'! An' all with God's help. May the Lord be praised! I said it before, an' I say it again – instruments, Emma, that's what we were, that's what we are and that's what we'll continue to be! An' I can see Ed lookin' down on us right now and smilin'. Bless his soul! Yeah, right enough, Instruments of the Almighty Himself! And the result, Emma? Luke will walk in the ways of the Lord. Amen!'

Emma smiled through all these declarations – she could hardly have done otherwise. But her smile was timid, like a little girl who doesn't know how to respond to a compliment. She wound her way home on that occasion, satisfied for the moment that she had done the right thing by Luke, while the Reverend, having no more to say, clearly felt certain that Luke had been set upon the path of white righteousness. The Reverend was as certain of this as he was that a triangle is a space bounded by three sides, and such certainty confirmed him in the conviction that if only the same could be done for all reds, the Indian Problem, such as it was, would dissolve away in the ether of divine ordinance.

Predictability being the constant companion of certainty, the good Reverend's reaction was a foregone conclusion when told that Luke had gained a student scholarship in white academia. The years had had as much effect on the Reverend as they do on men who are somewhat further removed from his version of God or less voluble in singing His praises. He now sported a substantial white beard, as if to further underline his faith in the supremacy of the white race, and, as he made these spiritual and spirited declarations to Emma, he looked all the world like some pioneering patriarch struck ever more deeply religious by the sight and sound of Custer's cavalry charging over the crest of yonder hill to the rescue of his good self and his dependents from red devils bent on wanton slaughter. For an instant, Emma thought she had gone back in time, as though stranded on the lonesome Plains, praying with the good Reverend for divine intervention, both on their knees. The crazy image came and went.

Ed, though a religious man of sorts, had been a poor joiner, questioning in his homespun way all orthodoxies, even the 'unorthodox' ones. He had never been able to take the Reverend very seriously – and that was when the Reverend had been a good deal younger than he was now. This was a fact that Emma was all too well aware of, since she had sometimes been at odds with what she thought was Ed's insufficient grasp of matters divine. But now, and try as she might, she found it harder to find comfort and certitude in the preacher's fervent and by now eccentric utterances, which she knew wouldn't have made the slightest impression on Ed. She felt uncomfortable with the thought. Smile and nod though she did, she could not wholeheartedly accept the notion that they were all the instruments of the Almighty and began to wonder what the words might really mean.

5

The Bright White Lights of Assimilation

'O Great Spirit, Grandfather, Tunkashila, in your wisdom you made everything in pairs, so every living thing finds a partner; even the eagle cannot fly with just one wing, and one feather cannot make a wing; so too for our children; they will find partners when the time is right, to build nests and find happiness.'

Lakota Sioux Wedding Prayer

~ ~ ~

As expected, Luke proved to be a model student at Billings, so much so that even his room-mate fretted, as Emma had done, over his intense devotion to his studies, though how much this concern was due to altruism and how much to sheer envy can never be decided. Luke shared a room with Simon Westgate, and it worried Simon that Luke was more attached to his books than the prospect of a little fun and relaxation in off-campus bars downtown, where the lights were bright and the girls were plentiful.

Not that there was no serious side to Simon's nature – not at all. There had to be a serious side to him, for he was majoring in philosophy and was imbibing the wisdom of the ancients on the nature of life and the human condition, as well as the beer and bourbon on Saturday nights. But, in his view, the wisdom of the ancients would not have countenanced Luke's habit of closing the blinds against the sunlight so that he could study without distraction between lectures and seminars. There were endless tussles between Luke and 'Socrates', as Luke nicknamed him, on that subject, and Luke usually lost out, having to concede that the pursuit of knowledge was towards and not against the light.

There were occasions when Socrates managed to persuade Luke to accompany him to a couple of downtown bars, where Socrates would begin by toasting the ancient Greek philosophers, one beer devoted to each in turn – 'Hail Thales!' 'Hail Anaximander!' 'Hail Anaxagoras!' Rarely did Socrates manage to get further than that; had he gone as far as the moderns, he would surely have succumbed to alcoholic poisoning, though whether philosophy would have been the poorer for that is debatable. On one occasion, though, Socrates went a little too far with his salutations, being incapable of saluting the cab driver Luke had called to take him back to campus. Only once did Luke attempt to join him in this game, but he swore there would be no second time, which was a promise he solemnly kept.

In this if in nothing else he took after General Custer at West Point, who was a 'once-bitten, twice-shy' kind of guy as far as intoxicating liquors were concerned, a subject on which the excessively religious might congratulate him. It was just a pity that the lesson learned was strictly confined to alcohol and did not extend to the fateful pursuit of the red man – a pursuit which, had it been in his favour, might have landed him in the White House. History would have been deprived of his Last Stand, and Libby, his wife, might not have written his praises so lavishly, the job being done instead by his own hand. Such reflections were not open to Luke, since he knew little about Custer and cared even less.

With his determination never to drink to excess again after that one time, Luke ceased to be a suitable drinking companion for Socrates, though he continued for some time to accompany him to the bars and play audience to his frequent questions and reflections about the nature of life, death, morals and politics. Luke considered most of his commentary half-baked and listened with only half an ear. Luke considered himself a practical man with practical ambitions, believing that it is the practitioners of this world that keep things moving, while philosophy was static and produced nothing save inertia since it was the very product of inertia. Luke's idea was that all questions worth asking could be answered according to the canons of good practical sense, and if philosophy came up with a few questions that could not be answered in this way, well that was more than enough reason to give it up – anyway, it wouldn't do to have stockbrokers and bankers, the very people who kept things on the go, to question the sense or validity of what they were up to, for then they would stop and the world would stop with them.

'Philosophy's a dead duck, Socrates,' Luke said one night, sipping a fruit juice and as sober as a judge. The salutations had already got under way. 'Oh, yeah?' Socrates replied, already the worse for wear, 'Yeah, well, maybe one day philosophy's gonna jump up and bite you in the ass! Yeah, you wait! You just wait!' With that, Socrates went to the bar for another beer, and made his way back to the table, almost knocking over another en route, then he sat down with a limp and unconvincing 'Hail Anaxagoras!' on his lips. As things turned out, that was the last time Luke and Socrates drank together; after that, Socrates would need to find another audience or give up drinking, whichever was the easier.

Luke himself stuck to college discos and sorority girls. Campus events were sane and tame in comparison with Simon's half-drunken ravings, and it was on one of those saner, tamer occasions that Luke met the next important milestone, apart from Jeremiah, Ed and Emma, on the circumference of the circle he was traversing. That fourth piece of masonry was called Caroline Hayward, an ample feminine complement to Luke's chiseled masculinity. It was a case of the all-American boy, white of course, meets an all-American girl, naturally very white, in Uncle Sam's gallery of proud national stereotypes – it was white-on-white!

Once bitten, twice shy. Once smitten, forever thine. That was Caroline, herself a student at the Business College, who knew from her very first kiss that Luke was hers in perpetuity. They would be together right through college and beyond, maybe beyond life itself and on into the eternal night of Simon Westgate's unfathomable universe. Indeed, Luke was well endowed by mother nature to grace any good lady's table: young, strong, yet supple of limb, and serious, studious, sensitive and, above all, capable of loving life itself and not simply a pale shadow of life dancing somewhere on some vague and inaccessible horizon – or, as Luke as already put it himself in contest with Simon, he was an eminently practical kind of guy.

And as if this catalogue of cardinal virtues wasn't enough, Luke was a stone-cold sober kind of guy who was not therefore subject to the temptations of drink. The Haywards regarded strong drink as the devil's brew; had they known it, they might have shaken hands with the Sioux medicine man John Fire Lame Deer on this matter. Lame Deer, in praise of the advent of the horse, said, 'For bringing us the horse, we could almost forgive you for bringing us whisky.' But the Haywards knew nothing about Lame Deer, so knew nothing about what he had said. Lame Deer was red. The Haywards were white. Luke was a good investment, and the Southern Haywards had always been red hot at sniffing out good investments – it was in their blood. But though their blood was red, they were every bit white; white through and through, from their heads to their toes.

Their investments had always paid off handsomely, and they were very much in credit, their bank balance constantly in the black. And now Caroline was on to a sure thing. Once again, the SouthernHaywards were about to strike gold in Caroline's choice of life's running mate. Her soulmate had arrived and she was dead set on snapping him up, and it couldn't be too hard to do. After all, Caroline didn't come to Luke with a begging bowl. No, sir! Her father was a successful company lawyer, and it's well-documented that where there is law there are greenbacks aplenty. Her mother had died when Caroline was in her mid-teens, and Robert 'Bobby' Hayward had spared no expense in playing guide and mentor to his only child. Rachel Hayward, who had come from a long line of good Baptists, had taught her daughter to take little or nothing for granted, and Caroline hadn't been difficult for her father to manage, except that when she had an idea in her pretty little head it was there for good unless she herself expelled it. Strong-minded and strong-willed was Caroline, just like her mother, which endeared her all the more to her father. Bobby Hayward had decided not to remarry; like his daughter, he was definitely the once-smitten type and continued to love his first choice beyond the grave. Besides, he had not met anyone he considered to be a sufficiently good investment. He was wedded to his highly successful career and he would raise Caroline in his spare time.

So it was that Luke met the love of his life in a college hop. He kissed for the first time those lips he thought he would kiss forever, during a slow number in that stuffy sorority room which reeked of cigarette smoke and every affordable cologne and perfume that Uncle Sam could produce or import. The affair was nothing if not civilised and sensible, tidy and clear-cut. Luke and Caroline would meet when, and only when, circumstances were right, and they were right when classes were over and academic assignments were completed. They were always seen together during leisure hours; their lives were full of the right ingredients and all in the right measure. Simon Westgate was the only casualty of their amorous liaison, left alone to ruminate about the fate of mankind and the nature of truth, justice and love – yes, those interminable mutterings about the importance of something he called Truth or the Oneness of Things

***

'Well, I … I must say!' said Emma, almost lost for words, when she met Caroline for the first time. During a college vacation Luke had brought Caroline to Rapid City to meet his mother, as is, or was, the custom in the world of the white man; they planned to stay with her for a couple of days before getting back to Billings, where Luke would meet Bobbie Hayward. So Emma, almost dumbstruck, stood in the doorway, and Caroline stood in the porch light, as if to celebrate her beauty. 'I've been looking forward to this ever since Luke wrote me about you and, Oh! Whatever am I saying, keeping you out here on the porch! Come in, my dear, yes come in!'

Emma's eyes followed Caroline every inch of the way, as she stepped inside Emma's humble abode through the door which Ed, years before, had only just managed to fix on its hinges and which only just managed to stay fixed ever since. But Emma had seen in the porch light all she felt she needed to see. Caroline was perfect, and further glances only served to confirm first impressions. Emma had to make the best of perfection while she could, for these lovebirds would be on their way back to Billings to a far more splendid homestead, to that planned meeting with Bobbie which would be far less homespun, and far less rustic, as was befitting the elegance and status of the Southern Haywards.

Right now it was Emma's turn, and the two days and nights of their stay were more precious to her than the promise of life eternal. There was only one family album made up of pictures which stuck there on sufferance, threatening to fall out all over the place. But she was at great pains to show Caroline all there was. Emma spoke mostly about Ed, not surprisingly; the thought even occurred to her of giving Caroline a photograph of Ed, but she somehow sensed she shouldn't, and kept the thought to herself. Pictures of Ed showed him prim and proper in jacket, collar and tie, his face inexpressive – a model of conventionality. 'Ma still visits Pa's grave every Sunday, don'tcha Ma?' Emma nodded and smiled. Emma didn't feel right about these pictures of Ed. People said the camera never lies. But Emma knew better. Ed wasn't in the least bit conventional, or prim and proper, and his face was rarely inexpressive – so just who did these pictures depict? Not Ed, that's for sure. A damned lie, each one of them. What they really showed was just the kind of man Ed didn't want to be. They showed a kind of template of 'the common man', and Ed was the most uncommon man she had ever known, Lord bless his soul! 'The common man is what the world wants; the uncommon man is what the world needs,' but she kept this thought to herself, too. Wouldn't it be nice to explain all this to Caroline? Caroline was perfect, but there were no explanations yet, not until the girl could be thoroughly trusted to understand, because looks are nothing to go by – you can never be sure what's underneath, just as you can't trust a picture to tell you everything.

Emma would have been delighted to tell her about the real Ed, but for now all the time-honoured clichés would just have to do. 'And this,' said Emma, picking out a faded picture, holding it close to her breast, and then presenting to Caroline like a Hollywood Oscar, 'this is Ed and me at our wedding.' 'I was an only child,' she later told Caroline. 'And so was Ed. And … and both our parents died before we had Luke.' This was in case Caroline should wonder why Luke's early photographic history failed to show him in the company of anyone other than Ed, Emma and the Reverend Jeremiah Bate. 'Yes, the Reverend Jeremiah married us and we had him baptise Luke. Such a good man.'

Emma wasn't given to lying, but she wanted to economise on the truth. She felt the less said the better about Luke's early beginnings, lest, the Good Lord forbid, Caroline should enquire further back about his origins – best to keep them dark and out of the way, because in unknown territory you just don't know what might lie ahead. 'Luke's an only child, too – so he's following in our footsteps, eh?' said Emma. 'I'm an only child, too!' said Caroline. Emma laughed a little nervously; Caroline smiled, with more than a trace of gentility. Emma needn't have worried about letting cats out of bags. Caroline couldn't have cared less about Luke's ethnicity, if only because she had no reason whatsoever to believe he was anything other than plain white – the whole thing was not an item in her consideration; no, her thoughts were elsewhere, and in particular on the imminent meeting between Luke and her Pa, Bobbie Hayward.

It didn't take long to get through the family album, thin and sparsely furnished as it was. Another white ritual was over and done with, and Emma was glad. The whole thing had achieved precious little – except it brought Ed rushing back to her mind without actually putting him back into her arms. But she thought it was a ritual obligation of the kind to be gone through when a son brings back his girl to meet his Mom. Besides, Ed couldn't meet Caroline face to face, so pictures of Ed played a kind of vicarious role. If only those darned pictures had told the truth, instead of a half-truth, because a half-truth was no truth at all. Next day, Luke showed Caroline the same fields and hills that he and Ed had enjoyed, and he told her how Ed used to make him laugh, which made her laugh, too; as though Ed's ability to amuse had survived him, with Ed poking his head above his grave and making fun of his misspelt name – 'And who in Creation is Ed Benon?!' But now Caroline would have had some difficulty fitting Luke's narrative with the man she'd seen in the pictures the night before – but the divergence never crossed her mind.

Bobby was waiting. Luke and Caroline drove away leaving Emma waving fondly to them from the porch. The smile quickly faded from Emma's face as she, now more lonely than ever, stepped back inside through the door she remembered Ed trying so hard and not altogether successfully to fix.

***

Other things being equal, which they surely seemed to be, it really only remained to tie the matrimonial knot, and then yet another step towards the bright lights of total assimilation would be accomplished. Emma was all for it. Luke was about to leave the nest for pastures greener – that's what his education was all about. In fact, he had already taken some practice flights by studying at Billings; soon he wouldn't return at all, having what people seem to delight in calling 'a life of his own' to lead. Ed was gone already, and her own health left a lot to be desired, and one thing she was, like most mothers, keen about was that her child shouldn't end up living alone ; he needed a partner, someone to love and be loved by, and that included children of his own. It wasn't natural, not what the Good Lord intended, that a man or a woman should live alone. In this, Emma and most whites would have agreed with the sentiments of the Sioux marriage prayer, that things exist in pairs and in relation to one another.

Yes, Emma was all for the match. So was Bob Hayward. 'Call me Bobby, Luke – everyone else does! I want you to feel at home, you understand me? Completely at ease now!' and these words were the first spoken to the intending groom on his first visit to the Haywards' estate just outside Billings. This was the first but not the last close encounter with Hayward during which Luke felt watched from beginning to end. He wasn't wrong about that. Hayward was sizing up his potential son-in-law with a company lawyer's eye for detail and advantage. His large, piercing blue eyes seemed all the more menacing behind his expensive horn-rimmed spectacles. The license to call him 'Bobby' was maybe a smokescreen for a more in-depth, business-like, assessment of Luke's pedigree and qualifications, more clearly discernible whenever Luke's guard was down. Familiarity is said to breed contempt, but it breeds other things as well, including false confidence.

This whole thing may seem sinister, but although Hayward was whiter than white, he shared with any red father the same kind of concern about the fitness of any would-be suitor for the hand of his daughter. Red suitors would usually need to demonstrate their courage in war or in hunting, which is one reason why red men tended to be older than the girls they hitched up with; red men needed to prove their fitness to look after the needs not only of their prospective wives but also of the whole family from which they came, so lame ducks were out. What's more, hopeful husbands were measured by what they could pay there and then for the hand of a girl – usually one or more horses with maybe some blankets and food thrown in, and sometimes many horses, and if these gifts were deemed insufficient and rejected, they would need to be supplemented, and, if not, the deal had failed to get off the ground.

A father would look well upon a man who had 'counted coup' on his enemy and come away with a scalp or two, or in some other way had proved his courage, bravery and stamina. Romantic liaisons were possible, but not the norm. Red marriages tended to have more in common with white dynastic marriages or inter-family rivalries, almost like those of the Tudors in England, or the Medici and Pazzi families of medieval Florence – having much to do with politics and social considerations, and not so much with whether the couples concerned really loved one another, the principal question being, 'If we allow you to get wed to our girl, what can you do for the family?' Anyhow, fathers had the last word, and if the fathers of two families wanted the match, it would happen and the girl concerned could either like it or lump it. Thankfully, divorce was permitted and relatively easy, but it had a sting in its tail with divorced women often being shunned by the tribe and not permitted to remarry.

Hayward's concern for Luke's suitability as a son-in-law had more than a little in common with red practice. He had to decide whether Luke was 'Hayward material', whether his face fitted; if Luke was successful, he would enter the family circle and would be in the immediate running for a job in the company and, maybe he would one day play a key role in Hayward, Inc., which specialised in business consultancy and company law. The question was: had Luke got what it takes? The customary, you might even say excessive, informalities of their first meeting were doing a bad job of masking the scrutiny that lay behind them, but Luke was destined to come out of it smelling of roses.

The fact that Ed had been 'in banking' was surely a good start. Hayward liked that. Ed might have had a modest position, but at least it was a position in a bank – so he had been in the right field of play. But it was just as well Emma hadn't confided too much in Caroline, just in case any of it got back to her father – discretion is said to be the best part of valour , but it's also the best part of diplomacy. Banking was respectable; Hayward liked what he saw and saw what he liked. Luke's parentage might have seemed as commonplace as tumbleweed in Arizona, but Hayward ventured no further questions about it. So one major hurdle was passed, or rather went undetected. Luke just didn't know how fortunate he was. The very notion that Ed had despised banking and bankers and anything that smacked of them would have been enough to jettison Hayward right up out of the black leather chair in which he was gracefully reclining and sipping his bourbon on the rocks, and Luke right out the door.

'Well, that's fine, just fine!' Hayward would say periodically, as if to suggest each time that Luke had managed to overcome yet another obstacle on the long and tortuous road to paternal consent. 'An MBA, you say? Well, now! That's fine. Just fine!'

The truth was, of course, there was no quarrelling with an MBA. If anything was a test of a man's business acumen, logistic talent and political sagacity, not to say moral rectitude, it was the attaining of an MBA, a degree which Luke was about to complete in quick time, and, as with the BA degree that preceded it, achieve summa cum laude. The store Luke placed on this much sought-after accolade achieved for him an immediate and very special place in Hayward's affections. If Hayward had been the head of a red family a century before, the MBA would have been comparable to the offer of 100 horses and 'Little Phil' Sheridan's very own scalp, assuming he'd had enough hair, in revenge for his having said that the only good Indian is a dead Indian. An MBA was mighty big wampum. Mighty big indeed. Luke had finally crossed the bridge that the big troll had straddled, and after that it was downhill all the way, for Luke could not have been better served if he had shown Hayward a Congressional Medal of Honour appended to a personal letter of recommendation from the President of the United States himself.

Hayward satisfied, it remained only to name the day for the nuptials. It was not immediate but was, according to the rules of good sense, to be just a little way off, after the lovebirds had feathered their nests at least to the extent that they'd both completed their studies at Billings, meanwhile securing the promise of suitable jobs. This little time would also function as a kind of cooling-off period, rather like the clauses found in any respectable insurance contract which allowed for a change of mind, or in this case change of heart. It was also an important time for Hayward, who would now be thinking hard about how to fit Luke into the scheme of things and take the fullest advantage of his very obvious talents. There were things to work out; a good position for Luke was good for Caroline, but also good for Hayward, Inc., and Hayward, like the meticulous lawyer he was, needed to scrutinise the proposed union with the greatest of care. 'Marry in haste, repent at leisure' was not an adage that Bobby was ready to put to the test. His daughter must have time to reconsider, and to withdraw with requisite dignity if necessary.

**

On one occasion, withdrawal was almost a possibility, but it turned out to be no more than the heat generated by an upsurge of passion and the threat passed away like a thief in the night. This is worthy of some explanation.

Caroline had all this time kept her virginity, a fact sufficiently remarkable nowadays to merit mention, believing, like a good Baptist, that to lose it before marriage was some kind of sin. In this she would have made a good red bride for a Lakota Sioux; among the Sioux, and tribes generally, promiscuity was frowned upon, and any would-be bride who lost her virginity before marriage, and especially to someone other than the prospective husband, was in no fit state to pray to Wakan Tanka, the Great Spirit. A young girl would not so much as look any man in the eye unless it were a member of her own family. She was expected to be demure, reserved and respectful, courtship was conducted with the utmost propriety, and interest in a man's equally demure advances could only be shown with the utmost respect for the rules of the game. An interested party might play his flute near a girl's tipi, and if she was interested she might walk past him without looking him in the eye, and if she walked in the opposite direction it would signify rejection. Maybe the Sioux would have made good Baptists if John had been around those parts and not somewhere else.

On the other hand, Caroline's view of such things probably owed as much to her mother's feminine insights as it did to religion. Rachel

Hayward had told her that she should try to keep her best assets hid up until the very last, and even further if necessary. She said, though not in so many words, that every woman should try to keep part of herself inviolate; her man should not, for example, see her washing her hair or manicuring her nails or doing any of those routine, personal things, household chores included, that didn't serve to put her in her very best light. Her man was entitled to view the final product, but it was inadvisable to let him in on the process of production; in short, a woman should preserve a sense of mystery, and be ever ready for her man, because, by keeping herself mysterious he would be ever ready for her. 'Remember child, keep mysterious and keep your man!' she told Caroline, who was at the time watching her mother painting her lips in an ornate bedroom mirror. She certainly sounded convincing, and she surely practised what she preached. She and Bobby slept in separate bedrooms, coming together only when Rachel was good and ready and not before. It worked, too. Bobby was on heat more often than he might otherwise have been, and although his career took first place in his affections, Rachel was sure as hell a close second.

Rachel had passed on, but Caroline was determined to keep her mother's worldly wisdom alive and kicking. So she laid it down with Luke at the very outset that all-the-way intercourse before the matrimonial knot had been securely tied was just out. Petting was in, as long as he knew when to stop, and the time to stop was when she told him to stop. The message was clear enough, but, unlike most other messages, this particular kind of message can lose a great deal in actual translation. Once, while the petting was heavier than usual, Luke felt obliged to put the message too far to the back of his mind; he was just a mite too feisty on that occasion and Caroline had to stop the speeding locomotive with a screech of the brakes – and this caused a rift which, thankfully, was patched up when Luke had finally cooled off.

Well, Caroline being what she was, and men being what they are, it stood to reason that animal passions would rise, like a red flame licking a barrel of dynamite tied up in a tall tree. But Caroline stood firm and in so doing had set the tone for future relations, one which might be rendered as 'I'll wear the trousers!' So the flame found its way home again, grudgingly waiting for the day when it could blast that barrel sky-high. During their courtship, Caroline's virginity kept Luke on a leash; she kept herself mysterious and made him wait, turning his passion to her own advantage and validating the principle she had so brilliantly imbibed from her mother. She sure as hell knew how to take advice.

***

So the wedding was never called off, and the big day arrived.

Bride and bridegroom looked no worse for waiting, and Luke was now in full possession of his MBA summa cum laude, though it made no visible difference to his appearance. Poor Emma looked as simple on the outside as she was on the inside, despite all her attempts to look special; in the company of Bobby Hayward and friends, she was just out-gunned. Ed would have choked on a tuxedo and stiff collar; Emma imagined what Ed would have done on getting home from the event – he would have ripped off everything with a moan and a groan, yet another act of defiance. Emma had seen Paul Robeson do that in an old movie, and when she told Ed about it, Robeson instantly became his hero. Bobby had arranged everything with a customary eye for detail. Emma cried in church. Bobby didn't. Then Emma stayed an uncomfortable night at Hayward's place, making the journey home next morning, after seeing off the newlyweds who were zooming off to Paris, France, for their honeymoon, courtesy of Bobby. Everything had gone off quick, smooth and very business-like. Emma was happy to get home, for home is where the heart is – her heart sure wasn't in Billings with the Haywards. Her own humble abode couldn't compare with the luxuries she had seen at Billings, anymore than the wedding could with her own, back in the day when getting hitched to Ed on a shoestring seemed nevertheless a surer thing than more sumptuous affairs with which she and Ed could never have competed either then or now. She wished the very best for Luke and Caroline – for Luke, especially, who had now taken one more gigantic step away from his origins and towards the bright white lights of assimilation. Luke was hitched to a white girl!

And as for the jobs that awaited Luke and Caroline on their return from the first flush of connubial bliss, Bobby had more than a hand in arranging them, too. Hayward wasn't the type to buy a pig in a poke; he believed in hedging his bets to the fullest possible extent. This explains why he made no real effort to find places for the two lovebirds in his own company. His idea was to test their mettle elsewhere. If they succeeded, he would feel a great deal better about giving them positions in which they had a very personal, family stake, the assumption being that if you worked hard for strangers you would work much harder for yourself. By the same token, if they didn't do well working for others, they might find an incentive working for him and therefore for themselves, in a situation where they had very personal ties. Neither Luke nor Caroline were entirely happy with this arrangement, and, in all fairness, Hayward's reasoning was a mite convoluted and far from evident but at least they were comforted with the thought that things would eventually turn out for the best and that they would one day soon be ecstatically welcomed through the portals of Hayward, Inc.

Anyhow, Luke was given a lower management position in a large and leading men's apparel corporation. Here he could feel his feet in the real world in a position that might lead skyward provided he played his part well and 'produced the goods' or, better, helped others to produce them. His MBA had given him a broad base as a starting position, and he saw himself as a marketer. So, there it was. In time all things might be possible, but right now he must prove his real worth – so said Joe Shapiro, his immediate boss and a close friend of Hayward's, and Jo should know, having sunk his life, and the lives of others besides, in Keever Brothers, Inc. 'Satisfy the Old Man,' said Joe, pointing to the ceiling which formed the floor which prevented the Old Man from falling down on top of him. 'Satisfy the Old Man, and there's nothing between you and...' Joe was interrupted by a hurried message on the intercom, from the very same elderly gentleman upstairs, to move his posterior in that direction pretty fast. Well, Joe was a fast mover when he had to be. He had acquired other skills, too. He could handle two, sometimes even three, phone calls and down a plastic plate of hot dogs and french fries all at one and the same time. It could not have been said therefore that his dedication to Keever Brothers, Inc. had proved fruitless.

As for Caroline, Hayward found her a job on the sub-editorial staff of a woman's magazine. He told her he wanted her to cultivate independence of mind and money. He was preaching to the converted, and well he knew it. She didn't believe in doing anything by halves, and she had a mind of her own, which she had already made up. Marriage, for instance. Well, a marriage without children, she decided, was like an experiment stopped halfway. She would have a child – only one, though. 'Daddy, I can raise a family and work at the same time!' That she could – especially if Daddy could dig a little deeper into his pockets and provide a nanny. The idea of a nanny was most appealing, evoking strains from The Sound of Music and Mary Poppins. A nanny was more than a person. It was a status symbol. She knew of some people who had employed English butlers. A nanny was about as English, and therefore as cute, as you could get. Bobby had nothing to say to the contrary, so it was a done deal. The more tedious, routine and objectionable work of bringing up a child could therefore be left to someone else. In like manner, the household chores could be left to others, courtesy again of the father, while for Caroline was reserved the more appropriate task of refining the décor of their new home, when she was at home, and pursuing her temporary career on the magazine when she was not. It must be pointed out that Caroline's staunch independence of mind did not extend to the refusal of golden gifts presented on golden platters – she would accept all the help that Bobby was pleased to give her.

So, offspring didn't have to wait, but could spring off the marital tree at the very time of planting. Caroline craved work experience, but craved it with discretion. She could have the experience of producing a child, without the inconvenience of bringing it up; she could experience running a home without the drudgery that is the common lot of womankind. She would be able to do these things and at the same time keep herself mysterious in the eyes of both husband and child, amply following her mother's sound advice. Meanwhile, she would be in a position to pass on this wisdom through the pages of a magazine should the opportunity ever present itself, and she felt sure it would. So, Caroline was all set to be a most rounded woman and a 'total experience' in her own right.

Where would the couple live? Bobby was at pains to convey the eternal truth that rented apartments were a bad investment. So, they would live in a small house on the outskirts of Billings bought with what Bobby smilingly called a 'loan' from his good self. The place was a picture – or so Emma thought when a picture of the frontage appeared unexpectedly in the mail one morning. The envelope contained no letter, only the picture with 'This is our place! – Love, Caroline and Luke' written on the back. These were Luke's words, but he had already begun the noble practice of putting Caroline's name first. The house was located in a quiet, respectable neighbourhood, because nothing less would have done, with a prim front garden and driveway, and with plenty of space to the rear for a grassy barbecue, or just stretching out on lazy Sundays, or even romps with an infant whenever circumstances permitted or inclinations suggested. It all seemed very appealingly quaint and English – only on a somewhat larger scale, which gave it its American twist.

***

Time passed quickly, chiefly because it was indecently ignored. Baby Benson slipped into the world on just one of those lazy Sundays while everyone else was stretched out. They, that is Caroline, named him John Henry, after his great grandfather on his mother's side. Luke had suggested the inclusion of 'Edward', but even he had to agree that 'Edward John Henry' or 'John Edward Henry' or 'John Henry Edward' struck a somewhat discordant note, so 'Edward' was dropped altogether without so much as a whimper of protest, not that Ed would have minded that much. So, John Henry Hayward it was, and he was known throughout his life as John Henry.

Caroline's mother had been the favourite child of the original John Henry, and Rachel had idolised him on account of it. In calling her offspring John Henry, Caroline was pleasing the dead and indulging the living, for Caroline herself idolised whomsoever her mother had idolised, and Bobby idolised his daughter – or at any rate made out he did. Everyone in this little circle of satisfaction was included, except Luke, who stood beyond its perimeters like an outsider; though he might have consoled himself with the thought that it was in his own interests to keep everyone as sweet as possible about as many things as possible for as much of the time as possible.

As we might have expected, the birth of John Henry was greeted by the Reverend Jeremiah Bate with characteristic zeal and spirituality. Emma had informed him of the glorious event, just as she had informed him of Luke's betrothal and subsequent marriage, and just as she had shown him the picture of their house outside Billings.

And it was Emma who suggested that Reverend Bate might perform the baptism of the little man and make the journey from Rapid City to Billings for the very purpose. Well,Caroline thought that having that rustic and eccentric figure perform the ceremony would be a quaint experience worth the time and effort to see it through. Even so, she wanted the babe immersed twice, once by Jeremiah Bate in Rapid City and once again by Reverend John Casey in Billings, Reverend Casey being a more stolid and, she thought, more representative vicar of the church than she imagined Jeremiah Bate to be. In this, as in so many things, she showed herself to be a chip off the old block; even in the world of the spirit she was hedging her bets, just like Daddy Hayward, and leaving as little as possible to mere chance; John Henry would be twice-blessed and his chances of entering heaven doubled – all thanks to his doting mother who, he would be able to say, was steeped in far-sightedness. Yes, Caroline never did anything by halves.

She needn't have worried too much about the sufficiency of the baptismal rites performed by Jeremiah Bate, for his zeal when he came to perform them can hardly be imagined. It was for him the climax of an almost unbearably long period of self-inflicted spiritual joy. If there was any moment in his life when that God-fearing man might have sprouted wings and flown heavenward in a cloud of ecstasy in the service of the Almighty, it was then. How he managed to conceal his elation as well as he did is one of the wonders of the world; as it was, he beamed, he positively glowed.

Whatever sort of creature he was finally to become, John Henry was at that moment a small, helpless being who was taken into the hands of Jeremiah as though he were the infant Jesus himself. As Jeremiah looked John Henry over and wetted his head, memories came flooding back of another helpless babe who had a long time ago been given up to the snow before he was given into the hands of Reverend Bate and baptised Luke Benson.

But this baptism eclipsed the first, for what the Reverend now saw in his hands was the final outcome of his cherished experiment. In his hands now was red-white Assimilation incarnate, solid proof and testimony that even the impossible could, with sufficient Christian dedication, be accomplished to perfection. Why, so complete was the process that the very concept of assimilation was swallowed up in its own realisation. When he spoke the words of baptism, it was as though the good Reverend was presiding over the coming-into-being of the great and solemn oneness of humanity, for who could look at little John Henry and see anything but an all-American product designed for an all-American market in an all-American world. The sheer whiteness of it all was blinding. This was just the kind of Manifest Destiny that could be justly defended.

Naturally, Caroline and Luke, standing close by, couldn't possibly have guessed why the good Reverend seemed so affected by the whole event; they both attributed his glowing countenance and the zeal of his oration to his natural bent for eccentricity. 'Brethren!' announced the Reverend, lifting both arms towards the wooden beams of the little church, 'Brethren! As this child comes to the Lord, I am bound to say, we are all the instruments of Divine Purpose!' These words meant as little to John Henry's parents as they did then or, for that matter, at any future time, to John Henry himself. But, slightly inclining his head, as if bowing before the eminence of Divine Providence itself, the Reverend cast a special eye towards Emma, who smiled knowingly in return.

6
Pride of Place

'I shall not see the sun go down behind the hills tonight.'

Bloody Knife, Sioux: Thamila Wewe, Arikara: NeesiRAHpat, Scout, 7th US Cavalry, 1876

~ ~ ~

As he got well into the whole business of settling down with Caroline, of making his mark in his job and of obtaining the wherewithal to bring up a family, Luke's thoughts had increasingly less to do with Emma. For all practical purposes, she began to join Ed, first as a creature on the periphery of things, then as a phenomenon of the past, becoming ever more vague, until at last, short of actually joining Ed in his grave, she was becoming a faint semblance of reality, a shadow on the wall of Plato's cave, a philosophical construction of which Simon Westgate used to make so much and Luke himself so little.

There was nothing either unique or very unnatural about this kind of drifting apart. It happens often enough. And, indeed, nothing could be more fitting than that the Eagle of Assimilation should stretch its wings to their fullest extent and finally fly its nest, becoming a creature in its own right, unencumbered by feelings of filial obligation, freed at last from the apron strings of dependency, able to stand on its own, proud and distinct, just like any other creature fortunate enough to have been born and bred in the Land of the Free. A bird that refuses to leave the nest will die, but Luke was determined to live. These were the very sentiments of the Reverend Jeremiah Bate, as he sat sipping Emma's coffee and inwardly wishing it was something infinitely stronger. These words of comfort and hope, a fitting response to Emma's now solitary and lonely existence, seemed straight and true enough, and all the more so because they flowed from the lips of one who now wore a much longer white beard, a sure symbol of authority and sagacity. 'Y'see, Emma,' Bate declared. 'It was kinda... kinda ordained! Y'know,' and here he became more animated, shifting his posture, 'as though you were another Mary, bringing a boy-child into the world for some greater purpose than, well, mere family ties! Why sure, and for a purpose which we hardly know our own selves. So, it's as though you were a kinda vehicle. Yes sir, that's the word – a vehicle of the Almighty!' – so adding yet another catchword to his litany of mantras .

Lord knows what the good reverend might have said under the influence of something infinitely stronger. Of course, Emma hadn't really brought Luke into the world at all, but she let it pass – because she felt that it was as though she had. As it was, he had said quite enough. And when he graciously took his leave Emma felt all the better for his having done so. She returned to her remorseless knitting, with thoughts of her own.

The fact is, and as Ed had remarked on one occasion, the Sioux had always respected parenthood. True, they might separate and travel considerable distances from their villages, to hunt, to kill, or just to see what was behind yonder hill, but they were mighty possessive and protective as far as their kinfolk were concerned. So, if a big white chief like 'Little Phil' Sheridan or 'General' George Armstrong Custer threatened a red village head-on, as it were, well, the whole game was up. Red men would rather surrender than see their families endangered and slain, for no Sioux warrior worthy of the name would risk injury to his kin, much less their lives if it could be at all avoided. He would kill to prevent the risk taking place, and he would kill to avenge the death of loved ones, but he would surrender rather than see his village wiped out. That's what Ed said – and he said he had read it somewhere, not being an authority on such matters himself. Men like 'Little Phil' knew that once a red village was taken the battle would be won, and the red men would come in like lame dogs, afraid lest the whites exacted revenge on their helpless kin. According to Ed, Sioux warriors might seem as macho as anyone can get, but when it came to family ties, or even the deep bonds of friendship, there was nothing to compare with them for dedication, loyalty or, if need-be, self-sacrifice.

So, why was Emma neglected? The Reverend had given an answer, but it didn't satisfy Emma. There's nothing like feelings when the chips are down, and no amount of words, even from a preacher, even a preacher with a long white beard, makes a dime's worth of difference. The thought came to her again and again that she wasn't Luke's biological mother; she had held him in trust, so to speak – well, really just as the Reverend had said. Well, perhaps that explained things after all. If she had been his blood mother, or was it just that the Reverend's 'experiment' had been too darned successful and Luke was no longer red at all, and so everything Ed had said about loyalties and family ties just didn't apply? But even white people know the meaning of such things, so why?

Emma was confused. Losing Ed had been so hard. Losing Luke should have been easier. But it wasn't. She found herself poring over the picture album, which, for the most part, meant scrutinising pictures of Ed, as though she was trying to communicate with him and trying to understand what it was she and Ed had accomplished by adopting Luke at all. She also wondered what she and Ed had had in common, for Luke had somehow held them together, and what had held them together wasn't that easy to understand anymore.

While Emma spent her tortuous evenings alone, and while she bent over her routine chores in darkness and in light, Luke slowly but surely climbed the proverbial ladder of success, one rung after another – which is to say, he succeeded in satisfying the Old Man Upstairs.

The Old Man was mightily pleased with the commendations Luke received from his colleagues and betters. But it must be said that luck played a large part in the unfolding of Luke's fortunes. His boss Joe Shapiro had himself satisfied the Old Man so well that he had at last been awarded 'unstable angina' to add to his peptic ulcer, a condition sufficiently serious to merit the accolade of early retirement, which, at 63, was not nearly as early as the beneficiary might have wished. Joe was already too washed out to enjoy retirement, especially retirement on a shoestring; he had been burned out for years, and it was his persistent pretence to the contrary that was finally getting the better of him and finishing him off. Pretence is a game more than one can play, so he was given a gold wristwatch in gratitude for his services.

On account of this dubious stroke of luck, Luke stepped smartly into Joe's job and sat behind Joe's desk as though it had been waiting for him all along. He was slow to learn that promotion at Keever Brothers meant more real work for less real pay, but promotion is promotion, and doing well at Keever Brothers stood him in good stead for a more lucrative and challenging position with Hayward further down the line, not that the idea of being taken into the family firm was all that attractive. He was making strides where he was and was content with that. What mattered was to keep the Old Man happy and keep on climbing, for there was something very pleasing about that. Luke respected the Old Man, admired him, not to say viewed him with awe – because everyone did, whether or not such feelings were well-founded. As for the inescapable fact that promotion implied more real work for less real pay – well, what's new? Luke was content therefore to devote himself to the consolidation and advancement of those conditions necessary for the maintenance and welfare of his family. But he was not the kind of father to John Henry that Ed had been to him. There was no eccentric ramblings over fields and hills, partly because there weren't any to speak of in the vicinity, but mainly because the idea hardly ever entered Luke's head, or, when it did, it failed to find a warm welcome there. Luke was just an all-too-busy provider. He was happy to bring his work home with him, sitting with it into the small hours; he would never question the rightness of that, never draw up a mental balance sheet to determine on which side it should be listed. His golden rule was never to take domestic issues to the office, yet he never hesitated to take work issues home. Things were not so fine and dandy. He began to be sullen and irritable, but never could understand why, being too busy to pay such things any mind. A sense of humour might have helped, but none of Ed's eccentricities had rubbed off on Luke. If pictures of Ed belied the man, Luke looked every bit what he was: a smart, good-looking young executive who had already come far in a short time and was destined to attain to even greater heights in the years ahead. Ed had been a model of eccentricity; Luke was a model of successful mediocrity, and therefore an embodiment of the American Dream.

Luke's mediocrity rubbed off on John Henry. The boy was totally run-of-the-mill and possessed as much eccentricity as a bar of candy. The child was a 'perfectionist', of sorts; if things didn't work first time they were discarded, if he didn't understand things first time he decided they weren't worth the effort. So he was pretty unexceptional except that he became, like his father, more irritable and sullen than most kids, as though he enjoyed aping his father, or as though his father's place on the ladder was somewhere worth getting to and required the cultivation of a moody and querulous disposition.It must have been somewhere around this point that John Henry was developing the skills that would later stand him in good stead in the world of business and commerce, by consolidating his brand of perfectionism. Despite Luke's later and belated attempts to reverse the trend, John Henry managed to retain the worst from his childhood and channel it into more adult forms of expression and was in consequence destined to become more feared than revered. As an adult, and in the years that would take us far beyond this present narrative into unchartered and unwelcome waters, John Henry was to acquire a reputation for business acumen and razor-sharp judgment, and become a man who would demand no less than complete loyalty and total commitment unto death from all those who served him, including the wives of his top executive directors. Those who failed to 'produce the goods' first time were summarily dismissed as a waste of space, and those who failed to understand first time weren't worth the effort to educate. Yes, compared with John Henry, the Old Man Upstairs was the Angel Gabriel, albeit a Gabriel permanently out of sorts.

Luke's visits to Emma during the first fleeting years of John Henry's childhood were few and far between. More often than not, when John Henry was halfway to his teens, he would accompany his father and play about in Emma's green patches, if annihilating ants with lightning jabs of his forefinger and administering the death sentence on snails with slabs of stone can be called 'playing about'. But boys will be boys, and Emma was mightily comforted by this well-worn tautology. Luke, with Emma's help, had learned the importance of studious application, and now he was encouraging John Henry to follow suit, with results that would eventually turn out all too fruitful. Study-wise, Luke seemed a hard act to follow, and Emma was just pleased to have John Henry around at all; but between them they must have got through to John Henry concerning the importance of study. Had John Henry been able to visit Emma more often and stay longer, who knows? He might have turned out milder and kinder and not just good at getting high grades. As it was, visits to his grandmother were confined chiefly to her garden, to the bitter regret of ants and snails, while somewhere in the background he might hear the occasional complimentary muttering from her concerning his schooling. 'He'll do fine,' she would say. 'Don't force him, Luke.' 'You forced me, Ma!' 'Yes, well, that was different. No, let him be, Luke. He'll be fine.' She was right. Forced or not, John Henry was destined for great things – but that's another story.

There were times when little John Henry actually felt he could get to like his grandma, and perhaps get to like her more than he liked anyone else. But visits had to be short and sweet, or so his father would say, so maybe John Henry was forced to impose the death penalty on his budding feelings before they grew into something more unmanageable. Visits to Emma were a kind of routine obligation, maybe for Luke and John Henry, the only sweetener for John Henry being that he could hunt snails and ants and kill at will. As for Emma, she would stand at the low wooden gate where the garden met the dusty road, while Luke and John Henry got into the car. 'Mind you come an' visit again soon!' Emma would shout, blowing a kiss to John Henry, who barely managed even a perfunctory smile in return, while Luke waved a hand briskly before turning the key in the ignition. Her words died on her lips even as the car door closed; it's doubtful whether Emma's acute loneliness was assuaged by these visits, serving as they did to accentuate it after Luke and John Henry had left. They became fewer and shorter, like sparks from dying embers.

'Be assured, brethren,' Reverend Bate told his small, humble congregation one Sunday morning. 'The Almighty bids us play our part, and it behoves us to play that part without question or remorse; all things that come to be will pass away, and it's no business of ours to question the purpose of the Lord.' Emma took no comfort whatsoever from these kind and profound sentiments – so profound indeed that no one, including the good Reverend Jeremiah Bate himself, could make either head or tail of them.

Meanwhile, during the early and so-called 'formative' years of John Henry's development, Caroline made her own mark by becoming sub-editor of her magazine, a publication which prided itself on feminine self-assertiveness, a concept which most red women would have found hard to grasp, not because they were hopelessly downtrodden and servile but precisely because they were otherwise – and so there was precious little 'issue' to confront, no 'cause' to champion. Some tribes were even matriarchal, but in every tribe the role of women, though different from men, was essential for survival and commanded the highest respect. But Caroline would no doubt have had the same kind of trouble understanding red women as they would have had understanding her.

In any case, the status of red women was not a subject that she ever called to mind. That said, she made great strides as a sub-editor of her noble publication, but it was not the only thing that benefited from her great strength of character. The marital home was also to feel her weight and prestige. Luke had left domestic matters to her, or, better to say, Luke had never been invited to take part in the decision-making concerning choice of décor, of ornamentation, or the colour and pattern of drapes, and such like. She did ask him the occasional question, 'What d'you think, Luke?' – but they were protocol only, just prefatory to her own statement of choice, which was final. She had no intention of waiting for an answer, let alone being guided by it. Caroline had no more idea of give-and-take than the average employer has of genuine consultation with his labour force. It got worse as time went by. First, the perfunctory question, 'What d'you think, Luke?' came only after things had got irretrievably done, and then the protocol was dispensed with altogether, cursory questions disappearing completely. The pretence of genuine consultation gave way to the reality of self-initiative, things getting done without reference to Luke at all, as if to say, 'Well, this is how things are, like it or lump it.' Things did not get done to escape comment, though. Not at all. They were done with an eye to their being irresistible conversation pieces between guests, and guests were arriving more frequently and numerously as time went on.

As Luke began to make his way inexorably up the ladder, the house with which they had started out gave way to a bigger and finer one, in a bigger and finer locality. Caroline flatly refused to move in until all the décor had been altered to her satisfaction, a process that she would personally oversee, and this entailed a small army of decorators and paper-hangers temporarily filling the premises. Then, after moving in, she would install the bits and pieces, which consisted largely of paintings and objets d'art from as wide a field as possible: Japanese ceramics, early-English reproduction furniture, Chinese and Persian rugs, and the odd Grecian urn strategically placed to produce the maximum effect, that effect depending as much on how and where things were placed as on what they actually were.

The effect was indeed intriguing and could hardly fail to impress even the most indifferent of observers – which was of course the raison d'etre of the whole exercise. Hat stands and statuettes would change position; what Luke saw in one corner on Monday would magically reappear in the opposite corner by midweek, while pictures would disappear from one wall to reappear on another, causing the unwary to feel temporarily unbalanced, even to the point of consulting their best friend or analyst, whichever was closer to hand. In order to collect the pieces for this fascinating exercise and to provide a satisfactory turnover of items for the sake of variety, Caroline would make regular downtown excursions to antique or oddment stores, and what could not be bought on the spot would be ordered forthwith. What she could buy there and then she would have sent up to the house. The interval between buying and receiving, and indeed the very act of moving from one house to another, gave her an excellent opportunity to practise and refine the art of achieving maximum effect.

Her collection of display items was a significant variable since, in the move, or on inexplicable impulse, she would discard whatever she had come to consider third-rate, and buy afresh; it was a kind of hobby, and one she couldn't shake off. She would have accepted this judgment – but not if you called it an 'obsession', for that would have rattled her cage and put you inside one. It was just after one of these moves into something bigger and better that an addition to her collectables was made that would function as a catalyst for a life-changing series of events.

First, it was arranged that the Old Man Upstairs and his wife would be coming to dinner. That was not all. As if the sheer presence of that great man was not enough, he declared that he would be bringing a present, something special, for Luke's good lady wife. Luke had mentioned her passion for interesting bits and pieces, and the Old Man said he'd had just the thing but hadn't let on to Luke what it was.

'Just the thing' turned out to be an early print of Otto Becker's lithograph of Custer's Last Stand. The original lithograph had been completed in 1895, and it was just as well that this was an early print and not a much later one, and just as well that the frame was older than the print and worth possessing in its own right; otherwise it might not have lasted very long among Caroline's collectables, or it might not have been given pride of place. For the fact is that Becker's depiction of the Last Stand is as commonplace and as American as apple pie, over-sweet apple pie at that. Copies of the print had hung in about half the saloons of the United States; it had advertised beer, decorated table mats and sweatshirts – in short, it was extremely popular, a fact which, in Caroline's by now expert discernment, stood very much against it. The Old Man might just as well have brought a picture of the Empire State Building and expected Caroline to fall into a stupor of enthusiasm and artistic appreciation. As it was, the age of the print and its fine frame saved it from premature disposal.

Of course, it shouldn't have mattered what the Old Man brought with him. The fact that he saw fit to bring anything at all was itself noteworthy. You just didn't look a gift horse in the mouth, especially if it had the features of the Old Man Upstairs. It was remarkable that he had accepted the invitation to dinner in the first place; it was the Bensons who should be bestowing gifts, since his presence was a gift in its own right. But, a present? Why, had Caroline kept a diary, and had she been born a century earlier she might well have done so, she would have carefully recorded the fact and in her very best hand. As it was, a few words of gratitude would have to suffice.

So, there it was. Becker's portrayal of Custer's Last Stand.

'Belonged to my father. Every house in the country should have one. Been in the attic all this time, gathering dust. A crime! Our walls are too crowded already. Thought you might like it,' declared the Old Man, who tended to speak in sentences devoid of their subject pronouns – perhaps a time-saving device, for time is money. 'Needs a good clean, though – frame too.'

Caroline was speechless, and said so – proving she wasn't. She thought much more of the frame than the picture, but couldn't say as much. She had to put up with it. Had she had a free hand, she might have replaced the picture and kept the frame. But who knew when the Old Man might condescend to call in on them again? She dared not change the picture. Feminine self-assertion, powerful though it was, dared not go so far. As common decency, or at least acceptable protocol, demanded, Luke and Caroline rested the heavy frame against the back of a large chair, and then stepped back to get a good, long view. The Old Man was gratified that his gift had been so well received.

Caroline's eyes skirted from the picture to the frame. Luke looked hard at the picture itself.

Becker's imagination depicted a battle scene which, like all such depictions, was far from the mark and more than a step or two from reality. Becker's Custer wielded a sabre, though history tells us no one carried one in that particular fight. Sabres were heavy and cumbersome, and they rattled on the march and might give the game away; they had been stored in boxes at the Yellowstone River. Becker has Custer standing in the geometrical centre of the picture, and Hollywood was later to follow suit in movie after movie, until it was safe to entertain alternative possibilities. The truth is still undecided and may never be known, but it is possible, according to some red accounts, that Custer was killed earlier, when he attempted to cross the Little Bighorn river in his assault on the red village. Becker surrounded Custer with red warriors, though, surprisingly, they are sufficiently obliging to give us a full and clear view of the hero, standing tall in a buckskin jacket, despite the fact that Custer had no doubt taken it off and rolled it behind his saddle bags, for Sunday, 25 June 1876, was a real burner – so much so that some cavalrymen, including Major Reno, had bought themselves straw hats back at the Yellowstone. Becker's Custer has long hair, and one of the names given him by red men was 'Long Hair', among others less flattering, yet Custer had his hair cut short before the battle. As an additional touch of unreality, Becker's Sioux and Cheyenne look more like Aztecs and Zulus and wield weapons unknown to the red men of the Plains. Becker's depiction therefore owes more to imagination than to fact, but Custer's destruction at the hands of those who were regarded as primitive barbarians required a heavy counterweight. He was hailed as a national hero and an embodiment of courage and tenacity; the country sought victory in defeat, especially since 1876 was the centenary celebration of Independence from the English Yoke. The country was in no mood for defeat and depression; somehow the Doctrine of Manifest Destiny had to be saved from the ashes of its own demise and rise like a phoenix to reassert itself anew. 'Little Phil' Sheridan's 'The only good Indian is a dead Indian' also found new and unbounded application, since after the battle all red men were fair game, whether Sioux or Cheyenne or anything else, and whether or not they had taken part in the fight at all.

Though it failed to satisfy the canons of historical veracity, Becker's lithograph gave some sense of the heat and unspeakable fear of battle and impending death. In this fight, Major Reno lost his head figuratively and was hardly capable of command. Bloody Knife, said to be Custer's favourite scout, lost his literally, and accounts have it that some cavalrymen surrendered their rifles up to red warriors but were killed anyway, while some others hid their heads under horse blankets, like children having bad dreams, and as though that would make them invisible or prevent their heads being cracked and their scalps taken. Red warriors took no prisoners that day. Maybe one red warrior stood out from the rest, his temper so inflamed that he fought like a man possessed. Yes, Gall (Pisi), a chief of the Hunkpapa Sioux, killed all his enemies with an axe that day, for the soldiers had already depleted his family with their carbines in the first assault. Gall had the physical stature of a grizzly bear, but his anger was shared by all red men. It was justly said that the Little Bighorn was as much the red man's last stand as it was Custer's; they had been pushed beyond endurance and would be pushed no more.

These were facts that Luke would come to know much better, but right now he looked hard at the picture, while Caroline silently assessed the value of the frame, at the same time adroitly conveying the impression that she was taking both frame and picture into account.

The Old Man, more respectfully known as William Keever Junior, glanced at the picture, then at the recipients, and was the first to break the silence. 'Yes, well, as I said, every good American home should have one!' This was said in no uncertain terms, which meant that it was time to put protocol and artistic appreciation aside and get down to the more urgent and satisfying business of dining. During dinner there were of course fairly regular references to the print, which would call forth from the Old Man remarks about America's 'fighting spirit' which, and here he attempted a joke, should be bottled and sold to countries which were not doing enough to maintain universal law and order and leaving everything to good old Uncle Sam; this commodity, he said, was not so much in evidence these days. 'If it was, profits wouldn't be so low and juvenile delinquency so high! What say you, Luke?' 'Oh, true, sir, yes, very true!' Luke's response was spontaneous and robotic. Truth was, he was still ruminating on Becker's lithograph, which seemed indelibly imprinted on the tabula rasa of his mind.

After dinner, the Old Man repeated his views, varying only in syntax and expletives, as he puffed on a monstrous cigar and with an occasional 'Humpf!' to ram his point home. Luke inferred that should the day ever dawn when his own fighting spirit was found wanting, he would feel the wrath of the Almighty in the shape of the Old Man. It would have been treading mighty thin ice to observe that for all Custer's fighting spirit, indeed because of it, he had lost the battle, losing his own life and that of many others despite the warnings given him by Bloody Knife, who knew better than anyone else what the outcome would be. Luke wisely kept such thoughts very much to himself. A contest with the Old Man on such matters would have been inappropriate. Besides, like most aging minor magnates, William Keever Junior was obsessed with the past, bored with the present, and fearful of the future.

'You should go,' said the Old Man, between puffs.

'I'm sorry?'

'The Custer Memorial – the battle site. You should go. Take young John Henry there!'

'Yes, Yes, I will. 'Had Luke known, he might have pointed out that while there were headstones marking the site of fallen cavalrymen, there was nothing to indicate the losses suffered by their adversaries; a visit to the battlefield and the Custer museum was an exclusively white experience, an imbalance that wasn't made good until many years later. But again, such a contest with the Old Man would have proved inappropriate – and very unwise.

***

Caroline not only kept the picture in its frame, she also found pride of place for it, between and above two large oriental vases which stood either end of the mantelpiece of a large mock-marble fireplace in the living room. As time went by, she even grew attached to it, a change of heart which probably owed something to the fact that, try as she might, she could neither discard it nor find a better place for it. It hung there in full and obvious view. She counted it among her most successful acquisitions; it was one of the most important conversational pieces, largely because she felt constrained to justify its existence to guests who were too polite to ask for a justification at first sight. So the picture continued to dominate the living room, like a loud, intoxicated guest.

7

A Key Witness

'The wife or mother, good or bad, is an individual significant by her individuality.'

J.L. Stocks, *Morality and Purpose*

~ ~ ~

About two years later, Becker's lithograph still stood on the mantelpiece, though the oriental vases had been replaced by tall, antique brass candlesticks, and they, in their turn, had given way to small statuettes of ancient Greek poets. Unexpectedly and uncharacteristically, Becker's work seemed to have taken up permanent residence.

It was then that news about Emma arrived. On Luke's last visit Emma had complained of headaches and excessive tiredness, but she had mentioned it casually, because she tended to brush all such matters aside perhaps in the hope that in so doing they would disappear of their own accord. Ed had never been one to complain; maybe she thought she should follow suit. Luke, himself seemingly impervious to the adverse effects of round-the-clock dedication to the Commercial Principle, the maximization of profit and the minimization of loss, was not predisposed to sympathise with Emma, and failed to question whether her complaint was understated.

The truth was that Emma had never recovered from Ed's demise. The notion of 'closure' was not something she would have understood. When people grow together so far and so deep that they become inseparable, so that life without each other is inconceivable, then one can't be taken without doing irreversible damage to the other, much like two trees whose roots are not only intertwined but have grown into each other and become single strands – uprooting the one will cause the other to shrivel and die. Ed was irreplaceable and unforgettable – or, to put it more simply, Ed was Ed.

Emma had had Luke to look after, and then there were the household chores, and she dedicated herself to them to a degree to which the casual observer would rightly consider well over the top. Particularly after Luke's departure to Billings, she attempted to assuage her anguish and loneliness in a superfluity of dusting and polishing and knitting. She would dust and polish over and over, and sit up nights knitting with a frenzy that had to be seen to be believed, and she polished the small dining table so much that it finally refused to take any more punishment and developed a matt surface as if in protest. Despite all the energy this pattern of behaviour required, she slept badly if at all. She would lie awake feeling her heart beating, as though she were in mortal fear, though she couldn't say for the life of her what it was that caused her to feel afraid. There she would lie, fearful, apparently over nothing at all, waiting for the morning light, when she would start her chores all over again, whether or not they needed to be done.Sometimes she would feel pressed to get up and wander from room to room in darkness until it was light enough to dress and begin the day. What she did, she did repeatedly; what she thought, she thought repeatedly. In the sameness there was both comfort and nausea. It seems strange that she should despise genuine necessity in a life so boringly repetitive, but she did. Every little thing that went wrong or needed attention, like a creaking door or a flaking window frame or a shower that dripped, was just too big to contemplate, though Emma herself had been more than capable of fixing such things herself when Ed was alive, or of exasperating the man with her advice in his own attempts to put things right. But now, when things went wrong, Emma thought it was near the end of the world and the smallest hitches occasioned in her morbid reflections about how different things would be were Ed alive to fix them.

Luke might have helped her out in all sorts of ways had he not gone off to Billings to further his education and advance his prospects, but this thought did not occur to Emma; he had not only gone with a mother's blessing but with her deepest hopes for his permanent and seamless salvation from the deprivation and hopelessness of a life lived on Pine Ridge, from the life of a red man in white America. Having completed his education, Luke might have visited more often and stayed longer each time, but the requirements of his job seemed too demanding. There is one thing he certainly could not have done: he could not have invited Emma to live with him, Caroline and John Henry – this was not a proposition that either Emma or Caroline would have entertained longer than decorum or polite protocol permitted. Even irregular and occasional journeys from Rapid City to Billings were arduous for an elderly lady feeling the effects of age – even if they had been politically desirable, which they were not.The bottom line, always implicit between Emma and Luke, was that Luke had a life of his own to lead; Emma was grateful for that and happier for him than he himself could ever have realised. If Emma was ever apt to wonder whether her gratitude was a mite misplaced, there was always the good Reverend Jeremiah Bate to reassure her with his zealous appeals to the unfathomable designs of Almighty God, designs to which he, Emma and the rest of mankind were, he repeatedly affirmed, merely instrumental.

***

One night, as Luke pored over some cost projections for the year ahead, the phone rang with news that could not be costed so easily. It was Louise, Emma's neighbour and at least ten years her senior, who was anxious to impart the news that Emma had suffered a severe stroke, paralysing her left side and making speech difficult. Louise, who really needed looking after herself, was minding the fort in the expectation that Luke would rush to Emma's side; she said another stroke might be imminent, and fatal. What could be done? The journey to the nearest hospital was too risky, the doctor had said. Not that Emma would have consented to go, as she hated hospitals, especially after Ed had been given his death sentence in one, with no chance of a reprieve.

Luke was quick to realise that the Commercial Principle had somehow and for some time to be set aside. The whole thing needed some thinking about. If Emma needed constant attention, and if hospital was ruled out, someone would just have to do what was necessary. That someone couldn't possibly be Caroline, who was much too busy and hadn't in any case formed a genuinely affectionate attachment to her. No, Caroline had to be ruled out, and a qualified nurse ruled in. Meantime, Luke would need to get to Emma as soon as possible.

Such were his thoughts, which, in the event were like seeds sown on barren ground. Emma suffered her second, and fatal, stroke, just as Luke was en route to her side; he was never to see her alive again. He stood looking down at her face, which he had uncovered, and what he saw was to stick with him burr-like for the rest of his days. It was his first encounter with the death of a loved one, or with death at all, for that matter. It shocked him and it grieved him. He tried hard to feel that the poor lifeless creature lying in that bed was the same wonderful Emma – his mother, his tutor, his guide. Her face was contorted and her eyes had not been closed, and now he could see first-hand what death really meant; he could see what death takes away and the nothingness it leaves behind.

He regretted uncovering her face. He closed her eyes, kissed her forehead gently and covered her up again. He later recalled one of those half-intoxicated lectures Simon Westgate used to give him in off-campus bars, and one of those quotations he was so fond of spitting out, something about the importance of a mother, something about her uniqueness – husbands and wives may come and go, but mothers are unique and too special for words. Even a very bad mother continues to have a claim on her children, like a mortgage her kids never succeed in paying off. But Emma was a good mother – the very best of mothers. Luke's sense of guilt was at last making itself felt, and would go on doing so for the rest of his life; a little less Commercial Principle and a lot more Emma should have been the order of the day. His real priorities were finally taking shape, with a most regrettable belatedness, as is often the case in the world of white men. The words, 'Mind you come and visit me soon!' suddenly took on a new, unsettling and everlasting significance.

As he left what remained of Emma in the semi-darkness of that bedroom, Louise, something of a crone but kindly enough all the same, put an envelope into his hand, with the words, 'She wanted you to have this.' Luke slipped the envelope into his pocket, where it was temporarily forgotten. He was stunned by events and needed to sort things out in his head; the envelope could wait. He didn't stay at Emma's that night, but checked in to a motel on the edge of town. If he could have checked out again early the following morning it would have suited him better, but there were things to arrange: the funeral, first and foremost, and then the disposal of Emma's house and household effects. He felt helpless, unprepared and unqualified, and, above all else, deeply distracted by the image of Emma's lifeless corpse. Anyhow, he busied himself as best he could with all that fell to him to do. At least he was alone and unencumbered, Caroline and John Henry being at home in Billings and therefore in a much better place.

Just three days later, Emma was laid to rest on a hill, in a plot she had already marked out and paid for. It was right beside Ed in a place which could hardly have been quieter six feet under than it was on top; not a sound was there, save for the occasional automobile or truck winding its way in the distance to God knows where on a poor excuse for a road on the flats below. The words over her were read by Jeremiah Bate's successor, the Reverend himself having retired from active service just one year, almost to the day, earlier. A handful of people came to pay their respects, most of them unknown to Luke. The whole thing was fast, smooth, well-ordered and subdued, just as Emma would have wanted. Louise was there, one of the very few Luke was acquainted with, and she herself was to join Emma before many moons had passed.

Maybe it was just too easy. The sheer pace of events seemed also to blur them, and Luke had hardly time to take everything in. Just after speaking to a lawyer, a For Sale sign was hammered in to the ground next the garden gate, and all Emma's furniture, such as it was, was auctioned off locally. 'I'm afraid it's hardly worth the trouble,' the auctioneer had said, after a cursory glance around. Caroline would certainly want none of it, which was just as well, for there was a strong case for pushing everything as far back into the past as possible and leaving it there – as far as that could be done, for as we all come to know, the harder we try to relegate a thing to the past the more it imposes itself upon us, refusing to stay down and lie low.

Emma's personal effects were simple and few: the picture album, and a box of knick-knacks, consisting largely of some fake jewellery, except for a 9ct brooch Ed had bought her as an anniversary present. He would buy her a few cheap things most times, saving up for something better next time round. The gold brooch was something better; it was kept apart from all the fake stuff. Emma had wrapped it up in brown paper when Ed died and put it in a box together with Ed's cherrywood pipe and diaries. Luke remembered the brooch and thought about taking it for Caroline, but she would never have looked after it, probably thinking it to be beneath her and of inferior quality to all her other bits and pieces. So Luke left the brooch where it was.

The box containing Ed's pipe, diaries, and the brooch still wrapped up in brown paper eventually ended up on a bonfire together with some unsaleable bits of furniture, having been opened in a perfunctory manner and thrown there by a young auction attendant thinking it to be rubbish and not fit to auction – he hadn't even bothered to unwrap the brown paper. Luke himself paid no mind to Emma's trinkets. All necessary arrangements concerning her effects and house had been left to the attorney; it was up to the lawyer to sort the wheat from the chaff and since he was told that he would be hard put to find even a single ear of wheat, he didn't even bother to look.

The evening of Emma's funeral, Luke sat in the small living room in Emma's place. He was taking a last look round before getting back to the motel and moving out come morning, leaving Rapid City altogether and intending never to return. He was tired, the place was quiet and the armchair was inviting. As he sat there the past zoomed before him under its own steam, invited or not, ideas stopping of their own accord, lingering and passing on again to make way for others – had Luke been a hard-drinking man he might have tried to blank them all out, but they came rushing in. Emma's funeral had reminded him of Ed's, and Ed reminded him of his childhood and … Well, he reckoned that no one should lose their parents, that losing them was one of the worst things life has to inflict on us all; parents should be set in stone and here for good. One crazy thought followed another in this quiet tempest.

He had to shake his head vigorously to bring this express train, which had gotten out of control, to a final stop. The experience confirmed him in his lifelong conviction that thinking is a dangerous thing and seldom beneficial to health – which reminded him of Simon Westgate. Every philosophy book should carry a government health warning. The thought amused him, and he got up from that old armchair with a smile on his face at last. He moved towards the door. As he did so, his hand slipped into his pocket to check for his keys, which would have to be handed in to the real estate office in the morning.

His hand slipped into the wrong pocket. He pulled out the envelope Louise had given him a few days ago. Now was as good a time as any to look inside, there and then in his mother's place, and then dispose of it or else pass it on to the attorney. Then he could get back to Caroline, John Henry and the Old Man Upstairs. He switched on the table lamp and sat back down in the old armchair, expecting anything other than what he was about to read, for, if Luke's head had been spinning just now, that was nothing at all to the shell-shock he was about to receive. It was a letter from Emma, written in her own and now faltering hand – the same but then steady hand that had taught Luke how to write the letters of the alphabet, long ago, in another world.

To Luke, our dear, dear child,

I'm writing this, Luke, for me and Ed. Ed and me, we knew the time would come. But the time had to be right, Luke. And now it falls to me to speak for the both of us. Just like Ed to leave all the important things to me. Ed loved you, and I know how much I loved him, too. Trouble was, he wanted the world to be much better than it turned out to be. If men were better, politics would be better, but men are what they are, and so politics is what it is. I guess Ed's expectations were way too high. Anyhow, he was such a good man and he'd want to speak to you now and not leave it to me – but the time wasn't right when he was with us. We'll both rest better in our graves for telling you something that maybe should've been said long before now. But maybe it had to wait this long so you'd understand better, so you'd know the truth when knowing it wouldn't do you any harm. I know Ed would agree with me, Luke. I've been speaking to him about this very thing though he's resting in his grave. 'Emma,' he says to me, 'it's high time you put pen to paper before you join me here.' So, there's something you have to know, Luke.

But remember all along, Luke, that you belong to Ed and me. You're our one and only child – as much a part of our flesh and blood as any kin could be. This is true now and always will be. Please remember.

But truth to tell, you weren't ours to start with, Luke. You were given to us when you were newly born. Your parents were Sioux Indians from Pine Ridge. But they died and you were orphaned, and Ed and me, well, we gave you a home, because you were left all alone in the world, and we wanted a child of our own to love and cherish. Ed and me we prayed for it and the Lord God saw fit to answer our prayers. You were the answer to our prayers, Luke. There's a lot Ed and me never got to know, but seems your mother's name was Ruth Plainfeather – but it was a long time ago and my mind's hazy.

Luke, we've loved and cherished you all these years. Now you can stand on your own, equal, no, more than equal, to anyone else on this here God's Earth – Ed and I would like to think we've played some part in that. We prayed to God we taught you right. You're a man now with a family of your own. But Ed and me guessed you'd want to know the truth just as we've had a big hankering to tell it. It isn't right to hold it from you. Well, right or not, something may happen to me pretty soon, and if it does this letter will have to tell all.

Ed and me both love you dearly, Luke, more than words could ever tell. You're our one and only child. Be happy and be good.

Your ever loving parents,

Ed and Emma

PS Reverend Jeremiah Bate knows more.

Luke had just attended his mother's funeral, and this letter told him he hadn't. A sledgehammer could not have delivered a heavier blow. Of all the things Emma could have said, this was the most incredible. She might have said the Earth is square contrary to received opinion, that she and Ed were foreign royalty fallen on hard times, that they were aliens dropped from a far-distant world and forever stranded on Earth, she might have said anything other than what she was really saying, and it would have seemed more likely; she might even have said that black is white – but what she was really saying was that white is red! No, it was absurd. Crazy!.

Naturally, Luke read and re-read the letter. If he could have turned it upside down or read it back to front he would have done so; first he disbelieved it, then he wondered whether it might contain at least a grain of truth, then he wondered whether it might be true lock, stock and barrel, then he dismissed any and every possibility that it might be true, and at length he returned to it. Stunned, he sat looking at that piece of paper as though it had been written in a tongue he could not comprehend – not knowing what to think of it.

If what Emma said was true, or at least true in part, it did seem to make sense of things which had seemed strange in days gone by: the way Emma used to watch him, follow him with her eyes, almost as though she couldn't quite believe what they told her. Ed and Emma used to whisper together sometimes, and he had vaguely felt they were whispering about him, and then there were the times Emma would speak with Reverend Jeremiah Bate – conversations held at some distance, with only partly concealed glances towards himself, which suggested that their mutterings involved him in some way, or that he was some kind of secret. It would make sense of the feeling he had often had that something was being held back. But, no! Impossible! Nonsense! Anyhow, it was very hard, when not impossible, to believe.

Luke even questioned the authorship of the letter. But it was written by Emma's own hand – as far as he could tell; worse than that, it certainly sounded like Emma, and reading it was like listening to her talk. It might be Emma's own hand, but was she in her right mind when she wrote it? Of course she was. Emma knew how to write, and you would need to be sane to concoct a story like that. Emma had become forgetful and the letter itself was a little rambling and repetitive – but there was nothing abnormal about that, and there are reasons for everything. Emma might have been on the road to senile dementia, but she had only taken the first few steps. There was no good reason to doubt her state of mind; the letter was well-ordered and said just about everything that needed to be said if the story were true. But was it in fact true? Simon Westgate, in one of his beer-driven philosophical moods, once put forward a what-if hypothesis: they were now sitting in a bar quietly sipping their drinks, but suppose everything started to rattle backwards and forwards and they found themselves in a train compartment hurtling forward to God knows where. He had asked Luke what his reaction would be. 'Wouldn't you be amazed? Wouldn't you question your own sanity? Wouldn't you wonder what the hell had happened? Well, that's what being a philosopher is like! You see, a philosopher is filled with wonder – how come everything is as it is? Other people take things too much for granted, but the philosopher...' 'Finish your beer, Socrates, and let's get out of here,' was Luke's reply. But now, with Emma's letter in his hands, maybe Luke felt a little of what it must be like to be a philosopher, wondering what everything was and how everything was as it was. He didn't feel he could trust his own name anymore.

All his doubts and questionings were ultimately irrelevant. It was what Luke was beginning to feel that would finally settle the issue in his own mind. The fact is, he was beginning to feel red, at least that he was different. He looked at himself in the long mirror in Emma's bedroom and saw himself in braids and breechclout. Luke had been brought up white, to think white, to feel white, which meant thinking and feeling in stereotype. That train Simon had talked about was well on its way down the track. His world had just turned upside down and inside out.

Feelings are one thing; his mind was still unyielding. Whites don't take easily to this sort of revelation. They don't take to it kindly, either. His white mind still doubted; still sought confirmation of what he had begun to feel. There was now no question of returning to Caroline and John Henry in the morning – leastways, not until this whole thing was cleared up and sorted out, one way or another. And this meant finding the Reverend Jeremiah Bate. If Bate sincerely denied all knowledge of this business, it might just throw some very welcome doubt on poor Emma's fragile state of mind and the fantasy she had entertained when she had put pen to paper. Or it just might, at a pinch, suggest that it was just some kind of crazy hoax or lie – though to what purpose God only knew. Whatever the outcome, he had to seek out Jeremiah Bate before he could move on, if 'moving on' was at all an option.

***

The harsh lights outside the motel did nothing to keep Luke awake that night. He had a surprisingly peaceful night and slept through until the morning, maybe because he had already suffered his nightmares on reading Emma's letter or maybe because he was exhausted. There were no nightmares about Sioux babes being ripped from their mothers' arms, or little red orphans wandering helplessly in the wilderness, changing colour, as they did so, from red to white and back again. His was a sound and dreamless sleep, giving him the kind of night, Simon Westgate might have said, quoting Plato in the Apology, that even the Great King of Persia would have coveted above all others. Even so, he awoke with a thick head, as though he had been on the tiles all night or had tried to out-drink Socrates. The trouble with such a sleep is that you wake up with a sharper realisation of your condition. He woke with a start; his heart was in his mouth, once again finding it impossible to credit what he had read the night before. His nightmare was a waking one and would not let him be.

He knew where Jeremiah Bate lived and made his way there without unnecessary delay. Bate was there, if not quite altogether. His daughter from a late marriage greeted Luke at the door. It turned out that Luke knew where Bate lived better than Bate himself. Emma might have escaped the cruel embraces of senility by passing before it could get a real grip; not so for the Reverend, for the old preacher was already in its grip, which was, said his daughter, tightening day by day. He had, she explained, quick bursts of lucidity, but they were getting even shorter and more infrequent; often he would just fumble about and lose track of what he was saying before he could finish a sentence. Sometimes he even failed to recognise his own daughter. Sometimes his long-term memory seemed intact, but he had problems remembering what he had for breakfast, or even where he was. He was still recognisable by his white beard, which was more unkempt now, but his eyes had a blank look about them, as though he was staring into the distance and seeing nothing. He spent all day in an armchair by the fireside, periodically being fed and medicated before being helped into bed at the end of the day – all this being done by his daughter, since her mother, she said, had already passed. She seemed a prisoner in that house, with little prospect of release any time soon.

So there sat the good Reverend Jeremiah Bate, hunched up in his large armchair. Luke was ushered into the living room by his daughter, who repeated several times to her father that he had a visitor called Luke. He said nothing – just continued to stare ahead.

'Yes, sir. That's right. Name's Luke. Luke Benson.' There was still no response. 'My mother, sir, is Emma, Emma Benson, and she's just...'

'Emma!' the Reverend beamed at the mention of her name, as though he had suddenly come out of some kind of trance, roped up and out of some deep, dark well. Sometimes he would respond squarely to what was said to him, but mostly he seemed to be talking to himself, and then it didn't matter who was there, or whether anyone was there at all.

'She said… she said you might know something about me.'

'Emma! How is that good woman?'

'I'm afraid…'

'A good woman! She's taking care of him, that boy! Yes, sir, she's going to give that boy a future – a white future! Yes, sir, I'll vouch for that good woman!'

'She said…'

'I tell you this – all you who wanna know – that woman … that woman is an instrument of the Almighty. Yes, sir. Saved that child from the snow! Abandoned he was – to die in the snow! And now? Why, if you could see what's become of that child. You'd get down on your knees and praise the Lord. Emma's teaching him letters! Yes, sir, I'll vouch for that woman!'

Then the good Reverend was silent, for what seemed an intolerable length of time. Then he spoke again, in more subdued tones, as though thinking out loud.

'Grief, I guess. Husband dead. Just wanted out. She lay… lay down with child in the snow. Didn't know any better. Bled to death. Emma takes the babe, to teach him letters. Yes, sir, I'll vouch for that woman. I'll, er…'

Bate's voice sank to a low pitch and began to fade away. His eyes closed and he fell asleep. The good Reverend had delivered enough information in staccato fashion to intrigue and frustrate; it couldn't have been more poignant if Luke had stood in front of a smoking machine gun. Nothing more could be got out of the preacher; Luke felt he needed nothing more, or couldn't take any more even if it was coming. Luke muttered a few perfunctory, even frosty, almost incomprehensible, words of thanks to Bate's daughter and then made for the door without further ceremony. Then something extraordinary happened. On reaching the door, Bate shouted out, 'Remember me to Emma, now, d'you hear, stranger!' When Luke turned round, Bate's eyes were still closed, as though those last words had come from unfathomable depths in that dark well of what remained of Bate's consciousness.

Luke left with those last words ringing in his ears. His visit had hardly helped. For how could you accuse a man who was losing his mind of lying? Such a man might be mistaken, but that staccato of his seemed to corroborate the little that Emma had told him. Bate's state of mind confirmed rather than disproved the veracity of Emma's letter. What Luke had wanted was a cold, reasoned rebuttal. It was denied him. Then there was all that stuff about snow and blood and wanting out and abandonment. It was all crazy and horrific. Worse still, it was crazy and horrific enough to have about it the ring of truth. If only

Emma had lived long enough to speak to him face to face. She would be a key witness. But now she was a key witness who could not be brought to the stand.

In these ruminations, Luke was not to know that even if Emma had been able to testify, she would have been unable to help him out on the question of snow and blood and wanting out and abandonment. The Bensons had not been told Ruth Plainfeather's story, the gruesome details of which Jeremiah Bate had carefully kept to himself.

Luke went away briskly, angrily and confused, while Bate, eyes open momentarily once again, muttered something about a Divine Plan. Luke left Bate's place so briskly that the preacher's daughter thought him ill-mannered and coarse, almost savage in his disregard for polite protocol.

8

Where My Father Once Walked, There Shall I Walk Also

'The soil you see is not ordinary soil – it is the dust of the blood, the flesh, and bones of our ancestors. You will have to dig down through the surface before you can find nature's earth, as the upper portion is Crow. The land, as it is, is my blood and my dead; it is consecrated.'

Shes-his, late 19th century, Reno Crow

~ ~ ~

After giving last-minute instructions to the real estate office and his lawyer, Luke headed home, although the thought began to grow inside his head that the idea 'home' was a fluid and unreliable one. What should we call 'home' when we don't know who or what we are? He was beginning to sound like Simon Westgate, and that brought a fleeting smile to his lips. En route to Billings he stopped several times at roadside cafes, not just for refreshment, but to read again and again Emma's letter, which seemed to be burning a hole right through his pocket; by the time he reached Billings that letter was partly torn and crumpled and began to resemble a historical document, having been read, handled and mishandled so many times.

The drive gave him plenty of time for reflection, mostly of an inconclusive, uncomfortable and unsettling nature. It seems unwise to dwell on the past, unless it can improve present and future prospects, but dwell on it we do. Luke was beginning to dwell on a past that was not his own; he was beginning to shake hands with a nostalgia that he had no right to feel – and that's something else altogether. For how is it possible to feel nostalgia for a past that is not your own? He wasn't red, he was white. That's what he kept telling himself. Yet he felt drawn to that past which was not his own, as though the letter in his pocket held a magic potion that, once read, was unleashed and whose power could not be subdued, come what might.

On the plus side, most people would want, at least in imagination if not in the flesh , to revisit the past and embrace those loved ones who had passed away, to apologise to them for what they did or said, or did not do or say, or to right wrongs, or just to embrace for one last time – a kind of second chance to put things right. It seemed attractive to be able to make a return to the past, ideally a fleshy one in a time machine, down through the portal of those misty visions of the past to give one last ecstatic greeting, one last, long grief-laden goodbye to all those who loved you and wished you well and are now no more. Memory and imagination distorts the past, sometimes opening portals through which we may be tempted to travel at our peril. Yet, sometimes we need to go backward in order to go forward, as when we've lost something and need to retrace our steps.

But after all this confusing concatenation of ideas, and when all these half-baked ruminations were burned out, Luke was still left with the intolerable fact that the past towards which he was drawn and for which he felt a creeping nostalgia was not one he dared to acknowledge, even to himself – let alone to anyone else. By the time he reached Billings, Luke was exhausted, mentally as well as physically. But there was nothing and no one there to help iron out the creases. It was late afternoon and Caroline was not at home. He found a note pinned to the ice box, reminding him that she was to give a talk to the newly formed Women's Executive Society, an organisation which she herself had had more than a hand in forming. Its business was to discuss and promote ideas inspired by their heroine Betty Friedan in her book *The Feminine Mystique*. Caroline and friends regarded the book as a blueprint of ideas which should be energetically applied to the world of commerce to the enhancement of the role of women in the direction of business affairs – in their view, the book stood to business as pure mathematics does to applied mathematics.

Caroline was building up her already formidable reputation as a shining example of what women could achieve once the shackles of male rule and convention were snapped asunder and feminine power was finally unleashed, proving beyond question that it was a man's world in name only, as it had always been, and that male dominance was an unacceptable illusion to be put down once and for all, like a rabid dog. To this end, meetings of the Women's Executive Society consisted largely of readings from Betty Friedan's book followed by commentary and discussion.

John Henry wasn't home, either. It was a school vacation part of which he was spending at Bob Hayward's. John Henry loved staying at his grandfather's place. His visits had become more frequent and lengthy as he grew older. He was now ten years old and as impressionable as ever, but he seemed more impressed with his grandfather than anyone else. The boy often returned with stories about how his grandfather had bawled somebody out over the phone, or had promised him a pony, or had had a room set up for him all his own, complete with pool table, television and video recorder. The relationship between grandson and grandfather was certainly close, even to the extent that John Henry was quickly becoming Hayward's personal confidant despite his years. Hayward would speak to him like an adult; true, any questions he asked him about adult matters he usually answered himself, but the very fact that he asked them at all would have been regarded by the casual observer somewhat eccentric and inappropriate, and therefore amusing. 'Now this investment seems the most promising of the lot – I've given it a lot of thought, John Henry, and I think we should go ahead. What say you, boy? Yes? Yes, I think so, and I'm glad you agree. Mighty glad.'

Hayward stopped short of offering the little fellow whisky and soda or the occasional after-dinner brandy, but in most other respects he addressed him as an equal, and John Henry himself seemed uplifted by it, even if the more business-type matters his grandfather addressed were mostly incomprehensible. 'One day all this will be yours – yes, that's right, everything you can see, house, land and all!' Hayward would say; there was in this no reference whatsoever to Luke, only to John Henry, and the boy never thought to mention his father – maybe he sensed that such a reference wouldn't be welcome, or maybe he was just too young.

From an even earlier age, John Henry was told to address his grandfather as Bob. So, it was Bob-this and Bob-that for days on end after one of these visits to Hayward. Luke seemed to have less and less to do with John Henry. The boy spent more time with his own friends and his grandfather than Luke liked. But how could he object? Luke was himself a busy man, and he knew that any colleague he might confide in on the subject would count him lucky to have the opportunity to get on with the whole business of 'getting on' by getting his kids born and out of the way as quickly as possible; after all, children are obstacles to ambition, and those who speak of the importance of quality time spent with their offspring must remember, when all is said and done, that time is money.

The whole household was mighty busy, what with both parents engrossed in their careers and a child who was growing up fast and was likely to show more interest in emulating the rich and powerful than in studying philosophers and poets.

So, on his return to Billings, it was up to Luke to smooth out his own creases. He poured himself a whisky and sat down. He had taken to an occasional whisky somewhere down the line; whether because it was some kind of career accessory or because it had become a personal requirement is hard to tell. Gone were the days when he would sit half the night with a fruit juice, as he used to with Simon Westgate. But a strong drink in moderation had become needful, and especially now after Emma's revelation; she had kept a closely-guarded secret, which she now passed on to Luke, and he knew that it was a secret that he would need to keep even more securely. Sitting down with Caroline and revealing all was not an option, and never could be. He was saddled with it, and the thought weighed very heavily on him.

He sighed, looked up and his eyes caught the picture, Becker's print, still residing in state just where they had put it. He stared hard at it. Had he been less tired he might have got up and approached it and taken a closer look. The picture had really been a present for Caroline, and Luke had learned to take only a casual interest in her things, for she would brook no challenge to her territory. But right now, he would most certainly have risen from his armchair and approached the picture had his eyes not resisted the suggestion so strongly. They closed, and he fell asleep.

Luke had never been one to dream much, if at all, or at least he could never remember anything very clearly. But he dreamed now, and he dreamed vividly. In his dream, he got up out of his armchair and walked up to and into Becker's picture, as though it were a portal into the very scene it depicted. He stood only a few feet away from Custer, who stood cursing his mouth off in the swirling gun smoke and shouting commands that no one could either hear or obey. No one seemed to take any notice of Luke, who, for a while, stood around like some journalist who had been caught in the thick of it – but a journalist with some kind of mystic diplomatic immunity, as everyone else shot and hacked each other to pieces. It was mayhem, sure enough. Gunshots and the unearthly yelling of red men mixed with the muted barking of orders and the groans of the dying, and, somewhere, the occasional sobs of a young white soldier hiding his head under a blanket, unable to believe even now that he had stepped off Ellis Island into something as far removed from paradise as it is possible to be – perhaps it would all go away if he refused to see it. Custer stood in the centre of a circle of bluecoats, their number diminishing by the second, and one or two of them just sat there, trembling with fear and paralysed into a posture of waiting, with expressions on their faces which seemed to say that they just didn't know how all this had come about and that they had nothing whatever to do with it anyhow. One bluecoat, somewhere in his 30s and sporting a neatly trimmed moustache, saw the blow coming seconds before it struck, yet he just sat there motionless, as though he himself was dreaming it all, or as though every rational thought had died before his body did. There's nothing rational about a war club wielded by a wild and screaming red man, unless you factor in the murder of his wife and child by bluecoats in their first preliminary assault earlier that afternoon. That bluecoat's face was smashed beyond all recognition, in poor recompense.

With the same kind of paralysis, another young bluecoat, who had just surrendered his rifle in a gesture of surrender and peace, allowed himself to be rolled over on to his belly while a red man removed his scalp. Luke himself was paralysed; it required great effort to move, and then he moved only in slow motion. All that suffering moved him, or seemed to. He suddenly found himself a participant in all this madness as he bent down on one knee to help a dying bluecoat, lovingly holding the man's head in the palm of his hand, but all the man could do with his dying breath was to call him names – 'Oh God, lousy redskin! Bastard! Bastard!' and these words seemed to be spat out of his mouth in a little fountain of blood. Luke released the man abruptly, maybe through disgust, his fine suit and white shirt-front soaked with blood and gore.

In the next instant, a fearsome-looking warrior, the upper part of his face painted red, the lower part yellow, and a buffalo hat upon his head, jumped on Luke, pinning him helplessly to the ground; one hand held his throat in a vice, the other held a hatchet which was about to descend and cleave through his forehead like a machete through an apple. The red man's eyes glowed like hot coals as he yelled, 'Wasishun! Hown!' But the hatchet descended in slow motion, 'You don't understand!'

Luke cried out in desperation. 'I'm not wasishun! Your friend! Washtay kola! Washtay kola! Your brother! Yes! Your brother!'. And with these words red man, hatchet, buffalo hat and all, just dissolved away into the smoke and confusion of battle, the clamour of which grew fainter and faded away, Custer's cursing being the last element in the furore to become indistinct and then inaudible.

'Your brother!' With this poignant appeal still ringing in his ears, Luke awoke in a bath of sweat, shook his head and made for the shower room. When he at last emerged, he poured himself another whisky and took a cooler look at Becker's print. There, sure enough, in the bottom right-hand corner, was the bluecoat who had obligingly awaited execution and was now in the process of having his hair removed; the redskin, his knee sunk into the soldier's back, tearing off his scalp in a fury. For one who seldom dreamed at all, and could hardly remember his dreams even when he did, Luke was stunned into silence, unable even to speak to himself.

From then on that picture was to loom ever larger in Luke's life. Leastways, it would be one of Caroline's things that would receive far more than casual recognition. Luke even took to cleaning the glass, all the better to see it. For him it became the centre of attraction and the focus of his attention; wherever he might be, whenever he thought of home, that picture would be the first thing to come to mind and the last to leave it. Even if his first thought were Caroline or John Henry, the picture would be the next – attracting his attention like a magnet. If the picture was one pole of a magnet, maybe Luke was the other. Opposite poles attract, for he was beginning to identify more with the victors than the vanquished, more with red than white, and, so, less with what the print was meant to convey.

In the eyes of the white man, Becker's depiction was meant to suggest the ultimate victory of the forces of white civilisation over the negative forces of primitive, uncomprehending resistance. In cruder terms, it represented what the Old Man Upstairs had called 'the fighting spirit'; he had not meant the fighting spirit of the red man but of the white man. The red men had merely resisted the will of God; like ignorant and wanton children, they had been wrong to resist, which is why their so-called victory was a hollow one at best. Ignorant and wanton children can do a great deal of harm and delight in it, thinking it to be righteously ordained, but they are ignorant and wanton, and therefore wrong, nevertheless. So, after the battle it was downhill all the way for the red men; they had resisted the 'Manifest Destiny' of the whites, and they had paid the inevitable price – which, incidentally, was sufficient proof for those who thought this way that Wakan Tanka, the Great Spirit or Great Mystery, was on a collision course with the Christian God and bound in the end to disappoint those who put their faith in him or it. All of which would explain why every respectable, right-thinking, law-abiding, patriotic white American was expected to feel proud to behold the scene Becker imagined. If it was a scene of carnage, the reds bore the brunt of the responsibility for that. But it was also a scene of civilised defiance over the primitive forces of evil; it was the birth of ultimate white triumph, presided over by its midwife-in-chief 'General' George Armstrong Custer – or, put more simply, it was the reassertion of that age-old and time-honoured dictum, Might is Right. True, in his more pensive moments, when sitting in an armchair before a log fire and sipping his favourite brandy, the Old Man Upstairs might well have conceded that the responsibility for past injustices should be shared more equally between reds and whites, freely admitting that there had been bad and greedy whites; though it would take at least another brandy or two before he would go so far as to say that the reds were more sinned against than sinning.

It was quite clear to any average white observer what Becker's picture was meant to imply. Luke had understood the Old Man's sentiment perfectly when he had said that no home should be without an Otto Becker. He had not only understood it, he had concurred with it. But now? After stepping inside the picture, things seemed to take on a somewhat different hue. If Emma was right, if he really was red, things had to be different. In fact, it began to seem as though he had never really stepped back out of the picture – as though some part of him was still trapped inside it. He asked himself, disconcertingly, if he was developing a split personality. Should he secretly see an analyst?

Visits to analysts were becoming as respectable and as commonplace as visits to downtown drugstores. But this was different. How could you tell an analyst you had a problem being red? The issue was more sociological than psychological. Wasn't it? He was beset with doubts and confusions. The problem was more on the outside than the inside. Wasn't it? Was it even a problem at all? If it was, whose problem was it?

Luke was analysing himself – in an amateurish and confused kind of way. In the process he was finding himself increasingly at odds with the white interpretation of Becker's picture. For instance, the warrior who was poised to kill him and then dissolved away - was that Luke himself acknowledging that he was red? He no longer wanted to cast doubt on Emma's revelation. If he was red, he was red – and that was that; to deny it would be like a kind of suicide, and the more successful that kind of suicide was, the harder it would be to live with whatever was left. That warrior had dissolved away, his dissolution symbolic of the dissolution of further doubts.

Luke was beginning to find his own analysis irresistible and maybe, he had learned something from Simon Westgate, after all; he was beginning to reason, to acknowledge a kind of reasoning that didn't belong to profit and loss and the untrammelled pursuit of the Commercial Principle. This kind of analysis wasn't comfortable, but it seemed forced upon him. He had embarked upon a process of self-examination and was in danger of validating the Socratic notion that an unexamined life isn't worth living. Maybe philosophy had jumped up and bitten him in the ass, after all. Nor would the bite be a one-off. A wheel had been set in motion, one which wouldn't stop until it was brought to an abrupt halt by something strong enough to resist it.

In some lesser respects, things returned to normality. For one thing, Luke never dreamed about that Becker ever again, either because he never dreamed at all, or because he couldn't remember whether he had. Still, the Becker hung over the mantelpiece and continued to be a conversation piece among guests, a topic that Luke did his best to stay out of – for people employed the customary clichés, which annoyed him, though he did his best to avoid his acute irritation.

***

That part of him that lived on inside Becker's picture grew stronger as time passed, and became more assertive, more demanding of time and attention. Caroline and John Henry took on different aspects, too. When Luke looked at John Henry he began to see the red in him, for John Henry was half-red; to an outsider, Luke might have seemed delusional, but his perception was well contained and out of sight. It was not of course something that he could talk about, or even dared think about for longer than the time it took to form the idea. But this private perception was there, all the same, and continued on its path. Yet when John Henry spoke, the red in him seemed to vanish into the ether of illusion, especially on those occasions when he would find nothing better to talk about than the promises made to him by Bob Hayward – then he was more white than red, less than half-red.

As for Caroline, she was seen as the white woman Luke had married and the mother of his sometimes half-red son. But what a woman! Often more man than woman, one who would suffer no criticism in or about her tipi, a woman who went about her life just like one who lived alone, indifferent to the basic attractions and conventions of family life. It was almost like being married to some big white chief. Underneath all that veneer there might yet be some soft folds of womanhood, but they were getting harder by the day to visualise; doubts as to her femininity were becoming easier to entertain. As Simon Westgate might have pointed out, doubt is food and drink to those with a philosophical turn of mind. Once again, philosophy was nipping Luke in the rear, as a sheepdog might goad reluctant and wayward sheep into their pens. It was promising to be a shaky kind of fatherhood and an even more dubious marriage.

On his return from Emma's funeral, Luke thought he would have some delicate news to break to John Henry about his grandmother's recent demise. But all John Henry could say was 'Yeah, I know!' having been told already by Caroline, she having been informed by Luke, who had phoned her only minutes after Emma's eyes had closed. True, John Henry did run upstairs, not to bury his head tearfully in his pillows, but to pack his things to spend another prearranged weekend at Bob Hayward's place. John Henry wasn't running from bad news, but in excitement and anticipation of the visit with his beloved grandfather. Not for John Henry a moment's respectful pensiveness, though he was old enough by now to feel the need. Not for him some remorseful backward glances to times when things were left unsaid or left undone.

Luke partly blamed himself for John Henry's apparent indifference. He had hardly set the best example, yet over and above that there seemed to be something lacking in John Henry's feelings, something for which he could not wholly account, maybe something for which he dared not try to account. The contrast between John Henry's attachment to Bob and his indifference towards Emma struck a painful chord in Luke's breast and served to remind him how he had striven so successfully to shorten the duration of his visits to her and make them increasingly infrequent. The distance between himself and Emma had widened, maybe in consequence, and maybe that accounted for the fact that she had felt better setting things down on paper instead of taking him aside and speaking to him face to face. Such thoughts were uncomfortably persistent.

Caroline, too, had little to say about Emma, with just 'I'm sorry, Luke,' before going through the usual motions of asking how the funeral had gone, as though it could have gone in any other way than the way it did. And then the subject was dropped, as though the loss had occurred in someone else's family and Luke had just helped out.

Meanwhile, and although Luke never dreamed again about the Becker picture, it continued to play on his mind. He would awake at night thinking about it, or thinking about it would stop him settling down, so that lack of sleep became an issue to be reckoned with. One night, Caroline, unable to sleep either, went downstairs to get a drink from the ice box, and found Luke staring at the picture from his armchair, an empty whisky glass in his hand. The brief exchange between them was suggestive.

'Got a sudden interest in art, Luke?'

'Couldn't sleep.'

'Me, too.'

'They say', said Luke, after a pause, 'they say he got the landscape right. Wouldn't mind taking a look for myself – going there. Been meaning to take a break, anyhow. One weekend. I'll take John Henry, maybe.'

'Daddy wants to take him to New York. Show him around.'

'Yeah, right.'

That was all. She just said goodnight, turned round and left.

He wanted her to say that it would be good idea to take John Henry, that it was good to give him a real sense of history, of culture – but most importantly he wanted her to say that he and John Henry should spend more time with one another and bond like father and son. It would have taken just a few more seconds to say these things, but all she could do was to talk about John Henry and Bob Hayward, as though it were a subject that would be activated by the least suggestion, all ready and waiting to be raised and revisited whenever an appropriate prompt was provided. As for Luke's reference to the picture and the landscape depicted, he was surprised she had not responded by praising the frame instead. Clearly, saying too little is sometimes far worse than saying too much.

The idea of taking John Henry to a battle site seemed off the cuff, and just something to say. But it must have come from deep down somewhere. In truth, he wanted to go to Last Stand Hill all by himself, not just because John Henry, a mere boy of ten, would probably have found the whole idea boring, and not just because some might consider the trip inappropriate, but because maybe he felt he had a ghost to exorcise, or maybe because making the trip had about it the air of a kind of pilgrimage. But he told himself it was just because he wanted to see if Becker really had got the landscape right.

And that's what he told the Old Man Upstairs a week later. Maybe the Old Man ought to have been delighted that Luke had taken such an interest in his gift to Caroline; wanting to make the trip to Montana showed appreciation and gratitude. Instead, a little bemused, he thought

Luke was just angling for a few days off with the lamest excuse he had ever heard, especially when Luke said he would be going without Caroline and John Henry. 'Well, guess we can spare you', he said. 'Been noticing you lately, Luke. Seems your mind's someplace else. Screwed up that deal not so long ago – didn't say anything at the time. Maybe a few days'll do you good – you and the business both! Well, enjoy the trip!' Ordinarily, Luke would have found it hard to enjoy anything after such a grudging form of approval. But this was a trip he felt he had to make – enjoyment had nothing to do with it. Compliments from the Old Man were so rare as to be totally unexpected. Most of the time he was in neutral gear, neither complimentary nor censorious. Neutrality was good news; it meant the Old Man was pleased enough to be nothing worse. But this reference to Luke's slipping was a bad sign. Luke even entertained the notion that a couple of days roaming the Montana hills might just stand between him and the Old Man's misgivings, just as a little absence is said to make the heart grow that bit fonder – probably an illusion, but it was worth a try anyhow.

The Old Man's doubts didn't lack substance. Luke had slowed down a lot ever since his return from Rapid City. His step had lost the agility you expect to find in someone who was going places with a will. He would stare blankly ahead, as though he wasn't listening to what was being said to him, almost like a lost soul. No wonder he had screwed that deal up. Bill Winters was not a man to be trifled with;

he was a head-headed dealer who wouldn't do business with anyone who didn't look him straight in the eye, and Luke hadn't. Winters was disappointed; Luke had been commended by others whose judgments he trusted. Winters hated the Soviets with a vengeance that bordered on the irrational, but there is one Russian dictum he would have taken very much to heart – don't trust the eyes of another, trust your own eyes, even if they're crooked. Winters trusted his own eyes and they told him that he couldn't trust anyone who refused to look into them. They told him that Luke was not someone to do business with. That was bad news for the Old Man, who had placed so much faith in him, and what was bad news for the Old Man was infinitely worse for Luke. His trip to Montana did nothing, of course, to allay the Old Man's misgivings – nothing to help Luke back on to the straight and narrow.

Luke made the tortuous journey, driving himself up Highway 91, parallel with Custer's route along the Yellowstone River, and then joined Montana 447, branching south and south-west, almost exactly following the route taken by Custer and his Seventh Cavalry on that fateful morning of Sunday, 25 June 1876. Luke was driving on the hottest day July had to offer and was enchanted by the spacious yellow land which seemed to extend interminably in every direction. He drove in to the small, dusty town of Busby and headed for the post office, the site meant to indicate the spot where Custer made his last camp before his attack and subsequent slaughter, a spot marked by a Pepsi-

Cola advertisement. Was it here that Blood Knife's warning was given and went unheeded? Beyond this and further along the state highway, Luke began the descent into the Little Bighorn Valley. From Reno Hill he took a narrow road towards the Last Stand, passing white marbles dedicated to unknown bluecoats, though none to red men, known or unknown.

Finally, he reached the slope which is the site of Custer's Last Stand. It was deadly quiet. There was a penetrating silence. No tourists could be seen; partly because the place was off the beaten track and hard to get to, the nearest town being Hardin, 15 miles north-west; partly because it was still early morning. But tourists had been there and would come again. Chewing gum wrappers, empty cola cans and cigarette butts littered the ground here and there, while to the north of the site was a motel, a coffee shop, gas pumps and a rodeo stadium – surefire indications of the victory of Manifest Destiny over primitive forces, and the settlement of the Land of the Free. The spot where Custer is supposed, largely by Hollywood filmmakers, to have fallen was surrounded by a black iron fence, the whole battlefield itself stretching to about 600 acres.

Luke took a good look round. Things had changed somewhat since Becker produced his version of events. Imported evergreens came later, for instance. No matter, it was clear to Luke that Becker had got the landscape right. The fact that he had got it right validated Becker's depiction, but there was much more to it than topography and the contours of the land. There were ghosts there, and Luke felt them, here, there and all around. They seemed to fill the air with the sounds of battle. It was almost as though he was inside Becker's picture again, but this time it was no dream. The portals of his imagination were swinging wide on their hinges, through which he saw a dying red man, struggling to release his last few words: 'Yes, white man, red man, it was like this. It happened like this. Too much pain. Can't talk. Can't breathe. Can't tell you. You imagine what I would say!'

The image was gone in a flash and Luke saw the bluecoats sitting with their backs against those white marbles – all dead men, sitting, waiting, and for what? And for how long would they sit and wait? Luke felt the sanctity of the place. Yes, the ground was consecrated. Lincoln's address at Gettysburg would do well here. 'We cannot hallow this ground,' Lincoln had said. How true; those who had died had consecrated that ground. The blood spilt at Gettysburg was for one nation under God, a free nation dedicated to the canons of equality, respect and freedom – Lincoln had said so with an eloquence befitting such lofty aspirations, and he had meant every word of it.

The blood spilt at the Battle of the Little Bighorn had consecrated the ground, but Luke wondered for what lofty aspirations it had been shed. Surely the Doctrine of Manifest Destiny had to be ruled out; as for freedom, for whose freedom had the battle been fought? The red man had won the battle, but he was destined to lose the war. Had not Might been victorious over Right? What moral high-ground could justify the spilling of red and white blood here? This was a battle that had benefitted no one – a hollow victory, yes, but hollow for both red and white.

The red man was to lose everything that made him what he was, and whatever the white man gained was hardly worth the trouble – the means could not possibly justify the end. At dusk later that day Luke walked round the Last Stand before heading back to the motel seeming to smell the blood rising from the soil; the blood enriching it maybe, but not validating what had been done – everything just a pointless waste of life, recalling Wellington's solemn observation, 'Next to a battle lost, the saddest thing is a battle won.' The litter, the motel, the coffee shop, the gas station, the pretty blonde in blue jeans who kept shoving cold beers across the bar – everything seemed out of step and out of place. If this was the achievement of Manifest Destiny, it just seemed absurd and crazy, even crazier than Emma's revelation about his red origins. That revelation he might, just might, somehow manage to live with. But all this incongruity was just too much. Life had never seemed so hopelessly inside-out.

He returned to Billings at first light the next day, wishing he hadn't come but wishing also he had a better place than Billings to go home to. The incongruity kept nipping at his heels like a troublesome dog, and Becker's picture, central over the mantelpiece and threatening to remain there come what might, kept the incongruity in full and persistent focus. He wanted to avoid the living room but could hardly do so. There was nothing wrong in being red provided you forgot you were. Becker's little masterpiece just wouldn't allow him to forget.

But did he want to forget? To say that his feelings were mixed is a huge understatement.

When Becker's print first arrived he took a mild interest in the history and fate of the red man, but now he read prodigiously. More than that, he studied the paintings and photographs of red men that accompanied the texts, and he began to measure the truth of the texts by what he could see in them; if the text lied, the picture proved it. Quannah Parker, chief of the proud Kwahadi Comanches, intrigued him most. His name itself suggested a neat blend of cultures, red and white. 'Quannah' is Comanche; 'Parker' was taken from his white mother, Cynthia Ann Parker, who had been taken captive by Quannah's father, Quannah being the result of the forced union. Quannah led his warriors relentlessly against the whites for years and was once shot from his horse by Billy Dixon, a young buffalo hunter, at the so-called Battle of Adobe Walls: apparently one of the best shots in recorded history, the bullet being spent after reaching the end of its trajectory and having enough punch left to concuss Quannah but otherwise leaving him unharmed.

Quannah concluded that the Great Spirit was not on the side of the red man on that occasion, and decided to give up to fight another day. Eventually, Quannah gave up fighting altogether. He learned to speak English, and then to write it with very few errors, and settled down to the life of a successful businessman, even living happily in a wooden tipi, though never once forgetting his origins and his identity. He sometimes wore a waistcoat and tails, but he also wore his hair in long braids. He picked up some business practices from the whites, but his face was as proud as ever it had been, exuding Comanche pride, not white pride, not pride at being like the whites, but pride at being different – pride at being red, and staying red, despite everything.

Luke was haunted by Quannah's face as much as by Becker's picture. Quannah stared out of the page at him, and Luke stared back so hard he thought the face had come alive, as though Quannah's lips moved in that stony countenance with the words, 'Be yourself above all others.' The message was defiant and inspiring.

It wasn't just pictures of red men that moved him. He came across a photograph of settlers moving west: a family consisting of father, mother, grandmother and half a dozen kids. They rested near their wagon, and one thing the picture seemed to convey was pathos – the pity of it all; these poor, wandering creatures, destitute, save for what they carried on their backs and the bits and pieces they carried in that ramshackle, slow, cumbersome wagon. The innocence written in the faces of those kids was striking. Did they all make the trip? Were some buried en route? Were they destined to be killed in cold blood by a pack of red bucks out for some scalps? The breadwinner might have been riddled with arrows before he had time to load his one-shot musket, lullabied into death by the screams of his wife and kids. Or they might have succumbed to disease, been bitten by rattlesnakes, or bushwhacked by fellow whites, their colour being the only quality they shared in common.

Was the west, if not the whole of the USA, built upon the dreams of such poor folk? If so, things had turned out for the worse somewhere along the line, for so many, for so long. The American Dream was interspersed with nightmares along the trails that led from east to west and back again. Luke surmised that the family with the wagon might have sat down with a Lakota Sioux family and got along just fine – if only all the vices could have been put aside, vices white and red, vices red and white. The best favour whites and reds could do now was to acknowledge their differences and live side by side – no colour being better or worse than another. Nobody could go back and change what had happened in the past but maybe they could retrace their steps along the way to make sure that what had happened before would never happen again. To do that, you had to acknowledge many things – what you are, your mistakes, what you did right and what you did wrong, your heritage, your origins. To go forward, you had to go back.

And there was every reason to go back, because men, of every colour, were making a trash-can of the world. It was time to think again. Time for the philosophy that he had told Simon Westgate was a dead duck.

As for Caroline, her husband's interest in books and pictures relating to red history and culture went largely unnoticed, and doubts about his origins were as far removed from her pretty little head as reflections on the contribution of the ancient Greeks to the philosophies of the western world. How Luke would have loved to talk to her about the battle raging inside him, but they were in different solar systems and there seemed to be no means of transport linking the two. They moved in different spheres, and Luke felt he was on a collision course that was unstoppable. And down that one-way track Quannah Parker was to loom larger than ever.

9

The Becker Incident

'O ye people, be ye healed;

Life anew I bring unto ye.

O ye people, be ye healed;

Life anew I bring unto ye.

Through the Father over all

Do I thus.'

Good Eagle Wanbli-Washte, Dakota Sioux Holy Man, late 19th century

~ ~ ~

It must have been a white man who said the camera never lies, though maybe few red men would have contested the idea. But no one picture can tell the whole truth; no picture can delineate the whole man. Many pictures need to be taken to make any start at all, and even then it's what is left out that might matter most.

There was more than one picture of Quannah, erstwhile chief of the Comanches, who had been shot from his horse while trying to drill holes in white men at Abobe Walls. One picture has him looking proud and every bit a red man despite the fact that he had taken to some white ways. He stands tall and proud before the camera in full chieftain attire, his long braids meticulously wrapped in beaver fur.

But that was just prior to an important tribal festivity, where nothing less than proud authenticity could possibly have been expected. Red men wanted to look their best in ceremonies and before the white man's gadget, just as they wanted to prepare themselves well before battle, not because dressing well would improve their performance as warriors or somehow give them courage, but because they needed to prepare for death. No red man would want to enter the spirit world looking less than his best, which, come to think of it, is not so far removed from the desire of living whites to dress their dead in their very best clothes. When that picture of Quannah was taken, he was already a well-connected businessman, just as likely to be found in suit and tie. And this fact intrigued Luke Benson, who was looking for something, but was unsure what it was, or was yet unable to articulate it to his own satisfaction.

Quannah had been a rising star, or what seemed like it, both to many whites and to many reds. Before his death in 1911, Quannah had mastered the white man's tongue to such an extent that he acquired a reputation for shrewdness in business undertakings that the proverbial Russian might well envy, and he was especially adept at hammering out deals which leased reservation lands to Texas cattlemen, who naturally were white. He even held a major shareholding in a railroad company, and he didn't feel out of place in Washington promoting Comanche interests. In short, he had managed to become 'a good Indian' without having satisfied the condition imposed upon all reds by General Philip Henry Sheridan, namely that he should die first.

Quannah's adaptation to white ways did not go unrewarded. He was given white honours, among which was a 12-room, show place, ranch house for him and his family. To some this might have suggested the wisdom of a policy of integration and maybe even a highroad to complete assimilation. Not quite. Despite white inducements, he didn't forget that he was Comanche. He was buried beside his white mother, Cynthia Ann Parker, but in the full regalia of a Comanche chief.

But was it not possible to blend cultures and at the same time do justice to both? This is the question that most appealed to Luke Benson in his ruminations, for he imagined that an affirmative answer was more than possible and that the grounds for such a welcome answer could be found in the picture before him. On one occasion Quannah was photographed sitting between two paintings; one of his white mother, the other of Jesus Christ complete with halo. He sat proud – there was no doubt about that. He was honouring his mother's God – her creed, and her culture, since then even more than now, her culture was steeped in her creed, in her God. He respected Christianity, but did not embrace it; just as he was respecting his mother but not embracing her, respecting her origins but not embracing them. But still, he sat proud between those two paintings. So, was he not happy to embrace both sides of his heritage? Being half-red, half-white might seem no more threatening than it does nowadays for whites to hold dual nationality, or even for a black to be half-white or a white to be half-black.

But when Luke started to factor in the colour black, he found himself on a highroad to despair, for there seemed little either in the past or in the present to fill him with hope. Spoken Garry, a Middle Spokane chief, had said a long time ago, 'We are black, yet if we cut ourselves, the blood will be red – and so with the whites it is the same, though their skin be white.' But he was quick to add, 'I am of another nation, when I speak you do not understand me. When you speak, I do not understand you.'

The colour of blood is the same for all peoples whatever the colour of their skin, and this observation rings down the halls of history, no doubt even before Shakespeare put a similar announcement in the mouth of Shylock the Jew, who said if you cut him he would bleed just like the gentiles. But, clearly, Luke could not ground his hopes in this kind of revelation, for history shows that the colour of blood is insufficient to break down the barriers of inhumanity. He needed only to recall the assassination of Dr Martin Luther King in 1968, an event too recent for him to forget, to see that whites had great difficulty coming to terms with blacks, despite the fact that the Civil War had been fought partly to free them from the scourge of racial inequality and contempt. More than that, the whites couldn't even tolerate each other when it came to mere sexual proclivities, as the Stonewall Riots of the summer of 1969 had even more recently testified in New York.

The inability to get on with differences wasn't confined to colour in the southern states, but extended east even when colour wasn't an item. The colour of blood was hardly a balm. The chief had said, 'When I speak, you do not understand me. When you speak, I do not understand you.' Did he just mean they spoke different languages, so that if you translated the one into the other all would be well? Or did he mean something else – something that couldn't be translated and just had to be respected, and, if not respected, at least tolerated?

Quannah Parker was also photographed at a long breakfast table in his ranch house, flanked by a handful of respectful reds and only one white, though we can guess the picture was taken by a white. On the table are the customary white breakfast things: coffee pot, cups and saucers, bottles and condiments; there are even posters on the walls advertising concert hall personalities. The reds who flank him honour their natural heritage by wearing braids, which emerge from under their hats or flow over their button-up vests; the white had only one culture to honour, and he honoured it superbly from head to foot. Luke wondered what they all found to talk about. Quannah is seated at the head of the table, as befits a ranch boss, dressed like a white man, but his braids are properly arranged as usual and he is proud of face; he's a Comanche chief still, straight, true and unbending.

So did not Quannah represent an ideal blend of cultures? Wasn't he a salutary bridge in the great divide – a promising stride at least towards assimilation? Luke thought so – until, that is, another photograph seemed to help put him straight.

In the last picture Luke looked at, presumably of a later date, Quannah had been honoured with the title and office of Judge. It was his business to adjudicate cases brought to him on the Comanche reservation, and in this capacity he was of immeasurable assistance to the whites. But he is photographed in a moment of repose, or so we are led to believe. He sits under a print of Otto Becker's version of Custer's Last Stand, no less, and wears an expression that can only be described as utterly lost and forlorn. Was it just a moment of indecision as to what his judgment should be in the case at hand, or was he unhappy with a decision he had already made, or was about to make in the next session? Or, maybe he was at odds with the white man's conception of law and justice. Or, maybe just unhappy with white men. Or, maybe unhappy with trying to be white. When red tries to be white, it ends up being pink – which is all right if you like pink, but not all right if you prefer red. A red man might be forgiven for appearing pink and not liking it one little bit.

It struck Luke as extraordinary that a once-proud chief should now be sitting under Becker's depiction of the Last Stand, himself a picture of total dejection. When Quannah looked at the picture, he wouldn't have recognised the reds Becker had tried to represent and ended up misrepresenting as Zulus. The Comanche hadn't taken part in that fight, but Quannah knew what the Sioux and the Cheyenne looked like, and they didn't look at all like Becker's reds. Becker was doing an injustice to red men.

But this wasn't what made Quannah look so morbidly pensive. No, Quannah's expression had much more to do with how far the mighty had fallen and how far this Horseman of the Plains had come, having to quit both the horse and the plains for a ranch house table and the ironic office of Judge, for he was not judging the white man, as justice might have demanded, he was judging his own. No matter that he sits with a white man's hat upon his head and in a respectable suit and a vest complete with watch and chain. Yes, his hair is braided, but written on his face is far more than braids could ever suggest by themselves. In that face is the colour red, all red, and nothing but red, so help him Wakan Tanka.

His dress is cosmetic and irrelevant, as though some wayward white men had caught him and dressed him up just to mock him, or as though they had managed to persuade him to don white garb just for the sake of the camera, forcing it to tell a monumental and malicious lie. Luke remembered the time when he was about five years old and Emma had put him in a little girl's dress and gave him a small tin drum to beat – just for the camera, just for fun. But Luke remembered how embarrassed he felt, and the photograph showed his discomfort in his little face, all screwed up and set to shed tears – thus far the camera hadn't lied. And thus far the camera wasn't lying now, either. If you looked carefully enough for long enough, you could see the pain in Quannah's face. Had they smiled for the camera, both the great chief Quannah and the little infant Luke would have been lying through their teeth, and might have deceived everyone; and had they smiled hard enough and long enough they might even have deceived themselves.

Both had their hair to hold on to; little Luke's was long when he was an infant, and maybe that's why Emma wanted to try him in a dress just for fun. And red men were mighty proud of their hair, which was the only thing the white man had left them, not because the whites were properly conscious of such proprieties on their behalf, but precisely because they were not.Incidentally, Luke had come across that photograph of him as a boy in a girl's dress; it was among some trinkets that were disposed of or destroyed. Luke's first thought was to rip up the photograph, but he left it intact, for Emma's sake, and it got thrown out by the auctioneer's young assistant.Quannah was a man brought down low. Luke concluded here was no cultural blend, happy or otherwise, any more than oil can blend with water; no mix that could possibly work. A mix had to have dignity, and an identity in its own right. Identity was a precondition of dignity, and there was no real dignity here. Quannah must have known; his face said so. He was an old man, disillusioned and washed out – defeated. Defeat is demoralising. But defeat does not belong to the outcome of battles alone. Defeat can be known when you no longer know who you are, when you have no identity to hold on to, or, what comes to the same thing, when you are obliged to play a double game – a double game is one you can never win. It's as crazy as trying to hedge your bets by playing both sides of a baseball game at the same time.

Chief Seattle once said, 'Our warriors have felt shame, and after defeat they turn their days in idleness and contaminate their bodies with sweet foods and strong drink.' His warriors were defeated in battle, and for some small consolation they turned to the white man's poisons, and the irony is hard to take. After defeat in battle they needed to be raised up in other ways, by being granted their identity and therefore their dignity – but in reservations, most notably later ghettoes like Pine Ridge in the mid-west, it was hard to look yourself in the face, with only the trappings and dregs of white civilisation to pass the time, like Toyotas and Pepsi-Cola and strong liquor. . Toyotas, Pepsi-Cola and strong drink, though pleasant enough in moderation, do not make a man. After defeat in battle, far more was taken away than could ever be given back. People can be stripped of their identity and dignity as easily as their clothes might been taken from their backs; just as the Jews, among many others, were stripped by the Nazis. And when you're brought that low, climbing back up, without hand-holds or assistance of any kind, is no mean task, and for many just impossible.

Anyhow, Quannah was a case in point. Here was an old man, disillusioned and washed out. That's how he appeared, leastways , to Luke – like the little boy with ringlets photographed as a girl. The fun was over and everybody had gone home; he was left alone, with the laughter still ringing in his ears. Where now his dignity? Better to have died with a Winchester rifle hot and smoking in his hands, whatever the odds. For no odds were greater than these. Quannah looked as though he was searching for something in his mind, trying to remember where he had left the young warrior who had plagued the whites. The Comanches were proud in the saddle, so much so that even the whites, slow though they were to bestow honours on mere savages, called them the horsemen of the plains. But now this tired old man could hardly sit astride a big American horse, let alone ride a pony bareback all over the plains on the wings of the wind while at the same time taking aim and blasting away with his Winchester from low under the pony's neck.It was more than just the bittersweet memories every old man, red, white, black or yellow, has of his past, more than just a feeling of irretrievable loss and inevitable decline, more than just a longing for the dead and a fear of dying. It was rather that, past or present, red and white were hopelessly incongruous, that the one could not be achieved without the destruction of the other; pink was not an acceptable option, for it was no option at all. Quannah had been given some of the playthings of the whites. He had played with them quite well, but now he was tired of them and wanted to give them back. Trouble was, during playtime something of vast importance had been taken away from him; just as when an adult takes something away from a child by first distracting his attention with some sparkling novelty, and then, when the novelty wears off, the child discovers his loss – the price he has had to pay for his amusement, which invariably turns out to be far higher than he would ever have been able to imagine.

***

So, for Luke, this last image of Quannah was striking and unforgettable, and the message in his face was unmistakable. The very idea that this red man should be sitting under an Otto Becker – a picture prized for its symbolic representation of faith in the Manifest Destiny of the whites over what was no more than a hollow victory for the reds at best – the primitives might have won the battle, but they would lose the war. No wonder Quannah looked so forlorn, so despairing, to think that it should all have come to this. There was a feast of food for thought here, whether or not that hapless red man, any more than the photographer for that matter, had actually intended to provide such cerebral sustenance.

If indeed it was true that red could never become white without self-destruction, Quannah was not seeking a gentle moment of repose from the burdensome task of adjudicating cases, of judging others in terms of what whites considered right and wrong. His reluctance, to put it mildly, of being judged a white red man, or a red white man, had become the bane of his life, a heavy mortgage that he could never hope to pay off. For whether he was judged a white red man or a red white man mattered little, as both meant that he was either an inferior white or an inferior red, and either one spelt shame and humiliation, with the all-important consequence that you can't stand on your dignity if you don't know where you should be standing.

Luke's premises may have been right or they may have been wrong, valid or invalid, for it must be remembered that unlike Simon Westgate he was a novice in a kind of reasoning that stood outside the realm of profit and loss. His conclusion was that if it was not possible to remain red on equal terms with whites, then assimilation had to be resisted tooth and claw. It was what counted with yourself that mattered most – what you could live with, and you couldn't live with the judgment that you were a white Indian, that you were only a pale reflection of yourself.

Luke was almost as concerned about John Henry as he was about himself. John Henry was his only son and only child. In his reading he came across the words of Robert Higheagle, a Teton Sioux of the early

19th century, 'It is strictly believed and understood by the Sioux that a child is the greatest gift from Wakan Tanka, in response to many devout prayers, sacrifices and promises. Therefore the child is considered "sent by Wakan Tanka", through some element – namely the element of human nature.' So it was not possible to turn your back on your own children, even if they turned their backs on you. No red father worthy of his heritage could ignore his offspring; on the contrary, his duty was to nurture the very gift Wakan Tanka had bestowed. This obligation belonged to being red, but if anyone had said that John Henry was half-red, half-white, Luke would have been strongly inclined to say that he was neither the one or the other. So it came down to choices, and right now Luke was convinced he knew which colour to choose: the more red Luke was inclined to feel, the closer he felt towards John Henry and the more frustrated he became, for where was the red in John Henry?

The red in John Henry was being bleached out, which might easily suggest that something should be done to restore it before the process had become irreversible. Such were the confused and labyrinthine twists and turns of Luke's thinking. He persuaded himself that John Henry's destiny was bound up with his own, that where John Henry went would depend on where Luke led him, and it was becoming clearer to Luke where John Henry should be led. It seemed clear from this kind of reasoning that he should be led away from Bob Hayward, and, if at all possible, much further than that. As for himself, he felt the red pigment lay near the surface, and nearer still as each day passed, and that it needed only the slightest encouragement to emerge into the full light of day. The more he read about the so-called Native Americans, the more he felt red, and the more he felt red, the more he read. Emma's letter was his bookmark, folded carefully into a strong buff envelope.

Along with all this, the Old Man Upstairs came to epitomise the whites with whom Quannah had conducted land deals, or with those who paid him dubious homage in his 12-room wooden tipi – homage, not because he was a respectable man called Quannah Parker, but because he was a red man making good, which is to say a red man conforming to white ways and losing himself in the process. Luke's respect for the Old Man declined noticeably. Unlike Joe Shapiro, he didn't respond with a sweat and a jump when the Old Man wanted him upstairs; not at all – he would drag his feet and be late for meetings, even the ones marked urgent. Tangential reproaches seemed to have no effect on Luke whatsoever, not that the Old Man was ever tangential – in fact he was always excessively direct, but Mrs Harper, Luke's secretary, took a kind of motherly liking to him and did her best to drop a few meaningful hints – all to no avail.

The Old Man didn't believe in giving subordinates the wrong ideas, or even the right ideas at the wrong time or in the wrong place. Mrs

Harper, a kindly soul in her mid-50s, had been allocated to Luke, the younger variety of secretary being reserved for the Old Man himself who, though in his mid-60s, considered himself 20 years younger than he was and still a catch in every possible respect. He was never slow to mix business with pleasure when the latter took the form of young, shapely secretaries, who were told to wear minuscule skirts as a principal requirement of the job, the rather delicate task of explaining this requirement being left to the Old Man's personal assistant, who regarded it as one of his most unseemly duties. The safest line taken by the PA was that the Old Man's natural and truly harmless eccentricities should best be humoured for nothing 'untoward' attached to the stipulation. Young, upwardly-mobile ladies were for the most part happy to oblige. Even so, some 'nice' girls had been lost in the process of explanation. Suggestively, some good secretaries had not.

Mrs Harper took a motherly interest in Luke. But these were delicate matters, so she tried to broach them tangentially by referring to 'a friend of a friend' who had suffered 'burn-out', or she would talk about someone she knew who was in the throes of some kind of mid-life crisis. Luke was too green in the job to be subject to such things; nevertheless, he might have been feeling the pinch after four years – some people felt it earlier than others. She even referred to a book she was reading, entitled *Psycho-Cybernetics*, by Maxwell Maltz, a popular treatise dealing with the ramifications of various forms of inferiority complex, which had been published in pocket-book edition. Maybe the book would have very little application to Luke. But the truth was, she didn't want to ask him personal questions straight out; roundabout hints of this kind were well worth a try, because something big and nasty was coming if Luke didn't get his act together. She came in from lunch one afternoon and found him laid right back in his leather-bound swivel armchair, facing the window, and with both feet on the windowsill – absolutely not a posture that the Old Man Upstairs would favour in any of his trusted underlings, though he himself was not averse to spreading himself around when no one else was looking. She found him lounging there, humming strangely to himself, unread files still lying untouched on the desk behind him. It was not at all like him. 'Taking it easy, hey Mr Benson?' she said, trying to sound as nonchalant and as natural as she could. He didn't even swivel round, but went on humming as if no one was there. It was worrying. She was relieved when at last he did swivel round, sighed and picked up the report he should have picked up days before.

The Old Man hadn't asked for the report yet – but if he had!... What intrigued Mrs Harper was that Luke's behaviour could not be described as cocksureness; she reasoned with herself that his attitude was inconsistent with the idea that he was feeling over-secure in his job and safe from reprisals or something worse, for that wouldn't imply an indifference as to whether the job was done at all. That was when she raised the subject of mid-life crisis, sounding as casual as she could, but at the same time knowing that the topic was surely in all probability irrelevant. All Luke did was to smile politely and nod sagely, before slinging his raincoat over his left shoulder and announcing that he was going out for a late lunch and that he would be back later, adding the word 'probably'. Poor Mrs Harper spent the rest of the working day, and a large part of the evening, repeating to herself the word 'probably' and wondering what it could possibly mean.

True, his behaviour was not always so devil-may-care, but it was frequent enough to worry Mrs Harper, whose day would be made simply on those occasions when he seemed almost normally engaged at his desk, though he would increasingly ask her to handle all his calls, despite the fact that he was not over-burdened and could easily have handled them himself. All Mrs Harper could do was to wait and hope that it would all blow away in God's good time and with God's good grace, for she was not one to leave her God out of all account in any matter that attracted her attention but regularly consulted him in private when occasion seemed to demand it.

The noticeable changes in Luke's behaviour were not confined to the office. He took less and less work home, until finally he took none. He took to lounging about in the living room instead. There was an almighty row one evening when he lunged in and out of one of Caroline's at-home seminars on the subject of feminine assertiveness, and she only just managed to control her temper until her guests had left – but she was a smouldering volcano, which was about to erupt. 'Quarrel' is not quite the right word, for it might imply joint participation. 'Outburst' and 'eruption' would be better choices, for Luke himself spoke not a word throughout. In fact, that was the most galling part; he was almost saintly in his nonchalance. He simply lounged in and out of Caroline's feminine assertiveness, too.

Naturally, she went through the customary list of clichés, beginning with a reference to 'plain bad manners', and going on to wonder whether he was 'losing his head' or maybe even 'losing his heart to another', saying that it wouldn't matter anyhow, because they were 'living separate lives' and adding that God could be thanked for that (what kind of God this could have been, one is left to wonder). She possibly forgot to mention in all this, though no doubt the thought was present, that her failure to check his behaviour in full flight might have been interpreted by her guests as a lack of feminine assertiveness, and so as an abject failure to practise precisely the principles she had been preaching. She had, she said, restrained herself, but now her guests had left and she felt, she said, rightly bound to speak her mind good and plain.

And Luke's reaction? Well, without uttering a single syllable, he just lounged upstairs, lounging down again a few moments later with what appeared to be nothing other than John Henry's baseball bat.

It must be said that for a moment Caroline thought maybe she had gone too far and that she would soon be closer to God than she ever wanted to be. She needn't have worried on that score. Luke lounged right past her, walked right up to Becker's Last Stand and delivered it a stout broadside blow, shattering the glass which continued to tinkle down to the hearth for some seconds later. Then, tossing John Henry's bat aside, he just lounged out of the living room and out of the house, with Caroline staring after him open-mouthed and paralysed with astonishment, all her precepts touching the hallowed subject of feminine assertiveness being in a state of temporary suspension – like a volcano which had decided to sleep a while longer, repose being the better part of eruption.

Caroline later rationalised the violent incident quite nicely, and in such a way as to keep intact her precepts concerning feminine assertiveness. Luke hadn't reacted verbally and rationally to her reproaches, because he hadn't had a leg to stand on; instead, he had resorted to physical violence, which was, she was pleased to affirm, a typically male response to be treated with the contempt it so richly deserved. Feminine assertiveness on the other hand was non-violent, verbal and perfectly rational – in a word 'civilised', and so should be contrasted with everything that was primitive and backward in men-folk. She was happy not to have compromised her precepts by answering like for like. John Henry was in his room at the time of the incident sorting through his collection of baseball posters; he had watched his father lounge in, pick up the bat and lounge out again, completing ignoring him in the process. John Henry then heard the crash and splinter of glass. He was a smart kid and had learned how to put two and two together to make six. After satisfying himself that the link between bat and crash was genuine and causal, he immediately assumed that his father had been uncommonly drunk or beside himself or both.

It is maybe to his credit that the Becker incident was one of those few things he remembered for the rest of his very crowded life – the night his father had purposely smashed his mother's Otto Becker, though he never in all his long years managed to attach any significance to Becker's masterpiece in its own right. His dad had just had it out on his mother, that's all – and having it out pretty ineptly, too. But John Henry made good use of that night's doings well before he was out of his teens.

John Henry's next visit to Bob Hayward was close on the heels of the incident, and of course he told his grandfather all about it. Bob was taken aback and wanted to know every detail – with a kind of childish enthusiasm, like a child who enjoys the comfort that comes with familiarity when the same story is repeated night after night. John Henry was more than happy to oblige, embellishing skilfully as he went along, furnishing choice details from his own fertile imagination for the effect, for the fun of it, because it pleased his grandfather's thirst for knowledge, and because he felt closer to Bob than he did to his father. He told his grandfather about the deathly look on Luke's face as he marched in and out of his bedroom, though Luke had lounged in and out and John Henry hadn't looked at him at all and so couldn't know what kind of expression he'd had on his face. 'Yeah, he rushed in and grabbed my bat and then rushed downstairs. Yeah, he was real mad and he smashed mother's picture – made a big noise. Smashed into bits! Then, then he stormed out of the house. She was scared. I slept in her bed and we put a chair under the door. What? No, she was okay. Nothing happened. But it was real scary.'

Of course, Luke hadn't rushed anywhere; and John Henry had most definitely not spent the night in his mother's bed. Caroline was far too independent – in fact she was so independent that she hadn't shared her bed with anyone at all, including most notably Luke himself, for many moons.

John Henry's exclamatory and embroidered account did very little to endear Luke to Bob, who said he'd felt from the very beginning and all along that something was amiss, that something somewhere would come unstuck. And that's what he told Caroline over the telephone as soon as he had sent John Henry out of the room and into the small stable out back. 'There's no talking to you when you've made your mind up. But if you'd listened to me...' Caroline, in keeping with her precepts concerning feminine assertiveness, interrupted him: she could handle it, and if things didn't work out right, she would know what to do. This did little to reassure Bob. The Becker incident gave him much to think over, no small thanks to John Henry, who felt even closer to his grandfather for lying to him to such good effect. Luke began to be the object of Hayward's deepest and most morbid suspicions; Hayward may not be permitted to come bluntly between his daughter and her husband, but he would sure as hell keep a close eye on Luke from now on – after all, anything, just anything, might happen! The Becker incident became a turning point in the painful history of the Bensons. Not even Luke's MBA could exonerate him from his psychopathic deed. Nor was it simply the deed itself. John Henry's embellishments had also included a more general account of Luke's behavioural decline from common standards of normality. John Henry had heard his mother grumbling about his father during a phone call to one of her friends. He just wasn't the same man anymore but slouched aimlessly about the house, and when he wasn't slouching his head was buried in books – she was so put out by this that she had actually taken the trouble to take notice of some of the titles, and even to peek inside the covers; books about American Indians, sometimes reading the same book over and over again, judging by the dog-eared pages and what she thought were his annotations, and what did any of this have to do with his job, his career?

Some women might be able to put up with this kind of irrelevant obsession, but not Caroline; this wasn't the man she had married, and whenever she asked him anything, he would just slouch away. It was maddening and driving her crazy, and if things didn't improve then no good could come of it. He seemed to be neglecting his job and instead of working into the small hours on something respectable like a file, he would fall asleep in the living room over one of his infernal books, or he would go to his study and fall asleep there; how could a man change so?

John Henry had understood the gist of this catalogue of complaints, and, after some further probing, remembered that this particular phone call had occurred before the Becker incident. As a lawyer, his grandfather was deeply impressed by the detailed attention to temporal sequence afforded by his tender protégé, who was thereby exhibiting the very stuff of which legal prowess consists. Bob was ready to read far more into all this than wisdom and caution might dictate. The inference he drew from the tender lips of his witness was that the Becker incident illustrated a dramatic worsening of events, with the corollary that no improvement seemed at all likely in the near future, and that a further incident was not at all out of the question, with the further corollary that next time someone, Caroline or even John Henry himself, might get hurt.

Bob was ready to expect just about anything. He was genuinely worried and didn't know what to make of it all. For one thing, the holding of a MBA was so incompatible with what appeared an excessive, and maybe explosive, interest in Indian affairs that his son-in-law might actually be going insane – for he knew enough about mankind to know that insanity may take many forms and that the form it takes in a particular case may be unpredictable and inexplicable. For another, hard-headed and strong-minded as Caroline might be, there was little protection against the explosively insane.

Hayward began to wonder about Luke's origins, not that he ever dreamed that Luke might be anything other than plain, bright white. But he now felt that he should have delved deeper into his background and not taken so much for granted – suppose, for instance, there was evidence of hereditary and criminal insanity? On the other hand, Caroline wouldn't like it one little bit if she thought her father was trying to meddle in her affairs on the assumption that she was too weak, too soft or too fragile to handle things by herself, thus revealing a typically male prejudice. So, he decided to wait. But if things didn't improve soon, he felt duty bound as father, grandfather and above all man, to take matters into his own hands. There again, he might decide not to wait. Like the good lawyer he was, he reached a workable compromise: he could at least have a word with his son-in-law's employer – a phone call, just to ask how Luke was getting on; what could be more natural than that? And after all, hadn't it been through his influence that Luke got the job in the first place?

Which explains why the Old Man Upstairs started to take a far keener and much less paternal interest in Luke, beginning to watch him more closely and critically than he might otherwise have done. One friendly, casual word had led to another, and Bob, in his capacity as dutiful father and concerned father-in-law, felt bound to relate the Becker incident. His account, though skeletal, was more than enough to alert the Old Man, who now felt a personal hurt on top of any doubts he might have begun to entertain as to Luke's suitability as a trusted employee or his standards of professional performance. Before Hayward made this call, the Old Man's suspicions were already on the hob, ready and waiting to be subjected to some heat. Bob now kindly lit the match under the pot, and the whole troublesome mixture began to simmer rather nicely. It only needed a few bubbles breaking out on the surface for the Old Man to throw the whole concoction down the drain, with Luke riding on top of it, destined for the sewers of the unemployed and destitute.

Meanwhile, Luke started to entertain a strange, novel and dangerous idea – the idea of reversing the whole process of assimilation to which he had been subjected from the time he had first seen the light of day. Madness, indeed; as though he could cheat time and live all over again. As he looked around him there was little encouragement to preserve the status quo. He felt he hardly knew John Henry at all; Bob had managed to bleach all the red out of John Henry, who was no more red than the Big Mac hamburgers which had recently flooded the United States and which John Henry loved to gorge himself on. At the same time, Luke was obliged to remind himself that a child was the gift of

Wakan Tanka and could never be ignored, but, on the contrary, must be embraced. So he wondered if he could rescue his son from white embraces before it was too late altogether – it was already very late.

As the for the Old Man Upstairs, he was just an old man with nothing to offer that could justify subservience. And Caroline? Well, she was not the woman he had married, if only because she was not a woman anymore – not the kind of woman a red man would understand. She was the vanguard or the epitome of some kind of new and incomprehensible creature, neither man nor woman, who found it easier to assert her authority than to make love. But he would have been the first to admit that he wasn't the man she had married, either – that man had had his insides pulled out so well that he failed to recognise himself. Luke felt much the same as Quannah Parker looked in that picture of solitude, dejection and despair – a soulless corpse, not now capable of paying lip service to the canons of white respectability and conformity. With his soul gone, there was hardly much point hanging round. Or maybe he could find his soul elsewhere. Maybe he could start the journey of life all over again, and, if Wakan Tanka willed it, he could take John Henry with him.

Not once had it seriously occurred to him to bring his true origins out into the light. Not once had he seriously entertained the possibility of sitting Caroline down in one of her more receptive moods, admittedly rare, and putting the whole matter to her, of showing her Emma's letter and talking things through. Maybe that wasn't the kind of thing a red man would do with a red woman. Such notions had been rejected in the time it took to articulate them, as though they had been formed only to be summarily dismissed. The distance between them had become unbridgeable on this and any other matter of significance – but this was the mother of all matters. He had struggled to be proud of what he now felt he was, and had just now managed it. But his pride was young and raw, and he had been shocked into it, while Caroline's was as deeply rooted as the tallest oak and just as unshakeable. Maybe it wasn't his being red that stood between them, but what the process of acceptance had entailed – a vision, a re-vision of himself and the world in which he lived. It was as though everything had to be re-assessed and re-evaluated, and so far, the world in which he lived had been found wanting. He began to long for another world, another self – a wholesale revision of everything. Maybe he could be reborn. But a phoenix must first burn before it can rise from its own ashes.

10

Circle Walker

'I am going to venture that the man who sat on the ground in his tipi meditating on life and its meaning, accepting the kinship of all creatures, and acknowledging unity with the universe of things was infusing into his being the true essence of civilisation.'
Luther Standing Bear, 1868–1939, Oglala Sioux Chief

~ ~ ~

The match had already been put to the fire that would consume the phoenix. The depth of Luke's revision could not be under-estimated. Luke was well in the process of peeling back and peeling off the layers of what the white man had come to regard as civilisation, just as you can peel off the layers of an onion, one by one, and not stop until you are left with nothing at all. It was all very well for Mrs Harper to rattle on about mid-life crisis, but Luke didn't think much of such talk, because mid-life crisis was largely a white man's hang-up, fed by superficial complexities of which the red man had no knowledge and with which the red man, together with a very few whites, would have little patience. When needs are simple, such hang-ups are few and far between, maybe even non-existent altogether. It wasn't that life for the reds was easy, for life in a 'state of nature' is anything but easy, but it had much more to do with keeping pace with the seasons than it did with keeping up with the Joneses, it was much less concerned with 'upward-mobility' and job satisfaction than storing up in the summer and getting through the winter.

Sure, simplicity had its drawbacks. It meant that such a life had fewer material things to offer, that those things that did exist were very simple, material options were limited, and there was certainly no advantage in having anyone die for lack of the white man's medical knowledge and his ability to manufacture supplies. Even so, the spiral of competition and the ensuing rat race brought out the worst, seldom the best, in white civilised man: a morbid obsession with self, epitomised in the search for eternal youth, in the psychological hang-ups that come with the stresses and strains of a form of life based on raw competition, to say nothing of internecine jealousy, envy and discontent, and the crimes on which they permanently feed.

To Luke's way of thinking, what Mrs Harper was complaining about was a white man's disease; mid-life crisis was no more than the economic growth of the individual run wild, a condition based on the crazy assumption that there could be no end to the returns on investment – just as people referred to productivity, thinking it to be an infinite possibility, so that when things looked inflationary, the insufficiency of productivity was alleged to be the culprit, as if to suggest that an arrow could be checked in its flight by giving it a further boost. No, there were limits, and they were easy to step over – but it wasn't so easy to step back. Greed and bad logic were the white man's problem, and Luke wanted none of it. That fateful combination of greed and bad thinking were responsible for man's inhumanity to man. Once again, Luke found himself reasoning, which would have delighted Simon Westgate, even if Luke's premises were open to discussion and far from watertight.

There were limits, not just to the world's resources, but also to the capacity for enjoyment, to material satisfaction and the enjoyment of acquisition. There came a time when things turned back on themselves and became a liability – like having too many coats and ending up with an anxiety complex because you could never decide which one to wear, and then, having finally made up your mind, reproaching yourself for the decision you've just made. If you stepped over the boundaries, things just started going backwards, joy turning to despair, an experience the whites encapsulated in the so-called Law of Diminishing Marginal Utility. The red man had never known what it was to cross the boundary of their needs – because they hadn't got that far, so couldn't make any 'law' out of it, either. Whatever hang-ups the reds had, that wasn't one of them. If only the best of what the whites had to offer could be mixed with the best the reds had to offer, Yes, but that wasn't permitted, because the worst in everyone always seemed to be too dominant. Simplicity wasn't allowable, let alone sustainable.

One of the more practical consequences of this line of reasoning might have amused the casual observer, had he failed to understand the reasoning that underpinned it. Luke took to cold showers and leaving the windows of the shower room open even when it snowed outside. White 'civilisation' had made him soft and he determined to put this right by refusing to use heaters in the shower room and refusing to heat the water; energy could be saved in this way, and Luke himself could toughen up. In his reading he had come across a Lakota Sioux who had said, 'We are not afraid of the cold.' Among all the fears, real and imagined, that white civilisation had brought about, fear of the cold was one that Luke was keen to dispel. Neither Caroline nor John Henry were aware of Luke's dedication to cold showers, though they both wondered why the shower room was bitterly cold and free of steam whenever Luke left it.

***

Less amusing was the fact that Luke and Caroline hadn't spoken since the Becker incident, a feat of non-communication that was not at all difficult to accomplish. Even at the best of times, they tended to see little of each other, except for brief periods in the evenings. Caroline had hired a housekeeper, whose duties included the preparation of evening meals, and it was during mealtimes that Caroline and Luke normally had the opportunity to exchange the customary marital civilities touching the affairs of the day. But since the Becker incident,

Caroline had instructed the housekeeper to leave off preparing dinner. She had decided to eat out, taking John Henry with her, in this way altogether avoiding Luke, who had taken for some time now to sleeping on the couch in his study – a habit which had started with his falling asleep over his work files, and continued with his books about red men. The outcome was that seeing each other was a weekend affair if it happened at all, and now it rarely happened, what with Caroline away attending conferences, which seemed very much on the increase, and John Henry regularly spending weekends with Bob Hayward, or in any case in and around his grandfather's house.

Two weeks passed this way after the Becker incident; there seemed little hope of reconciliation any time soon, for the sun had gone down and given place to a hard and icy atmosphere, impenetrable to everything except the sharpest of ice-axes wielded by the most determined, and there was a marked lack of determination on both sides of the frozen divide – in fact, on all sides. Even the kindly Mrs Harper was a mite distant. Whether she had consulted her God on the subject of specifically male hang-ups and had found he had little to offer, or whether she now thought it somewhat dangerous to be seen to be leaning too far towards Luke, must remain a matter of guesswork. Phone calls weren't coming in as thick or as fast as before. Luke suspected that Mrs Harper, seated in a small outer office, was handling calls herself or even putting them through directly to the Old Man Upstairs. The phone just didn't ring so much these days.

Every way he looked, Luke sensed nothing but hostility, an attitude of cold indifference creeping slowly but surely towards him like the gradual icing-over of Lake Michigan in mid-winter. It was about the third week in November and a bite was in the air. The trees were leafless and pointed skyward like cold skeletons in postures of pathetic appeal. Caroline had had her Otto Becker removed since the incident, not bothering to replace the glass. Luke guessed it was in the attic, but couldn't have cared less. Maybe Caroline had seen a silver lining in the cloud of the incident, giving her an opportunity to deposit the picture in the trash can. Anyhow, the picture was all the more conspicuous for its absence. Every time Luke passed the spot, Becker's Last Stand stared after him and followed him through the room; that blank space became the most significant and oppressive in the whole house – though it was no more than a piece of wall.

But it wouldn't concern him for very much longer. As November was coming to a close, he decided to move out – probably, maybe, for good – and head for Pine Ridge. If Emma was right, that's where he had started out. He kept his intention to himself – well, who was there to tell? He just packed a canvas bag, and left. He wasn't leaving on a weekend, either, but a working day. He said nothing to Mrs Harper. And as for the Old Man Upstairs, he could just go to hell, if he wasn't there already. Luke was going AWOL and was very much past caring.

Pine Ridge, as Luke's researches had by now revealed to him, could hardly be said to live up to the salutary, rustic, not to say romantic, image evoked by its name. Chief Seattle in his speech of 1854 waxed lyrical against the clatter of white cities, 'The Indian prefers the soft sound of the wind darting over the face of a pond, and the smell of the wind itself, cleansed by a midday rain or scented with the pinyon pine.'

But poets would be hard put to find inspiration anyplace in the vicinity of Pine Ridge. Consistent with Luke's reading, the place oozed poverty and deprivation, solitude and desolation, especially now that hard winter was setting in; Pine Ridge looked like Hell in winter. It consisted of a series of scattered wooden huts, against a hilly background devoid of much natural vegetation save scrub. On the crest of the hills were clusters of tall evergreens, which stood out like the few remaining hairs on a balding head. Nearer the base of these hills stood the occasional pine, as though in forced exile from those above. Forced exile it would have had to be, for the flats down below had little to commend them. Among the poor excuses for dwelling houses, which were no better than half-dilapidated wooden shacks, were a general store which also functioned as a bar of sorts. The store and bar seem to serve each other, each a focal point for the wretched folk that dwelt thereabouts, who might sit or stand about in groups of two or three, talking long and slow about nothing in particular, since there was never anything in particular to talk about save the slow, stultifying decline towards eternity. Since the sale and consumption of alcohol was not permitted on the reservation, the store served as a cover for whatever could be smuggled in or made; anything, even a disinfectant called Lysol, was better than nothing to mitigate the pain of lives wretched and pointless.

And wretched they certainly were. Young kids played with dogs that seemed to belong to no one in particular, looking as under-fed as they did, both no doubt finding some solace in each other's company; old men sat about with wizened countenances, the human counterpart to the barren ruggedness of their surroundings. Sure, it was the onset of a bitter winter, but it was hard to believe that the place offered much more in the height of summer, and now the skies were a cold and indifferent grey. The barking of dogs, the playful shouts of children, the occasional baby crying for its feed, and the roar of an engine as the key turned in the ignition, broke the otherwise unearthly silence of the place. In better places and in better times, silence may well be golden, but on Pine Ridge in winter silence was fraudulent currency, an incitement to depression and intoxication.

While residents slept at night, that silence descended like a heavy shroud, as fires, lights and candles went out, each in turn, and the whole scene was hidden from view, when, with a little luck, a dream or two of better times temporarily lightened the load. But in the broad light of day it was hard to reconcile Pine Ridge with images of the Promised Land; even the ghettoes of New York, Los Angeles and Chicago compared very favourably with Pine Ridge. The difference was that the destitution in a metropolis was hidden in among the weeds of a concrete jungle, but there was no place for Pine Ridge to hide during the light of day, only the darkness of night offered a temporary respite from a scene that disappointed the eyes and destroyed the soul.

Luke turned his car up the long asphalt road that led between the crude wooden tipis, straining to see where he might park without offence and get a room. He pulled up outside a general store which looked anything but inviting; the wooden frontage hadn't seen a lick of paint for years, and the sign about the door was lop-sided. There was no sidewalk outside the door, just a row of wooden planks which shook and creaked when walked upon. It was approaching midday and he had been driving since the early hours. He reckoned he would rest up and brush up and take a look round later. As far as he could see, there was nothing that looked even vaguely like a hotel or motel anywhere on the reservation; the place had few visitors, and none were expected. Prisons have parking lots but there were none on Pine Ridge; you just chose a mud-caked space and took your chances, no questions asked.

'Room? Maybe,' said the portly red man who doubled as storekeeper and tight-lipped 'barman'. 'How long you staying?' He offered a room, of sorts, for one night, which Luke was obliged to accept, there being no earthly alternative. Jim White, a name truncated from Jim White

Antelope, was a man of few words, and he sure as hell had little to say to a wasishun; at the best of times he wasn't much good at conversation, he just provided a venue for it. But there was little of it going on in or around the store at the time Luke appeared. Maybe it was just one of those days. He was a new guy, and new guys were few and far between, especially those who wore decent clothes. Luke had had the sense not to appear on the reservation dressed as though he were attending an interview for a bank job; he had dressed down and wore casual clothes topped with an anorak with a fur collar, but the clothes were new, at least they seemed that way to the residents of Pine Ridge. White guys were expected to dress that way, and one reason why they were despised was the way they were expected to dress. Three guys were in the store. Two sat together at a small table in a corner, drinking some vile concoction; whatever they drank, it wasn't fine grade whisky, and the third guy, maybe in his 20s, leaned up against the makeshift bar or counter. They all looked the worse for wear, but that wasn't in the least unusual at Pine Ridge. They were all naturally suspicious of Luke, and their eyes followed his every move. He smiled as best he could, but to no effect; it seemed that nothing on earth could move their fixed expressions of doubt and reserve. Maybe they thought he was some kind of federal agent come to check the place over and write yet another report for some Congressional sub-sub-committee. Maybe it would be on living conditions, which would be filed away with all its predecessors and forgotten – a process as relevant to the residents of Pine Ridge as the presidential elections in France.

To the guys in the store he was just another wasishun. Luke felt the same way – entirely out of place, if not out of time. The fact that he hadn't shaved for two days and dressed down, and against the cold, didn't seem to matter a jot. It wasn't a good start; cold, grey skies on the outside were complemented by the dingy, icy atmosphere on the inside. Jim White nodded and showed him to his room out back, which was just big enough to get into and out of the bed that formed its only focal point. There were no windows and no electricity. Jim left him in semi-darkness and a few moments later returned with a candle; when Luke closed the door of his room, which was hardly much bigger than a cupboard, he would need it. Luke was grateful. Jim nodded and said, 'Twenty dollars.' He then turned and walked back into the store. Luke followed him. 'I'm not white. I'm Sioux,' he said. 'I don't speak Lakota.' Jim just stared at him blankly, as though he hadn't heard a thing. He was just about to walk away when Luke spoke again, 'You know anything about an Indian child given to whites called Benson? Ed and Emma Benson – Rapid City? Long time ago.' Jim looked at him as though he were either drunk or insane , and then he said, 'Don't know. Crazy Jack might – if he's tellin'. Been round a long time. Mighty long time.' 'Crazy Jack?' 'Yeah, hangs round the store, every day. Stick around. You'll see 'im later.'

But it was a long wait. Luke tried to manage a short sleep, but the bed was uninviting. Luke got up and walked outside. He looked to the hills stretching to the sky behind those poor excuses for dwellings sprinkled here and there, including a car carcass or two which unbelievably looked lived in. All this was so far removed from what he had known all those years; it was hard to believe it was still the same country, only a few hours' drive away from Rapid City and Billings beyond. The most desolate spot in Queensland, Australia, would seem consistent with this. Yet, here he was in the United States of America in the age of the business computer and the MBA, waiting for a guy called Crazy Jack. It was the mother of all eccentricities, but no one, least of all Luke, was laughing. The ground was cold and hard, and the sun was a heatless spot far removed from the doings of that place; it hung high, out of reach and out of step. Luke turned his back on the scene and returned to the store.

Crazy Jack finally shuffled into the store, taking his usual place in one of its dark corners. Jim White came over with the usual concoction and placed it on the small table in front of him, and no words were spoken. Crazy Jack just sat there, an aged, wrinkled, crumpled old man, with a hawk-like nose and long white hair; he had stood tall once, but was now bent over like a broken arrow. He had been someone sometime, but was less than nothing now.

Crazy Jack was irony on two legs, because the most important thing about him was something Luke was never to learn: Crazy Jack was none other than Jack Red Hawk, Ruth Plainfeather's father and Luke's maternal grandfather. The whites had let Crazy Jack out of jail years ago. It could be said that he had been freed for good behaviour, which is true. But if he was well-behaved, it was because he was crazy, saying little and doing little all day save for sleeping and eating, just a big, harmless zombie and quite beyond the help of whites or reds. He had proved himself incapable either of much good or of much evil his whole life through.

Whites are not partial to this kind of insanity; they prefer the variety which speaks a common language and runs for Congress with a will. Jack Red Hawk, though, had assumed a wordless sitting position in Cell Block D of the State Penitentiary for so long that nobody knew what he had been incarcerated for. The wordless insane can live just as well outside the penitentiary as inside, the decision depending, as always, on which option is the cheaper. Since the cheaper option was pretty obvious, Jack Red Hawk was set free, and, after some indecision, he finally arrived back where he had started, at Pine Ridge, just as the homing pigeon, however labyrinthine its flight, is likely to make it back home.

Jack Red Hawk's time in jail did, though, confer on him the benefit of another name; he was known on the 'inside' as Crazy Jack, a name that stuck on the 'outside' for the rest of his days, affording him the additional advantage that with a name like that nobody was likely to expect much from him, which was just as well for them. When Crazy Jack did finally make it home, no one recognised him, or maybe they just preferred to say they didn't. But he was an old Sioux with a smattering of Lakota, two attributes which somehow jail hadn't managed to remove. God knows what might have passed through Crazy Jack's mind during those long years of confinement; we can be reasonably sure it wasn't the love songs of Hiawatha, yet, through it all and crazy or not, he remained a Sioux. When he got out of jail he was essentially the same who had gone in, except that he was no longer capable of what the whites call 'connected discourse'. After jumping a few freight trains and landing awkwardly in the process, Crazy Jack made it back home to Pine Ridge, not much the worse for wear, and older but no wiser. His craziness was no pretence, it must be said. He would spend his time sitting in dark corners muttering insanities to himself; on cold days he would stay in the store, out of the way, and was allowed to sleep on the floor at nights. At first he was just tolerated, but in the course of time he became something of a local institution. Pine Ridge would never be the same without him. Young kids followed him about on his ramblings, sometimes sitting round him, but they never jeered at him, or thought any the less of him because he was crazy; they treated him like some kind of old sage who was temporarily out of order and who might suddenly come back to himself one day in a puff of smoke and overspill with pearls of wisdom gleaned from another world and another time. For a few years he whittled bits of wood, but now he whittled no more.

So if he was crazy, he was also respected, and it was infinitely better to be a crazy red respected among reds than a crazy white ignored among whites. That's why a small table and a rickety chair was reserved for Crazy Jack in a corner of the store, where he could sit with as much pride as his insanity would allow – all by himself, between about midday and late afternoon, accompanied by a scrawny mongrel, which would lie flat, resting its head on its paws and yawning from boredom and punctuating its resting hours with an occasional reconnaissance out of doors in search of scraps – which were few and far between in Pine ridge. The dog would growl protectively when strangers approached, though such expressions of ferocity were largely nominal, the poor, emaciated brute lacking the strength to gnaw convincingly on a bare bone. Both dog and master were on the low road to eternal rest, and her together they bided their time, clinging to what little they had left.

Luke had done all the looking around he wanted or dared to do, and he had lain on his bed in a long state of disbelief, before Crazy Jack and his mongrel took up their places at the small table in the corner, Jack on his chair, his mongrel under it. True to custom, Crazy Jack had been up early, shuffling with his dog all over Pine Ridge, singing or whistling to himself, his meaningless dirge well-known and expected by all in the vicinity. When Crazy Jack was heard, it was time to get up and greet the day as best one could.

Crazy Jack's chair was creaking when, with a nod from Jim White, Luke made his way over and sat down facing him. The mongrel growled purely for form's sake, closed its eyes and grunted itself into a feigned sleep.

'The name's Luke. Luke Benson. Thought maybe you'd know something about an Indian baby adopted by whites called Benson.' He might as well have addressed the mongrel for all the response he got from its master, whose chair continued to creak in the shadows with every slight movement.

'Ed and Emma Benson? Y'see, I'm...' But Luke was stopped short.

'Jack knows!' cried Crazy Jack, and his mongrel growled, as if to validate the claim, and then closed its eyes again.

'Yeah? Well, I...' Luke began, with great expectations.

'Oh sure, sure. Jack knows! Long day. Long day coming. Time to sleep.' With that, Crazy Jack just settled himself back in his chair and closed his eyes, as if to follow his mongrel to the land of dreams.

The old fella was as capable of rational discourse as his mongrel was of chasing conies. Luke looked hard at him; he was half-hidden by shadows, a wizened old coot who had no doubt been born into the world once upon a time and who'd had a mother and a father, and maybe even a good-looking girl to caress and plan a future with. But that must have been a few millennia ago, for these things were hard to guess from the poor creature that slouched before him in the shadows now.

'Jack knows,' mumbled Crazy Jack, sleepily, as Luke turned away. Next instant, Crazy Jack was snoring in unison with his mongrel, leaving Luke with as much idea that that heap of old bones was his own grandfather as Crazy Jack himself.

So far, Luke's visit to Pine Ridge had been even less fruitful than his trip to the Custer battlefield. It was more depressing, even; for he now knew more clearly than ever that the process of red humiliation that had set in after the Battle of the Little Bighorn was making further progress towards a total annihilation of dignity despite the pious sentiments sometimes expressed in the corridors of power back east. If Luke had lost his soul, he sure as hell couldn't find it in Pine Ridge. The only thing to be found there was desolation and decay, with as much soul in the residents as there was left in Crazy Jack – a living corpse with no future and a past that was increasingly hard to recall.

Crazy Jack, fast asleep now in that shadowy corner, reminded Luke of a picture he had seen of Chief Big Foot as he lay dead, in a sitting position, in the snow at Wounded Knee in that bitterly cold December of 1890; in fact, Crazy Jack could have been Big Foot himself, disinterred and placed there in the corner of the store as a monument to posterity. Big Foot was an old man and wore a tattered scarf round his head against the merciless cold. Already expiring with pneumonia, he was killed by a bluecoat bullet in the head as he attempted to rise in hopeless defense of his people. Now, once again, how the mighty had fallen. The Chief died and froze where he fell, in that sitting posture, as though reposing on a bed of cold, white linen masquerading as snow – his eyes closed in death and a faint smile of resignation on his lips, an expression which some whites might be pious or fool enough to call 'peace'.

Faced with the desolation of the whole place and the cold reception he was getting, Luke just lay on that bed in that dusty, dusky room and allowed his thoughts to wander on a long leash. He had not been welcomed. Why should he have been? He was just another crazy wasishun who wanted to be red for a while until the novelty wore off and he came back to his wits. He fooled nobody in his good clothes and his European car. He couldn't speak Lakota, not even a single phrase convincingly – except 'washte kola' (good friend) which he had heard in a movie. He could produce no evidence that he was anything but a crazy white; instead, he had about him all the trappings of a white tourist, or maybe he was some kind of reporter or researcher out to make an impression. What he had hoped to gain from his visit to Pine Ridge wasn't really at all clear – confirmation of Emma's claims? But not just that. He was maybe hoping to receive a welcome home, But this was not home, nor anything like it. Home was with Ed and Emma Benson and everything that belonged to an irretrievable past. And as for anything before that, well no one seemed to know, let alone care; there again, neither was he over-anxious to find out.

Emma's claims may have been genuine enough, but he couldn't make them relate to anything. He couldn't give them any depth and they were like a plant without roots to hold it down, just tumbleweed blowing in the wind. Emma's letter was just a series of statements without authority apart from the authority Emma gave them; the letter might just as well have been a recipe for homemade cookies.

Luke resolved to relieve Jim White of his embarrassment at agreeing to accommodate a wasishun. He decided to leave for home, towards which his thoughts were now more firmly swaying; for home now was in Billings and with Caroline and John Henry. He would return because that's all he had to return to, and that at least justified his visit to Pine Ridge. True, with Caroline and John Henry he had little, but without them he had nothing at all. Maybe, with greater effort and in the fullness of time, he could exert a greater influence over John Henry. If John Henry was now all wasishun, Luke decided to try and make him into a good wasishun and to devote his energies in that direction. As for Caroline, there was no changing her, but maybe one day he would try and tell her all about this: about Emma's revelations, all about his thinking and doing, and she would understand, or understand a little of it, or pretend to understand, which would be just as good. The Old Man Upstairs might leave a lot to be desired, but he wasn't the worst wasishun. And, as for Bob Hayward, he was just doing his best to play the part of grandfather – what more could be expected of him?

Luke wasn't entirely convinced by this line of reasoning, and, in his cooler moments, he might have called it panic-thinking. But it was also a question of cutting his losses, and pulling back and pulling out from everything in Pine Ridge that led to nowhere. Better to go back to Billings and be a little boat in choppy waters than an ocean liner in a maelstrom. And Emma's letter? He would keep it, but he would forget all about it. He would put it by and he would try to live – to live in spite of it. It would be his secret. Didn't everyone have a cross to bear? And one day, the truth, the whole truth, might be told, without ambivalence, without the kind of soul-searching with which he had so far tortured himself, and maybe even with a touch of humour. The plain fact is that Pine Ridge was so dead, it had the effect of making the impossible appear more feasible.

So, Luke would have left Pine Ridge with this jumble of thoughts, mostly defensive and even apologetic, floating around his mind. He would have left if it had not been for a remarkable twist of fate; yes, if Jim White hadn't approached him and said, 'Didn't get much out of Crazy Jack, eh? Didn't think you would. You did well to get as much as you did. Must have been one of his good days.' Luke thought this was a joke, but not the slightest flicker of a smile attended it. But then Jim went on, 'You should speak to Running Deer. Big medicine man – old as Crazy Jack. Older, maybe.'

***

Jim wasn't kidding. Running Deer was old. No one knew just how old, least of all Running Deer himself. He was the same medicine man who had said prayers for Robert Eagle-Sees-Him; he must have been in his 60s at the time, though he looked older even then. Now he was most likely in his mid-90s; wizened, with wrinkles deep as the Grand Canyon, but calm of countenance and clear of speech, when he took to talking, that is – and, it must be said, he opened up to Luke more than he had done to anyone else in a very long time.

They sat on the floor, facing each other, in the back room of a two-roomed wooden shack, with a small window which let in more cold air than light. Luke found him easily and was surprised how welcoming the old guy was, allowing him to come close and sit down and take his ease. Luke explained Emma's letter. Running Deer listened and then told Luke about his father Robert Eagle-Sees-Him and how he had fought and died in the white man's war against the yellow men. He spoke about Ruth Plainfeather, too, but he said nothing about Ruth's intention to do away with herself and her baby. It's likely that he knew nothing about that. He just told it as far as he did, adding that Ruth was 'wichinchela' (a pretty girl).

'I don't know Lakota,' Luke said.

'You can learn. You're a red man – like me!' Luke was warmed by this, like a cold man warmed by a log fire.

The room was full of smoke from the pipe Running Deer smoked; a short, curved pipe which bore little resemblance to the chanunpa (the sacred pipe) of the Lakotas.

'A white man's pipe,' said Running Deer, holding it out. 'White man's tobacco, too. Easy to get, easy to light, easy to keep lit. Try it?' He offered the pipe to Luke.

'Thanks, no I don't smoke.

''Pity. Keeps you sane. Keeps worries down.

''I don't know why I came back, but...' Luke started.

'You came back. That's all.'

'Yes, but...'

Running Deer pointed to the smoke rings which floated upwards from the bowl of his pipe.

'You know about circles? We Lakotas know about circles. White men like squares with corners which pinch and hurt. Circles have no corners. The tipi is round and so are the nests of birds. See? Everything is round, like the Earth itself. Orbits are round. Sky and stars, all round. No corners! The wind blows round and round, and the seasons move in circles, always going back to where they started. And the day follows night and night follows day, round and round. That's how the world works – round and round.

'We, too. We are born and grow old and go back to the earth. The fears of a child are not so different from the fears of old men – fear of darkness, judgment and extinction, of being lost and never found. The child just born becomes the child of old age. This is the power of things. You came back. You are Circle Walker! We all go back. Even white men. They called us savages and primitive because we are simple. But maybe even the white man will need to be simple, to stop him destroying the Earth. If he destroys the Earth he destroys for us, too. The white man needs to go back, and start again – no mistakes this time round! Even white men say "what goes around, comes around" but they don't care what goes 'round, so they don't know what's coming 'round. White men will walk in a circle, whether they like it or not.'

Running Deer's pipe had gone out. He relit it, producing great clouds of smoke. 'Simple. Simplicity,' Luke muttered to himself.

'Simple, sure. That was the way of the red man. We loved nature, we respected all life and we treated each other truthfully and generously, our dealings were honest and we did not lie, everyone was equal and we were a brotherhood. We could not kill the buffalo without love for the creature we killed, and we honoured our men with its name and its qualities – like Tantanka Iyotake, which the white man translated as "Sitting Bull" – and many white men made fun of his name, but no red man could. No man would go hungry, no woman or child without protection. The white man knows these good things, too. But somewhere along a straight line he has forgotten them; now he needs to bend the line and turn it into a circle; he needs to go back – just like you! Simplicity may save him, after all. Who knows?'

To say that Luke felt revived, and that he felt reborn with these words of an ancient medicine man, is a vast understatement. Simon Westgate might have learned a thing or two, and even the wisest of men through all the ages of man might have benefited from a few timely reminders. Luke knew that to go forward it was often necessary to go back. Before his meeting with Running Deer he had decided to go back to Billings. But was Billings the place to go back to? The words of Running Deer had given him a new determination and, with it, a new direction. Perhaps in his own mind he had achieved simplicity at last; perhaps the way ahead would be simpler than he had ever imagined it, and it was all down to Running Deer, who had been a welcome balm to open wounds. He took his leave of Running Deer and Pine Ridge with the name Robert Eagle-Sees-Him buzzing in his head, with thoughts of the hell of Iwo Jima to accompany it, and with a long road ahead.

The thing about simplicity is that it needs to be cultivated and nourished, otherwise it's apt to get lost and forgotten in the weeds of complexity, just as weeds can hide and suffocate a delicate plant, so that what seemed simple may cease to be as simple as it once appeared.

Right now, though, Luke was about to start the journey back to Billings feeling mighty proud of his new name, Circle Walker. It had about it the kind of wisdom that white names lacked. There was much more in a red man's name than in a white man's name, and his new name seemed to confer on him a new and deeper identity, a kind of validation of Emma's revelations and a justification for all the angst that these revelations had caused him; it spoke to him in a way that the name 'Luke Benson' could not, and on this he ruminated.

After all, it is possible to walk a long way, sometimes with a skip and a jump; sometimes stumbling and falling and picking yourself up again, maybe cut and bleeding, but with renewed faith and hope. It is possible to walk the road of life, without knowing that the road you're walking with such an intense sense of duty, or else in obedience to a stultifying routine, is merely the circumference of a circle, so that each step taken, whether painful or elated, gets you no further forward from the centre. Traverse the circumference of a circle long enough and you arrive at the point at which you started, and the sameness, if it strikes you at all, might naturally prompt you to reflect on the circularity of all great journeys, the most important of which is the journey of life.

11

Simplicity, Whisky and Slush

*'Do you know or can you believe that sometimes the idea obtrudes...
whether it has been well that I have sought civilisation with its bothersome
concomitants and whether it would not be better even now... to return to the
darkness and most sacred wilds (if any such can be found) of our country
and there to vegetate and expire silently, happily and forgotten as do the
birds of the air and the beasts of the field. The thought is a happy one but
perhaps impracticable.'*

Ely S. Parker, 1828–1895, Seneca Iroquois sachem Brigadier General,
US Army

~ ~ ~

What seemed simple with the words of Running Deer became somewhat
less so as Luke's journey back home to Billings progressed. Ambivalence
crept in despite his new name and the wisdom that went with it. Like
a demon rising from muddy waters, there was a vague expectation that
somehow things would work out back in Billings, with Caroline and John
Henry; a idea that somehow what had been the status quo could not only
be reinstated and preserved but vastly improved, that any questions or
misgivings concerning his behaviour in general, his trip to the Custer
battlefield and this trip to Pine Ridge in particular, would either be
answered and settled or else would just dissolve away of their own accord.

Equally vague were his images of telling Caroline all about Emma's letter and of John Henry excitedly asking questions about this or that, and even of Bob Hayward taking a renewed, sympathetic, not to say fatherly, interest in him, and even of the Old Man Upstairs inquiring after his health with genuine solicitude. But such comforting thoughts would also be succeeded by their contraries, while these in turn would make way for yet another bout of hazy optimism, all the more pleasant and credible for being foggy and not thoroughly thought out. The contest between these contrasting moods seemed never-ending, almost as unsettling as the thoughts of a man with a fevered brow, half-sleeping, half-awake. But it was just as well that in his less pessimistic reflections he had not pictured Caroline, John Henry and Bob Hayward standing together in the doorway to welcome him home with open arms and hot coffee, or that his mind hadn't settled on the picture of John Henry running down the pathway to greet him like a prodigal father, or on that of Caroline holding him in tight, loving and everlasting embrace.

Just as well, because Luke found the house empty and he had to let himself in.

There was no sign of either Caroline or John Henry – or for that matter of the housekeeper, though that was more explicable. Luke made for the living room and slumped into an armchair, looking up again at the blank space where the Otto Becker used to hang so imperiously. He was hungry and exhausted, and the house was cold, the heating having been turned off for longer than usual. He checked upstairs and found Caroline's wardrobe with much less in it than usual – all her heavy, thick winter clothes had been taken; the same was true of John Henry's wardrobe, and his posters of baseball stars were missing. Then he checked downstairs, thinking there might be a note of explanation. There was none, which might have meant that Caroline despised him so much that she thought he didn't deserve any, or just that she and John Henry had gone away for only a day or two, a sort of tit-for-tat response to his own unexplained absence, a two-can-play-at-that-game reaction – which tended to be a recurrent feature of even those marriages which are said to be made in heaven. But, no – that wouldn't explain why John Henry's baseball posters were missing.

He would call Bob Hayward. Or, should he? There were several aborted attempts to call Hayward before he actually went through with it.

Things had been moving apace in Billings since his uncomfortable sojourn at Pine Ridge, even in the short space of 48 hours, which was highly suggestive of the state of the union of this couple whom the white God had seen fit to join together, a union which no man could break asunder but which had broken asunder anyhow. . Hayward's call to the Old Man Upstairs had prompted the latter to resolve that Luke's next move, if only a hair's breadth short of perfection, would be deemed gross and unforgivable and would see Luke right out of the door, sure and permanent. Failing to find Luke at work, he had called home and had been told by Caroline that he'd left for Lord knows where and that the Devil himself may care – which further prompted the Old Man Upstairs to demand an explanation, and, since one was not forthcoming, he decided to furnish one of his own, which had something to do with taking far too much for granted, in particular his own goodwill, which had now run the full length of its lariat and was irredeemably exhausted. So he decided to carry through his resolution, especially in view of the state of the marital union, because no man can give of his very best if his heart, like charity, is not best served at home, and since he could be satisfied with nothing but the very best, there was nothing further to discuss. Caroline, maybe to anyone else's astonishment but the Old Man Upstairs, agreed, 'Truth is, things haven't been right for a long time now. No, no, I don't blame you at all. You've given him the best chance a man could ask for, just as I have.'

She went on a mite longer, not forgetting to make reference to her beloved Otto Becker, which she missed more than words could tell; she said Luke had known how to hurt her when he busted her Becker and that she hadn't been the same since and never could be again – which prompted the Old Man Upstairs to promise to get the glass in the picture replaced, or maybe, even better, replace the whole thing, lock, stock and barrel, with a bigger and better one. Such behaviour, he commented, was inexcusable and was either the result of a misspent youth or a serious mental condition and, in any case, a sure indication of a man who didn't deserve such a fine young lady as Caroline, even less to marry her and least of all to keep her. The exchanges between them were so amicable that it might not have come as a surprise to anybody listening in if a proposal of marriage had ensued; conditional of course on a divorce from Luke and the continued good health of the Old Man Upstairs. Caroline was firm but cool throughout this conversation, like a seasoned and highly successful lawyer addressing a sympathetic jury, confident of the outcome, but not likely to be thrown off course even if the decision happened to go against her, for there would be other cases, always more clients and certainly other triumphs in abundance – this time it was a triumph for feminine assertiveness.

Following this call, which served to cement the relationship between the participants even further, the Old Man Upstairs called Hayward, as a kind of double indemnity, to apologise for having disturbed Caroline at a time like that; but, he said, he felt obliged to put the cards firmly on the table, and Bob, he was sure, would understand perfectly. Businesses exist to be run, they don't run themselves, as Bob above all people would surely appreciate. Luke had disappeared without a by-your-leave, not even having the decency to obtain permission, let alone to say where he might be found in case of dire need, for, as Bob knew better than anyonerisk was essential to good business practice, and where there was risk, emergency had to be allowed for. Luke's behaviour was intolerably irresponsible and, as proof positive that Luke was being grossly unreasonable, it turned out that even Caroline, his own wife and Bob's precious only daughter, didn't know where he was, either! And if this wasn't a clear sign of unreasonableness, then the Old Man Upstairs was bound to ask what was. By the time the Old Man Upstairshad finished, the case for the defendant's mental unfitness and moral decrepitude had been thoroughly researched, drafted, signed and witnessed.

Hayward didn't need convincing. He had already made up his mind, but the bleating of the Old Man Upstairs certainly added fuel to a fire which was already getting red hot. Bob called Caroline to relay what had been said, at the same time citing the Old Man Upstairs as a prime example of reasonableness incarnate and as one who possessed heartfelt concern for both Caroline and young John Henry. 'This time I won't take no for an answer. Pack what you need and come stay with me. No, no, no! Not this time! This time, you'll take your father's advice!' Well, maybe just this time. Besides, he was adamant. A father is a special man, an individual significant by his individuality, as someone had once said about a mother, so didn't pose the same kind of threat to a daughter's feminine assertiveness. His 'advice' was that there were things to be done that she had already decided on, and that they were best done away from the marital home, especially since Luke might return at any time, and this time there was no Otto Becker to wreck, as her father had been at pains to point out. In the absence of an Otto Becker, Luke might turn his violent attentions elsewhere and there would be the Devil to pay. Best get out now – the time was right.

Caroline had by now and for some time past a creeping fondness for the prospect of divorce. Her own study of feminine assertiveness had convinced her of late that no woman of substance really needed a man over and above the occasional fling, or maybe just to expel a spider or trap a mouse. A woman of substance was more than capable of leading a meaningful life, and a woman of true discernment would choose to do just that. It was just as well if the time ever came for women to have children all by themselves. Women could do just as well, even better, without their male counterparts; nature had deceived them for quite long enough. It was a question of successfully passing through stages, each stage more illuminating than the last, each issuing in an increasingly refined sense of judgment until, at last, the grub, as it were, becomes a fully-fledged butterfly, capable of mind-blowing self-flight. She had made it plain enough in one of her seminars on the subject, 'The trouble with the average woman is that she allows herself to get trapped in the earliest stages of her psychical development, thanks to conventional notions of femininity heavily sponsored by the more dominant males.'

Matter of fact, she considered it a fine sentence and probably one of the best she had contributed on the whole subject. She did not say it in so many words, but it was very clear to her that she was anything but the average woman; whatever the average woman was, she was not to be considered a role model for others to follow. It's a wonderment where in the spectrum of conventionality she would have placed Ruth Plainfeather, had she had any notion of her having existed. What, in any case, did white know of red, or red of white? Straight after Custer's defeat, red women, in defiance of Sitting Bull's warnings of ill omen, walked around the battlefield stealing bits and pieces and hacking at the bodies of dead cavalrymen, chopping and cutting arms and legs, so that they would be unable to mount horses or use weapons in the next life, and relieving bluecoats of their genitals so that the dead could have no children in the land of the White Buffalo. Maybe Caroline would have hailed this a shining example of feminine assertiveness. But of course we can never know.

Caroline had considered herself a butterfly for a year or so by now, fluttering no further than the glass walls of her marital cage, just waiting for an opportunity to liberate herself and reach heights which had until then been inaccessible. What her mother had taught her was by now bearing fruit in abundance. Now was as good a time as any. Where better to fling off the marital yoke than away from the marital home, with all its past conventional pretences of domestic bliss and harmony – pretences which had surely convinced no one. No doubt Bob would be pleased that she had finally come to her senses.

He was. 'Tell you the honest truth, I never did feel right with that fella – always seemed to be holding something back. No, you're doing the right thing, no doubt about it.' Bob was not one to mend bridges once they were down or suggest peaceable alternatives in times of drama. He enjoyed drama – thrived on it, even. He had always admired hard-headed lawyers, for he was one of them. Yes, he was pleased, but it was now a question of what exactly he should say to Luke should he call the house, which he was almost sure to do – let alone what he should say if he actually showed up at the door. He needn't have worried. When Luke called, all Bob said was, 'What? Oh, yeah, they're here.' He didn't have to say, 'You've got a hell of a nerve – they don't want to talk to you!' He didn't have to get his dander up, because Luke just hung up. Hayward felt let down as he later pondered that call. As a lawyer, and a hard-headed one at that, Hayward was not given to roundabout phrasing; he preferred straight talking, and Luke's hanging up, pure and simple, had deprived him of an opportunity to deliver some straight-talking venom. No doubt there would be other chances. Neither did Luke follow up the call by showing up at the door.

The next morning, a Monday, Luke decided to put in an appearance at the office. Arriving at the same time, Mrs Harper gave him a curious look, as if to suggest that of all the places he could show up in the office was one of the least advisable. She proceeded to unlock the door of his office, still giving him awkward glances, and attempting to exchange the customary civilities in a natural manner, and failing badly with a stutter and a stammer. 'Been away for a while, Mr Benson?' He smiled. 'I'm afraid there's been some changes around here and...' she began, but just then, and as if to offer tangible proof of the changes that had been made, a smart young man bounced into the office, nodded to Mrs Harper, sat down smartly at Luke's desk, and spoke briskly, 'What can I do for you, sir? Does the gentleman have an appointment, Mrs Harper? Because I don't seem...' Luke stormed out of the office and out of the building before he could hear anything else. Mrs Harper began to follow him, but she wasn't as nimble as she used to be and Luke was already driving off. She returned to the office and told that new incumbent that someone had got the wrong building. She brushed down her skirt and was asked to take down a memo for the Old Man Upstairs.

One door having been closed in his face, Luke decided to drive that evening to Bob's to talk things through with Caroline. After being washed down the sewer by the Old Man Upstairs, he had returned home, and saw or heard nothing of Caroline or John Henry all day, and further calls to Hayward only put him through to an answerphone. It was a long, hard day, and one drink led to another, and it was amazing how easy you could take to the stuff when for years past you could either take it or leave it and, for the most part, found yourself leaving it. Firewater among the reds had caused many problems, and some chiefs had done their best to advise their young braves against it, because they couldn't hunt buffalo with optimum efficiency or kill their enemies and defend their homes and families if they imbibed the white man's concoction to excess. But the stuff caused problems for whites, too. It had even been said that some of Custer's men were high on firewater and that this was a contributory cause of his defeat at the Little Bighorn fight. Maybe. But there's nothing like a fight for your life to sober you up with the speed of lightning, so the allegation might be taken with the customary pinch of salt. Custer himself was teetotal – and that didn't help him any. The story has it that one personal humiliation at West Point was enough to ensure his lifelong sobriety; and he sure was hard on men in his regiment who overstepped the mark by imbibing one over the eight.

Luke was putting one whisky away after another and making up for lost time. He reckoned it was time to sort things out while there were still things to sort. He could get another job – and Caroline would be supportive, maybe. All he and Caroline needed to do was to stick together, and then something would turn up. A fresh start was what was needed, a clean break, a new understanding, a new footing, a new chapter, if not a new book. A lexicographer would have been in his seventh heaven to creep inside Luke's mind and hear all the clichés Luke employed in his struggle with ambivalence, because Luke was unsure whether a clean break just meant a new job, in a new place maybe, or a break with Caroline and even John Henry, or a break with ... and here he just didn't know what kind of break a break with everything could possibly be. Some things were thinkable, and some things weren't, some things conceivable and some not, some things possible and some not, some things he wanted and some he didn't, some things he needed and some he didn't – and he just wasn't sure which was which. If only his mind could be made up for him. Despite the much-vaunted warming effects of whisky, Luke felt bitterly cold that evening when he turned his car into Hayward's wide driveway. Leaves cracked underfoot, dark grey clouds hung lifeless above the frozen, immobile skeletons of pines. Hayward was inside, enjoying one of his rare and expensive brandies when a loud, sharp series of bangs on the black iron lion-headed door knocker arrested his attention and immediately suggested the visit he had been expecting and dreading. Luke had been unwittingly burning a hole in Hayward's psyche for long enough now and of late had become a monster of almost inhuman proportions. But, you just never knew, some monsters may really be pussy cats at heart; there was no way of telling until the chips were down, and the knock on the door meant that the chips had landed. So Hayward wasn't quite sure what to think and what to expect, and so hadn't known, despite three large brandies, quite how to prepare himself for that knock.

'This is not a good idea,' Hayward said firmly, as he opened the door and stared a somewhat bleary-eyed Luke in the face. 'Caroline does not...'

'It's okay, Dad.' Caroline stood behind Hayward and whispered the words into his ear.

Luke made to go in. 'No,' said Caroline, 'we can do all the talking that needs to be done here, right here.' She certainly sounded matter-of-fact and unshakeable. She was resorting to cliché as everybody does who find themselves involved in domestic conflict, or for that matter any other kind of conflict, as though the cliché becomes a walking aid – something to lean on, or maybe some peg on which to hang your pride. Words are part of the game – one step, two step, and bullseye. It had already struck Luke that it wasn't the kind of game red men played – no wonder they had been up against it when faced with white negotiators and the verbal minutiae of peace treaties. 'You white people speak too much,' one red medicine man had said, though those who are counted wise among the whites complain that they don't speak enough. 'I've had to go away for a while,' Luke began. Snow started falling behind him – very lightly at first. He turned up his coat collar as he spoke, almost reflexively; he sure as hell wasn't being invited inside.

'I've filed for a divorce,' said Caroline. 'I want it soon – and John Henry comes with me. It's all in process. I've got no more to say.' She moved back a little into the hallway, making to close the door on Luke.

'This is crazy – we've got a lot to sort out, that's all...'

'I'll tell you what's crazy – it was crazy of me to expect so much from you in the first place – losing your job, and...'

'How d' you know about that? Can't we talk about it?'

'There's nothing to talk about, Luke. It's just too late. My mind's made up, that's all.

'Is John Henry with you?'

'Yeah, and that's where he stays,' And, with that, she closed the door, leaving Luke on the outside and in the cold, in more senses than one.

Sometimes you sense things are worth pushing further, that the desired result may yet be just around the corner and that a little more patience will see the job done; and at other times you sense they are not achievable – Luke felt this was one of those times, it was time to back off.

Caroline had said all she had rehearsed. As she had said to her father, she wanted Luke to know where he and she stood – and she believed herself to have accomplished just that. Her phraseology might have been cardboard, but the job was done and that was all that really mattered. She believed herself to have been sufficiently forthright; had she had her usual audience it would have been a masterclass in feminine assertiveness. Now only the formalities remained. The snow began to fall more thickly, but not so thick as to restrict Caroline's view of the road that now lay before her.

And Luke? First, he backed out of the doorway and into the driveway next to his car; he then backed up the car and, in the process, crashed into a large white, clay pot, which normally held spring flowers. He then accelerated forward into another pot which had been twinned with the first. The noise of breaking pots prompted the immediate thought that he was driving through the front door and into the living room, as though he had decided that Caroline was well worth a frontal assault and that the talking wasn't yet over by a long way. Hayward was relieved to be mistaken, as Luke drove down the driveway venting his spleen on the engine. The shock prompted Hayward to shout after him from the safe side of the living room window, 'Damned crazy fool! Better not darken these doors again!' together with one or two imprecations which decorum and common decency preclude us from recording here.

Things seldom end where you expect them to. Hayward felt angry and afraid enough to place a call to Mike Harding, the chief of the police. He didn't want any action to be taken. They were only garden pots, and Luke was still his son-in-law. Hayward just wanted to get matters off his chest while at the same time giving someone, almost anyone, a graphic account of events. During his conversation with the chief, he was at pains to point out that this particular event was not the only piece of evidence which pointed to Luke's emotional instability, and this was the cue for an even more graphic and embellished account of the by now famous Becker incident. Caroline had made a once-for-all decision to file for divorce and had told him so in no uncertain terms – now what was so bad about that? Would anyone think she was being unreasonable? And Caroline said she could smell whisky on his breath while they were at the door. Now that wild idiot might drink more than was good for him and he shouldn't even be driving in that condition.

The bottom line was that Hayward would be most grateful if Chief Harding could arrange to keep the place watched and provide a little police protection, or, at least police awareness of a possible situation. It was better to be safe than sorry. The upshot was that Chief Harding agreed to have the place watched, especially late at night, at least until Luke cooled off. Chief Harding, who happened to like Hayward no more than he did any other company lawyer, or for that matter any other lawyer, was ready to oblige, if only to get the man off his back.

Hayward felt much better for having alerted the police; he congratulated himself on thinking of everything as usual – on his ability to leave as few loose ends as possible in every conceivable situation. Caroline said she couldn't care less what Luke did, and probably meant it.

***

For the rest of that night, Luke was slumped in his armchair in his living room, having started another bottle of whisky, not that the stuff was having much effect in sending him off to sleep. How could he sleep? There was too much to think about. Or maybe that was the problem – maybe there was nothing to think about at all. Everything seemed to be decided already. Caroline had decided, and she had said that she had nothing more to say. There was just nothing to think about except nothing, like the blank space on the wall in front of him where once the Becker had loomed. There had been nothing at Pine Ridge, and there was nothing here, either. Nothingness may be a state of mind to which some in search of nirvana aspire to. But nothingness is hard to live with for those without any such kind of aspiration at all. Luke had climbed down from some sort of height to speak to Caroline, even though he had doubted whether she was really worth the effort that communication entailed. But now certainty had chased doubt away, and there was the certainty of nothingness. Maybe the whisky was having some effect after all – he was enveloped in a cloud of nothing.

The whisky had tasted good at first. After a while it didn't taste much at all, just like his life right now. He stared at the blank space on the wall as the Becker seemed to reappear and disappear at will. He asked himself what Quannah Parker would have done in his place. Whatever else he did or did not do, Quannah was at least buried in the way a red man should be, true to his race, in the end. Was being buried in full Comanche regalia a kind of confession? Was it a protest? Was it a last stab at fixing his identity, of finding himself in death? It was a useless thing, of course, if measured by its result.

But such things have never been intended to have results. The whole point was in the act itself; the dignity.. There was something of grace in it, an expression of self-respect, a self-affirmation of a kind; though life's candle had been snuffed out, Quannah himself had not; somehow he had managed to remain intact. It was important not to judge things as whites did, by their results, as though everything is supposed to have either a pragmatic value or no value at all, or as though everything was to be judged as a means to an end somewhere beyond itself. The whites had wanted the red man's country, not because it was beautiful, but because it was a means to an end; land was something to be developed, not left as it was. Was there any land more beautiful than Blackfeet country, with its rivers and forests and dark places where the silence was holy? But white men always wanted to do something with it to make other than what it was; they would not rest until they took up the roots of sacred trees with their caterpillar tractors, so that the holy silences were broken forever. The whites hadn't managed to change Quannah; if a man's death fixes him in eternity, Quannah had decided to fix his own as a red man rather than a red-white businessman with connections in high places.

By now the whisky really did taste like water.

Ed and Emma had made him as white as they could. They had been well-meaning folk, but if only they could have spoken to him when a child, he might have been able to tell them something about Quannah, with the 'Parker' left out. But it was too late now. Too late for him.

But was it too late for John Henry? Luke loved his son, or craved to love him, but what he despised was the whiteness in him, because it left no room at all for red. He would not attempt to do in reverse for John Henry what Ed and Emma had done for him. There was no way Luke wanted to make white red. But he could tell John Henry about the red in him, and maybe the red would somehow co-exist with the white. Red and white could be not blended, but maybe bridged, and then John Henry could learn to be proud.

If red and white could not be blended, whisky could surely be blended with anger and feelings of rejection, with frustration and despair – a fateful blend if ever there was one, and, no doubt because of it, an idea grew rapidly from seed that Luke should rush to John Henry, whisk him away, and explain the red that was part of him – and then Wakan Tanka would be pleased and appeased, and Luke's luck might turn. He would do for John Henry what Ed and Emma should have done for him and not leave everything to time and a letter from a dead hand. He was John Henry's father. Bob Hayward had played his part in the bleaching process, now it was time for Luke to play his and set matters straight. Luke's own father, Robert Eagle-Sees-Him, fought for the white man in his war with the yellow men, but that hadn't made him white; nor should the work of Bob Hayward forever hide the red that was in John Henry. Red must be brought to light. Luke had work to do.

Out of this stupor of half-baked ideas came the resolution to go again to Hayward's though it was approaching midnight and the small hours. But what did time matter? Time was a white man's construction. Luke had something to say, something of great importance to share with his only son. Would Quannah have left things rest? Would Quannah have remained silent on such a matter as this? And for how long? This was as good a time as any.

Luke stumbled into his study and dug out Emma's letter, which he had kept so carefully inside a copy of Dee Brown's Bury My Heart on Wounded Knee. He put the folded letter in the inside pocket of his jacket; it would be proof, or at least it would suffice for the moment, of John Henry's connection to the world of the red men, the Native Americans whose land the whites had usurped under the banner of Manifest Destiny. One day he might read Brown's book and feel the red in him and be grateful to his father for making it known to him, and maybe then he would ask the kind of questions about what the whites called 'civilisation' that so few whites were capable of asking themselves, let alone answering. Luke could almost see Simon Westgate smiling in astonished approval.

Important though his mission would be, driving wouldn't be so easy with so much firewater inside him. Many red men at Pine Ridge had come to a bad end driving with too much firewater in their blood. He would need to take as much care as he was capable of, but at least it had stopped snowing, and a thin white carpet of the magical stuff had stuck all around on roofs, trees and vegetation, except on the highways where the constant flow of traffic had reduced it to a grey-black slush.

God damn that whisky! He had to blink every few seconds to keep himself alert on the highway, and the wipers on the windshield were sticking every now and then, making visibility worse. But eventually he made it back at Hayward's place. It was dark, but the snow carpet seemed to illuminate the driveway, and there was still a light in the window of the large living room window adjacent to the main door. Luke's car sped up the driveway, because it was driven not by Luke but by whisky, although not in anger, because Luke was glad to have arrived and was dead set on completing his mission. The screech of the brakes brought Hayward immediately to the window.

It also alerted the two white cops sitting in their car in the shadows who had arrived a few minutes before Luke. They were cold, tired and in no mood to stick around long. They had received their orders from Chief Harding, and such an instruction was not to be ignored. He had said something about a possible demonstration of violence; it was, he said, a 'domestic' and interference in domestics was considered off limits, so long as no one broke the law. So if anything happened they were to keep out of it as far as possible. Chief Harding hadn't given the matter much thought – it was really little more than a sop to Hayward, something to keep him sweet. 'Stick around an hour or so, then head for home,' the desk sergeant had told them – and that was as much as they could so on a night like this, bitterly cold and with a stillness in the air which was strangely off-putting, though, after a while, a light wind was beginning to make itself felt. 'Snow's okay in a picture.' 'Yeah.' And this was just about the only remark that passed between them.

They expected nothing, least of all Luke's car as it came grumbling and zigzagging up Hayward's drive and stopped with a thud and a screech of the brakes outside his door. They hadn't expected the driver to get out of the car with a heavy stagger, which they later said was aggressive behaviour. And they certainly hadn't expected what followed, either.

Luke banged loudly on the door. There was no answer. The two officers just sat and watched in the comfort of their car, wishing the guy would get back into his and drive away like a good boy, and then maybe they could follow him and book him for careless driving – or maybe just let him go with a warning and then get off home where they belonged. Hayward was determined to keep the door of the house shut tight and locked. Luke moved back from the door and looked up at the bedroom windows, which a few moments ago were lighted and were now in darkness.

'Caroline!' Luke's frenzied shouting exploded in the cold, crisp air, as though it had no right to be there and was offending the silences of nature. There was no response. Luke picked up a handful of snow and small stones and threw them up at the window. The officers looked at each other nervously. Things were heating up. But they stayed put.

'Caroline! John Henry, I wanna see John Henry!' The air exploded again with another broadside. This time he unintentionally picked up more stones than snow and hurled them at the window above with a force that cracked the glass. But Luke was undeterred. There was more shouting and there were more stones, and this time some fell short of their target and cracked the living room window. More shouting, more stones. More broken glass. He just wouldn't give up.The two officers decided to leave the comfort of their car and intervene. According to their report, they thought they could talk him back into his car. They approached Luke. By now he was back at the door and ready to give it another almighty bang. Luke stood in the porch under the light, which was always on through the night.

They shouted to him, 'Hey! You there!' Luke turned round in the porch and through his bleary eyes saw two uniforms approaching. In his fevered imagination, fed by firewater, he might have imagined he saw two cavalrymen out to give the coup de grace to a hapless Lakota. But this we shall never know. What we do know is that he reached for the letter which was in the inside pocket of his jacket – we must presume he was determined to explain his mission to these two officers so that there could be no misunderstanding, and then he could explain everything to John Henry.

***

It was just as well that Emma wasn't alive to be told that her letter would be the death of her adopted son. She must have turned in her grave, though, and be turning still. We are all from time to time subject to the most bitter of ironies. The policeman who went for his gun and used it to such good and final effect explained later that he had been taught to react reflexively, that his reflexes were based on a split-second appraisal of the situation, and that his assessment right there and then was that Luke was going for a gun concealed inside his jacket. His colleague could do nothing but agree, for his own gun was already out of its holster and in his hand at that exact moment when Luke went down, but it just happened to be his partner who pulled the trigger first. The officer who had brought the curtain down wasn't a bad guy, nor was he gun-crazy – even though his most prized possession was a replica Winchester .44-40 calibre rifle, Model of 1873, the so-called 'gun that won the West'. Those white cops had no idea that Luke was red, let alone that he belonged to the same tribe of red men who had defeated Custer at the Little Bighorn fight. Cynicism might suggest to some that, had they known Luke's true lineage, their consciences would have been a mite relieved, but they did not know, because the colour of blood is red for all of us, despite the crazy fact that in the eyes of many the colour of your skin must dictate the colour of your blood.

The man who pulled the trigger was just cold, tired, hungry, nervous and afraid – and, above all, he was just trying to do his job, which, his superiors all agreed, he had done competently, even though he'd had the reputation of being a lousy shot. Maybe similar things were written in reports of many incidents of a similar nature, maybe even after Sitting Bull was shot by a nervous policeman – a policeman who happened to be of his very own tribe. Be that as it may, the incident was over and done with.

And Luke? He staggered several paces out into the snow before eternal darkness descended, Emma's letter falling from his grasp. His body was removed within the hour, and it was mid-morning before Hayward and Caroline received a courtesy visit from Chief Harding. The wind that had started to make itself known had picked up into a temporary frenzy, and Emma's letter was first blown away into the cold bushes that in part formed the perimeters of Hayward's driveway; from there, it drifted into the spaces far beyond, the ink finally blending into the slush on Highway 87, and was never seen again.

One thing that had not blown away was the blood that had penetrated deep in the snow on Hayward's driveway; that had to wait until the snow melted or was otherwise shifted. But pretty soon further snowfalls covered the spot until red on white was no more and all was white, the purest white, once again.

12

Epilogue

'Do you know who you are? Yes, but is who you are also what you are? Are you at one with what you are? Is there doubt? Come, then! Read this book of dreams, this book of life, turn its pages, and choose a dream, and be that dream, if only for a day; choose a dream that takes you above and beyond those petty differences that form barriers between men, far beyond the barbed, steel fences that hold us in and separate one from another – beyond colour, creed and tongue, so that we can finally know what we really are and not just what we appear to be.'

Luke Benson, Journal, undated

~ ~ ~

Yes, sir, I am proud to quote the words of my father.

My name is John Henry – John Henry Benson, to be precise, son of Circle Walker, and the year is now 2020 AD. I have chosen to give this epilogue the dignity of a chapter, and I have numbered it chapter 12, after the 12 apostles, after the number of hours on the face of a clock, after the 12 months of the year, and after the 12 chromatic notes of the octave. Twelve suggests a completeness, so that the foregoing story of my father, Luke Benson, can be complete, so that the story can turn full circle and be a mirror to the name he was given by Running Deer. I myself am not now the John Henry my father once knew and no doubt feared I might become.

I was 12 years of age when my father passed at the hands of a nervous police officer. Strange how time moves on relentlessly despite everything we do to slow it down – it's a wonderment; strange, too, how the greatest wonderments are taken so fully for granted until we stub our toes on them, obliging us to acknowledge them. Yes, time sure passes.

I am proud of my name. After my father passed I was given the name of my maternal grandfather, and I was known as John Henry Hayward, and this was how I was called through school and college, and even later in my first job. But then I began to read and take seriously what my father had written in the journal he kept, the book he scribbled in, just like his white father Ed. My father read about red men, and he kept notes about what he read and about his own feelings as he set out on a journey to discover what he was as distinct from who he was. And on this journey he felt devastated by what he discovered about the history of the red man in these United States of America – as did I, in turn; though in truth I had to hide the full extent of the devastation I felt so that I could go on in spite of it.

The foregoing account was based closely on my father's notes, jottings, remarks, because I wanted to record as truly as I could what he really was, in the light of what I believe he would have wanted me to know about himself and his people – our people. I have furnished further details which owe everything to what I have been most privileged to discover for myself about the Lakota Sioux that is in me, and the rest is owed to my own poor and deficient imagination. If you call a man red, he is not just a colour, any more than a language is just a code or a cipher. The colour of a man does not even begin to delineate what he really is, any more than the words a man speaks must necessarily tell us about the soul of the man who speaks them. That is why his colour alone cannot make him either good or bad, and is also why his colour alone cannot excuse the evil that he does, nor yet justify the good he does. His language is the element in which he lives, as is water to the fish. It is the life around him and his own life within, but many may speak the same language for different purposes, some good, some bad. A man may speak his language well and without fault, but the words he speaks may come from a heart that is filled with hate. Words can be uttered just as well by the soulless as they can by the saintly; and then there are those who may be unjustly condemned because they cannot articulate their own defence and are consequently outdone and undone by those who have the temerity to stand in judgment over them.

My father had issues with his identity because he lived in a world which insisted that he should. Sadly, but predictably, things have not changed. They have not changed for those living and half-living on Pine Ridge. The place continues to be the poorest in these United States of America, and it's a sad reflection that while much is said, and quite rightly said, about the colour black, the colour red is missed out of account altogether – as if to suggest the absurdity that in the eyes of a loving God one colour is more important than another.

Much is said, quite rightly, about the Jewish Holocaust of the Second World War, but very little is said about the Armenian genocide that preceded it and which was indeed alluded to in the insane attempt to 'justify' murder en masse. How would it sound if it were said that one soul is more important than another, one human being more important than another? There are those who have dared to say such things and even to act in accordance with them, and their names sadly live on, but rightly in infamy.

Some changes are good, some are bad. Some things never seem to change for the better. As time passes, the world moves on. But it can move forward in some ways and backward in others – both ways at one and the same time. If there were a physics of morality it would boggle the mind and challenge the imagination. It is my solemn hope that when bad things don't change for the better, some good people will challenge them, and that when things change for the worse there are at least some good people who refuse to change with them – standing fast for what they believe when what they believe is right.

I have said all I can say for red, white, black and yellow. Yes, it's true, blood is red for all men, whatever the colour of their skins; but when they speak together they do not understand one another; their words fly away, like little birds too frightened to linger long on open ground.

This must change. We have much to achieve and, before that, much to endure. Time passes quickly; a human life is fleeting and man runs before it like tumbleweed in a prairie wind. There is much to do; but let us not forget to begin.

John Henry Benson
Son of Circle Walker